Of GUARDIANS and ANGELS

THOMAS WADE OLIVER

ISBN: 0615866182
ISBN 13: 9780615866185

Library of Congress Control Number: 2013948526
Substance Press
Los Angeles, California

ACKNOWLEDGMENTS

Some of the most important pages of our American history can be found in the Slave Narrative Collection of the Federal Writers' Project. This collection of over forty-one volumes consists of interviews of former slaves conducted in the 1930s by writers employed by the government's Works Progress Administration. As heartbreaking and painful as many of them were to read, I poured over hundreds of the interviews to assure some degree of authenticity to this book. To those now deceased who participated in the project by sharing their stories, I am most grateful.

Books by Thomas Wade Oliver
To Watch the River
Valor's Measure
Best Story

-for Marianne

INTRODUCTION

This story is my pride and joy. It began to materialize several years ago after I completed the research for my Civil War novel entitled, Valor's Measure. To capture the authenticity of the war era as best I could, I spent several years touring Civil War battlefields, visiting war-themed museums, and engrossing myself in the study of nearly every aspect of American life in the mid-19th century. When Valor's Measure was completed, I found myself a man with a wealth of knowledge concerning a particularly tumultuous period of American history, yet I had nowhere left to go with it.

What I found most fascinating about my research was the humanity and sense of dignity among the common people who, in one way or another, created the foundation for what we are today. I wanted to explore that even further after Valor's Measure was completed, and I thought the best way to do it was to capture a single encounter and allow two ghosts of our past to come alive.

One of the most compelling stops during my research was at a large plantation in Southwest Mississippi. On the property remains a large antebellum mansion that continues to serve as a private home. The residents were gracious enough to take me on a tour, which

I found both remarkable and haunting. At the conclusion of my home tour, the owner walked me to the back of the house and suggested I roam the rest of the estate at my leisure. It was at that time that he informed me an old slave cabin could still be found not far off the path to the rear of the plantation where cotton was once raised. It would be concealed among the trees so I would have to take care not to miss it, but he assured me it was worth finding.

I located the simple dilapidated shack in the woods about a half mile into my walk. The moment I saw it I felt as if I was being drawn to it. The front door hung sideways, barely clinging to a single rusted hinge. Vines covered most of the exterior and the roof was covered with nature's debris. I decided to climb through an open window instead of maneuvering past the fragile front door. Once inside, I sat on the windowsill for fear I might fall through the rotting raised floor if I tried to walk on it. As I sat and absorbed the musty space around me, I began to feel both the sensation of complete peace and the over-whelming presence of history.

I closed my eyes and listened to the sounds and tried to imagine what may have transpired in and around that slave cabin prior to the Civil War. I imagined the grueling labor of being a field slave, and how the tiny cabin may have been the only sanctuary for its occupants. I tried to envision those slaves as individuals, and how they would have reacted to the news that Union soldiers had reached Mississippi. And in those moments of allowing the ghosts of our past to touch me, this story was born.

The first thing an author must do before they begin to actually write their manuscript is determine the voice of the narrative. For Guardians and Angels, I chose to approach this story from the eyes of the main character, John Sexton IV.   But John is a contemporary character and much of this story takes place several generations before his birth. When you reach that point in the story, you will find my writing style has changed to a third person narrative voice. I did this to make the change in time more pronounced. It also allows me to interject some historic commentary that some of you will certainly appreciate. It is a quite unorthodox approach, but one that I believe fits this story perfectly.

I can't tell you how proud I am of how this project has finally come together. With that in mind, it is my humble pleasure to present this latest novel to you. And as always-I hope you enjoy the story!

Tom

CHAPTER 1

THE GIFT

Probably the first thing I should clarify is the fact that I have no idea what I'm doing. I'm not a writer by any stretch of the imagination, and I have no ambition whatsoever of attempting to create the next great American novel. I'm just a man with an incredible story that needs telling. And that leads me to the second thing I need to clarify before we get started- this story is complicated. Believe me, I wish it was something I could share over dinner and a bottle of wine, but it is way too big for that. And, well, it's just complicated.

To begin, I'm going to have to set up the story and that will require I talk about myself, which is one of my least favorite things to do. I'm not only average, but if you lined up all the average people in this world, and then created some formula to determine the average of the average, I'd be that guy right smack dab in the middle. I figure if you understand just how middle-of-the-road I am, it will help explain why I reacted the way I did to some of the things I'm going to tell you about.

But don't get me wrong, I'm not a necessarily boring person either. On the contrary, it seems as much as I've tried to avoid it, my life has been one soap opera after another ever since I graduated from college.

I would have to say the one thing that keeps me anchored in my averageness, is that I'll do almost anything to avoid unnecessarily stressful situations. It has nothing to do with an inability to handle stress. I'm actually pretty good at that. My problem is I don't feel a sense of relief when it's over like most other people do. I feel more like some of my life has been sucked out of me. It's strange I know, but that's just the way I am.

Physically, I'm a forty-year-old, white, relatively healthy male. I stand six feet tall, weigh anywhere between 190 and 200 pounds-depending on if it's right before Thanksgiving or right after Christmas-and I'm lucky to still have a nice full head of brown hair. Science says I can thank my mother's side of the family for that so...thanks, Mom. I won't make a very handsome bald man, that's for sure.

I may wear a tie to work five days a week, but if you ever found me in anything other than a pair of jeans and a simple cotton shirt during the weekend, something way out of the ordinary would be going on. I'm sure there are some people who think I only have one pair of pants and two or three casual shirts. The truth is, my closet and dresser are stuffed, there's just not much variety in there. If I find a shirt I like that fits me well, I tend to buy three or four and don't feel compelled to buy a bunch of different colors. Blue or white is generally fine. I like to think my style is kind of ageless.

I live in an old, olive-drab craftsman-style home on a street overlooking Puget Sound in Seattle, Washington. I ended up here when my roommate at Cal struck gold with a couple of other guys from school. They created some software technology it turns out works pretty well in cellular phones. You talk about being in the right place at the right time. I knew those geeks were going to either hit the mother lode one day, or end up spending their lives in their parents' garages, smoking dope and playing video games.

The day the Japanese came calling with buckets of money, my friends needed someone they already trusted who knew something about numbers. I majored in accounting and had just started regretting it when my phone rang. Thank God I was nice to those guys when we were in school. They told me they were being offered a king's ransom for their software and the two pending patent rights that went along with it, and they were legitimately afraid of making a really bad decision. Luckily for all of us, I got in their ears before they signed anything.

I scolded them, "You guys aren't even thirty yet, and you're going to cash-out and retire already? Do you have any idea what this is going to cost you in taxes? With this kind of money you're going to spend the rest of your lives with investment bankers, stock brokers, and guys like me doing everything they can to get a piece of you. And knowing you guys, you'll all go broke before you have your first gray hair!"

I then showed them how much they could make if they formed their own company and simply leased their technology to one of the big shots instead of selling out to them. We called in a couple lawyers, and they set up a deal with an American billionaire software executive, who I won't mention by name, but will confess he was about our same age.

The next thing we knew, it was raining money. But even better, those knuckleheads still had a job to go to where they could play on their computers and figure out new and exciting ways to make even more money, which they did.

After their first contract was signed, the guys took me out to dinner and offered me a position as their Chief Financial Officer. I wasn't even two years out of school, I had just gotten married, and the most complex accounting I'd done at that point was help a wealthy old woman unravel some estate tax complications after her husband died. How the hell was I going to oversee the finances of a brand new multi-million dollar company that was founded by a bunch of kids whose greatest interests were comic book collecting, and debating which was the best Star Trek movie so far? I remember distinctly those exact thoughts floating in my head when my old roommate, Dickey Schaefer, handed me a slip of paper and said, "Maybe this will help you make up your mind."

My initial reaction at seeing a check in my name for two hundred fifty thousand dollars was to look around the restaurant and see if I was being pranked. I was sure a film crew would be appearing any moment to record the big gag at my expense. But I was wrong. Dick told me the first hundred thousand was for the work I'd already done, which was basically offering some old college friends a little advice, and sitting next to them during a couple negotiations and meetings with lawyers. The second hundred fifty thousand was my first year bonus in advance, to help pay for my relocation to Seattle.

"Why Seattle?" It was a question, but my tone was much more a condemnation of those guys making another questionable decision.

They took turns bombarding me with some surprisingly well thought out reasons for moving up the coast. I was actually surprised. Their ability to come together and make a sound business decision

4

without having someone else step in to hold their hands impressed me. *Maybe this actually will work out,* I thought.

The only other stipulation of the job offer, was that I couldn't call my old roommate "Dick" or "Dickey" anymore. His real name was Richard and, with his newfound wealth and respectable position in the world of computer technology development, he thought his real name was more dignified than the A.K.A. his parents had actually given him as a child. I looked at the other young entrepreneurs seated at the table and asked, "Seriously?"

One of the other guys answered, "Can you at least try? We're all doing it."

"Dickey," I growled with a scowl on my face. "There's no way in hell I'm going to be able to do that, and you know it. In front of other people, I can probably manage to call you Dick, or maybe with a few years of practice even Rick. But me being able to remember to call you Richard isn't gonna happen. C'mon, man."

Dickey shook his head in contemplation for a few moments and then professed, "Well, I gave it a shot."

We all laughed and when we settled back down I asked a few more questions about the offer and imagined what the future might entail. Even if this new venture tanked after a few years, I wouldn't be any worse off than I was now. And this new job would allow me to put some money away that I could use to start my own CPA practice, which was what I thought I wanted in the long run anyway. Yep, it just felt right.

I said, "Okay, let's do it!" and we all stood and shook hands like real businessmen do.

Then we all got drunk on the nastiest tasting, yet most expensive champagne in the house, like stupid young men with too much money do. Other than the day of my wedding and the day my kid was born, that could have been third on the list of the greatest days of my life. Instead it made my life very complicated, and like I said before, I'm not really wired for that kind of stuff.

As far as what I do professionally, I still work for those guys and we do make an awful lot of money- I'm almost embarrassed to say. Only one of the four founding partners landed himself a bona fide gold-digger, and spends his money like there's no tomorrow. The rest of us are just normal guys living in normal neighborhoods, driving regular cars, and have the same old problems everyone else has. Of course these days a big chunk of what I make goes to my now ex-wife.

Today, it's just me and my deaf chocolate Labrador retriever, Roger, who happens to be sitting beside me as we speak. He will undoubtedly be my sounding board and occasional distraction throughout the writing of this story. It's important to introduce you to Roger because he really is my best friend. The old guy was with me during some pretty dark days a few years ago, and he was always there to climb up next to me and let me know that at least *he* still loved me. That's kind of a sappy thing to admit to for a grown man, I guess. A few months ago I wouldn't mention it, but Roger and I have changed a little bit since then.

I always had dogs growing up and I got really attached to all of them. But Roger and I are especially close because I think he knows I basically saved him. This young dumbass at work bought him as a puppy expecting he would make a good guard dog. Clearly being deaf was going to be a problem, so this moron, after raising Roger for a year, decided to get rid of him. I'm not sure how much effort he put into finding Roger a new home, but he posted a flyer in the office break room that said he was going to drop him off at the pound if no one wanted him.

My daughter, who was three at the time, was getting into stuffed animals so I thought I could bump it up a notch and bring home the real deal. And to tell you the truth, I was ready to have another dog in my life. So I told the idiot, who no longer works for us by the way, to bring Roger in and I'd take a look at him.

I'd never had a Lab before, but everyone said they were great dogs and good with kids. That was certainly a big consideration, but what sold me on old Rog was the way he basically trotted up to my desk and picked me. I swear to God he sat down and handed me his paw without anyone saying a word. After spending some time bonding in my office, I decided to take a chance and I took him home to the family. As fate would have it, and in the spirit of no good deed goes unpunished, that decision resulted in me learning that not all surprises, regardless of intentions, are welcomed surprises. My darling spouse was furious!

Roger was nothing but a lean ball of energy at that age, and boy he did about everything he could to piss off my wife within the first couple hours of having him home. Even I was thinking I'd made a horrible mistake. I spent that first night on the computer researching Labrador retrievers and how to train them. At some point it became clear that I needed to fix him if I wanted to reduce some of his testosterone-driven energy.

I wasn't anticipating breeding him or anything, so I made an appointment and had his 'man-parts' removed the first weekend we had him. I'll never forget the forlorn look on his face when I got him back home. I have no idea if he thought maybe he'd done something wrong, was just in pain, or maybe it was the medication the vet put him on, but the poor guy had the saddest look in his eyes. Being the other man in the house, I shared some of his despair and spent the next few days sitting next to him, gently stroking his head and telling him he was a good boy. I think he never forgot that.

When my marriage went south and we moved out, he repaid the favor over and over again, snuggling up to me and letting me know I still had him to come home to. Sure, if anyone breaks into our house and ransacks the place he'll sleep right through it, but he's still a great dog. Without question he's my best friend.

So about a year ago, October 18th to be exact, I came home from work, got the mail, and was met by Roger at the front door. Of course he didn't hear me. He just knows about the time I come home every night and more importantly to him, that's his dinner time. It was my birthday, so I had an idea the package leaning against the wall next to the front door was probably a gift. I was also pretty sure it was from my parents.

I'm not a terribly emotional person. Actually, when people get emotional around me it tends to make me uncomfortable. When someone starts crying about something for instance, no matter if it's for a good reason or they're sad, my first instinct is to look around and find an escape route nearby. I just don't like that stuff. If someone is legitimately injured or seriously needs assistance, then I won't hesitate to help, but just crying...nope, not for me.

I think the reason I got married when I did was because that was the first time I really felt emotional about someone. It was such a strange and overwhelming feeling, I thought, *Ah ha! So this is what love is.* I'd had girlfriends before I got married and even some decent relationships, but I'd never met a girl I thought I couldn't live without. As best as I can recall, the day I decided to ask my ex to marry me, was the day I realized she was the most important thing in my life. For a guy like me, that was a very big deal.

Anyway, the only other people I ever really cared about are my parents. They are truly the best and they just keep getting better with age. My mom has always been a great mom- steady as a rock. She was always around to straighten me out, but also allowed me to learn things the hard way when I needed to. There was never a day when I didn't think I was the most important thing in the world to her, even when I was really mad at her. My dad was a former military man, kind of a manly man if you know what I mean. He liked guns and football, and my mother actually allowed him to have a Playboy Magazine subscription for a few years, which pretty much made me the most popular kid in school when I was able to prove it to my friends.

One of the greatest things about my dad is that he evolved with me. Unlike my mom, who was the same nurturing mother all the time, my father would teach me things and treat me differently as I matured. There was nothing else in my life that stood out more clearly as a gauge of my growing up, than my dad either teaching me how to do something, or just hanging out with me. Sure, he whooped me a couple times and there were plenty of restrictions and stern warnings about misbehavior, but I always deserved it and knew it. I can remember sitting in my room after getting in trouble and thinking, *Man, I hope my dad still likes me.*

It was important to him that I understand the values of respect and character. To my dad, my occasional lack of both was always the root of my trouble-making. No matter what I did, he would always bring it up when he was dispensing some form of discipline. He'd lay into me about the specifics of what I had done wrong, and then he would soften up and start talking about my lack of judgment and character and how, at the end of the day, it reflected on the entire family. Boy, did that always make me feel horrible. I don't recall ever a time getting punished for something and not feeling like I'd disgraced my entire family. It takes a special kind of parent to be able to punish their kid and get them to truly feel bad about what they've done.

As much as I credit my father for the way he raised me, I have to say he's also probably the reason I'm not a very touchy-feely kind of person. He certainly isn't. I don't recall ever telling him I loved him until a certain point during my rather ugly divorce when my parents were really helping me out, and I finally realized how important they were to me. I was leaving their house in Palm Desert, California, and I was about as emotionally exhausted as I'd ever been, and I just kind of blurted out, "I really love you guys."

My mom answered, "We love you too, honey," but my dad was awkwardly speechless. I remember thinking about his reaction on the drive home, and how I'd grown up to be just like him. He loved me to death and spent his whole life proving it. He just couldn't say it. I guess it was more important that I was the one who actually said it first, because I'd never been able to show him how much he meant to me.

I mentioned earlier that I assumed the package left at my door was from my parents because it was my birthday and they always sent a gift of some kind. My father had fairly limited input in the gifts, which was always obvious. On the rare occasion when he did involve himself with the gift selection, he would call with a detailed explanation why he thought I could use whatever it was he sent me, as if I may need convincing I really needed whatever it was.

Up to that point, the neatest gift they'd ever given me was when I turned eighteen, and my parents gave me a plaster statue of Auguste Rodin's *The Thinker*. I didn't know who Rodin was, but I did recognize the naked man sitting on a large rock was a replica of a famous statue located somewhere in Europe. My Thinker was made of heavy plaster painted bronze, stood about a foot tall, and weighed a good ten pounds. I don't remember many birthday gifts I've received throughout my life, but I'll never forget my Thinker statue.

I cherished it immediately because I thought of the statue as the kind of gift you would only give to another adult. After all it was a naked guy sitting on a rock thinking, for Christ sakes. Who would give something like that to an immature kid for their birthday? With that in mind, I interpreted my Thinker as recognition by my parents that I had crossed the threshold into being a fully fledged adult, and now my thoughts and ideas mattered. I was there. I'd kicked through the double-doors of manhood as dramatically as sliding into home plate for the winning run in a World Series game number seven. Of course that isn't the way the world works, but when you've just turned eighteen, you sure think that's the way it does.

I still have my Rodin statue. It followed me to college at U.C. Berkeley, and sat on the desk in my tiny dorm room looking down over my homework with me, as if he were as engrossed in my studies as I was. And when it was time to put the books aside, there were many evenings when Dickey and I would fire up a trippy purple lava lamp he brought from home, and then we would share a few hits of marijuana from a bong we'd purchased at a nearby head shop our second day together as freshman roomies. Future millionaire Richard Schaefer would then place headphones over his ears and privately escape to the sounds of Pink Floyd or his favorite Rush CD, while I'd lie on my bed in silence and stare at The Thinker...and think.

I never actually asked my parents why they bought me that statue. After a few years of philosophizing about it, I'd pretty much convinced myself my parents thought it represented my becoming a mature adult. And even maybe to some degree, recognition of my potential to become quite intellectual. I was a smart kid growing up and I did ask a lot of questions. The difference between me and most other kids was that my questions weren't about things like, "Why is the sky blue," or "How do birds fly?" My questions were more along the lines of, "How come we keep getting in wars with people who aren't actually attacking us first?"

My dad liked talking about that kind of stuff with me, and we almost always agreed on his point of view. Back then, I truly believed he knew just about everything and I trusted him. The older I got, the more he allowed me to come to my own conclusions about some of the deep subjects we used to talk about. He would ask me what I thought about something going on in the world of politics, and even though there were times I sensed he disagreed with me, he wouldn't say it because he wanted me to think my opinions mattered. At least that's what I believe he was doing.

By the time my Thinker arrived, I was convinced I was on my way to becoming a fairly intelligent man myself, and the statue was my parents', my father specifically, acknowledgment of the same. How disappointing would it be to learn otherwise? If I found out the gift was nothing more than a last minute grab from a clearance item shelf at K-Mart, that would have been very disappointing...more like devastating. Anyway, that's a little history of my parents and their gift-giving. As far as that Thinker statue goes, it's on my desk now, just to my right, totally engrossed in watching me try to tell this story.

When I was somewhere between eighteen and nineteen was also right about the time in my life when I decided it isn't always best to know everything. I didn't have a traumatic childhood, or experience some life-altering event that scarred me. It had a lot more to do with the fact that every time I started having problems in school, it was the result of distractions that had nothing to do with my studies. It just seemed to me there are some things I'm much more comfortable not knowing about because the second I know about them, I have to care about them. I'm still very much of that opinion.

When I was married it seems like all my wife and I did was sit around and find ways to make our life together more complicated. It was like we were unknowingly possessed with the idea that we had to create a mountain of stuff we had to care about. I finally cracked when I realized that if you're healthy and have a decent job, why stress yourself about things that don't really matter? I just don't get it. Unfortunately, people like me really irritate those who thrive on having drama in their lives. When my former spouse woke up in the morning, I swear her first thought had to be, *How can I make something difficult and complicated today?* At first it was cute because she was cute. Later, it wasn't so much.

Anyway, so there I was a newly minted forty-year-old with a UPS package from my parents delivered to my door. I set the plain box and a handful of junk mail down on the coffee table, and gave Roger a quick ear massage and pat on the head to subdue his almost hysterical display of relief that I had returned home. He then followed me into the kitchen where I asked how his day went while I prepared a can of food for him. As he devoured his dinner, I returned to the living room and plopped down on the couch to open my package.

I had a suspicion the gift was a photograph. The box was shaped like the kind that would contain a large frame and the weight was about right. During the last visit to my parents' retirement home in the desert I'd suggested they take a new professional studio picture, because the last one they'd taken was way back in the day when we still drove station wagons. I never liked that old picture. My mother was wearing an awful yellow blouse with a big bow on the front of it. And my dad, with his desperately thinning ear-to-ear comb-over, was wearing a smirk on his face that said, "I've got a hundred places I'd rather be right now."

To me, the people in that old photograph looked nothing like my parents today. Both were wearing seriously unfashionable eyewear in the old photo. Lasik surgeries had since taken care of their poor eyesight so no more glasses. As for my dad, he'd since lost the rest of his hair, and actually was a more handsome man without it.

It wasn't hard to convince my mother it was time for a new picture. My father seemed indifferent to the idea. Based on that and the weight and size of the package, I was pretty sure my birthday gift was an updated studio photograph of my parents, and that was cool with me. The old one really needed to go.

Once the wrapping paper was torn away and the tape was ripped from the sides of the box, I carefully opened the package to see what it contained. Pushing aside some pieces of shredded newspaper, it was clear it wasn't a framed photo at all. It was a white vinyl notebook with a cover sheet that read: *The Genealogy of John Sexton IV.* That's me, by the way.

I flipped through the pages and studied the different chapter titles in amazement. It didn't take long to realize it was an incredibly detailed compilation of formal documents, graphs and charts, and even copies of handwritten letters, all detailing what at first appeared to be my entire family history going all the way back to the middle ages. *Wow!* I thought to myself. "Roger, come check this out!"

The dog didn't hear me, but he knows what I mean when I wave him over and pat the space on the couch next to me. He gladly leaped up to my side and snuggled against my thigh, completely unaware he was no longer a puppy and every time he jumps up next to me he damn near knocks me over. We then took a closer look together.

I didn't know a whole lot about my family tree beyond the days of my already deceased grandparents. I never spent any time growing up with the few cousins and aunts and uncles that I had, so I rarely gave any thought to my family history. It just wasn't important to me. As far as I knew, I was simply the end result of a hodgepodge of various East and Western European inbreeding, and at some point a distant relative immigrated to the United States. By the time I came along, I felt like I was just another non-distinct white American male.

The only time I specifically recall my ethnic heritage being mentioned within the family, was after I got kicked out of school for a few days for fighting. I was in the 7th grade, and I got in a fight with another kid after he hit me in the face with a dodge-ball, the velocity of which I took particular offense to. My dad was the one who showed up to take me home from the principal's office and man, was I terrified of what was coming next. Much to my shock and disbelief, he chatted briefly behind closed doors with the principal and then escorted me to the car. There, he calmly provided me the opportunity to explain myself and then made a comment like, "That other kid probably won't be throwing any more balls at your head again, will he."

That was it. No lecture, no guilt, no punishment, nothing. We didn't even talk about it anymore. When we got home I remember sitting in my room trying to figure out how the hell I'd escaped the wrath of my father's anger, when I heard my dad tell my mom, "I guess that was just the Scots-Irish in him."

I went straight to the encyclopedia and looked it up. Sure enough there it was- an absolutely clear as day explanation for my instinctive rage and merciless attack on another who had first shown violence against me. For the next few days I was standing a little taller, for I was Scots-Irish dammit, and my people were not the kind to mess with. Kicking ass was in our blood. It was in *my* blood.

A few days later, I confessed to my father that I heard him make the comment about there being Scots-Irish in me. I can't tell you how disappointed I was to learn it was only a small fraction of my lineage, and the rest of me was made up of so many different and uncon-firmed nationalities, it was probably best to just think of myself as an American and be really proud of it. After that, I never cared to try and break down my ethnic bloodline into fractions. Did it really make any difference if I was one-eighth German or one-sixteenth Irish?

I knew my parents would wait until I'd had time to eat and settle in for the evening before they called to wish me a Happy Birthday. But I realized there would be a lengthy discussion about this particu-lar birthday gift, so I decided to not wait and gave them a call instead.

My mother answered the phone, "Well, hello there, Birthday Boy!"

Unless I was standing in front of her and she could actually see I was a grown man, I was convinced my mother always pictured me as her little twelve-year-old.

She continued, "Your father is right here. I'm going to put him on speaker phone."

My father's voice then came over the line, "Hello Johnny. Happy Birthday."

"Thanks, you guys," I answered. "Hey, I opened the package you sent me and, wow, this is pretty cool. I just briefly flipped through it and... this is some really detailed stuff. How'd you put this thing together?"

Now here's the thing with my dad. When he was a younger man and while I was growing up, everything he said had a specific purpose. If he asked you a question, all he wanted was short specific facts. He didn't want to hear about the weather or your feelings. He just wanted you to get to the point. And when he had a comment or something to say, it was just the same. Everything was brief, deliberate, and had already been processed through a filter in his head of what was actually worth saying, and what was just superfluous fluff. As some might say, "He weren't no talker."

But that all changed when he retired and decided the rest of his life should be spent commenting on current events, and reflecting on those lessons he's learned during his life that he thinks are worthy of sharing with others. It doesn't make any difference who you are, if you give my dad the opportunity, he is going to talk your ear off.

At first I really enjoyed listening to my father talk about his days growing up in the Midwest. And it was particularly interesting to hear some of his Vietnam stories that weren't appropriate for my ears when I was younger. When he retired, and once I became a man, I liked sitting down for a nice long chat with him when we got together. But now, just about every conversation is a rerun, and they aren't nearly as interesting the second and third time around.

To avoid what was becoming painfully long story-telling, I figured out the best way to prevent becoming trapped in my father's audience is to be cautious about what you actually ask him in the first place. For instance, it's safe to ask my dad why he went to the store, because there are few pearls of wisdom he can interject into why he needed to go get fresh batteries for the TV remote. Ask him what he thinks about gun control, or ask him why he chose the Army instead of the Navy or Marines, then you better have a comfortable seat, because getting to that answer might take all afternoon and continue through supper. But when it came to my birthday present, I truly wanted all the details. Whose idea was it? How'd you do it? How long did this take?

Well, I tell you what, I don't know if there was ever a birthday my father enjoyed more than my fortieth, and that includes his own birthdays. After allowing my mother to share about five minutes with me to discuss a general idea of what they'd done, my father then spent the next two hours going through the entire notebook cover to cover. Long after my mother had gone to bed, he was still on the phone synopsizing every page, pointing out noteworthy relatives, and telling me stories about how he and my mother came upon the information.

The basic idea was that a few years earlier, my parents had begun passing their retirement hours surfing the internet, which was a habit they developed during the summer months when constant hundred degree temperatures made it impossible to go out and play golf, or want to do anything really. It was at some point during one of those hot lazy days of having already seen all the recent releases at the local movie theatre, and having nothing else to do, that they stumbled onto a website that assisted people in tracing their family bloodlines. For a small fee, my mother made some initial half-hearted enquiries and soon became obsessed with investigating her lineage. My dad, a man who loved American history, also joined the project, lending historic perspective to the time periods my mom was targeting. Eventually, they were networking with several different genealogy organizations and accumulating data that compelled them to go beyond the e-mails and the relatively vague information they were accessing online.

I was relieved when my parents decided to start doing some extra traveling a few years ago. I was afraid they were becoming too sedentary in their lifestyle, and I knew sitting around all day doing nothing was going to accelerate their aging. I had no idea those trips all over the country were actually fact-finding missions. I just thought they were trying to get their money's worth out of their RV. But like a couple of old gumshoes, they were off investigating leads to possible family ties to our ancestors, with hopes that some unknown distant relatives might be discovered.

Their secret project took two years to complete, and the final result was an amazingly thorough documentation of my genealogy. There were charts, handwritten stories from distant relatives, copies of archived newspaper clippings, and even official legal documents, all assembled into kind of a doctorate-level thesis confirming who I am.

Before that night, I was happy just being an American. It's not that I didn't care about my heritage. I was just totally satisfied with who I'd become. If I was a full-blooded Irishman, did it really matter?

I could drink green beer on St. Patrick's Day with all the other drunks, and be part of the in-crowd for that one day once a year. Big deal. If I was German, I could do the same during Oktoberfest. And if I was Italian, I don't know..., but I *would* know if I was Italian. That sort of thing just didn't matter to me.

But what I discovered, while looking through the notebook for the first time, was that it wasn't necessarily where my ancestors were from that made a difference to me. It was learning who they were. Time and place, and what they must have lived through fascinated me. I instantly cared about them and wanted to learn more.

After I got off the phone with my dad I spent a few moments selecting a nice bottle of wine from my small collection, and then insured Roger I'd be back in a couple of hours. It was my birthday after all, so I decided to treat myself to a quiet dinner alone where I could relax and read through my gift with a couple glasses of wine, and maybe a big steak.

It was raining outside, which is one of the few things that still really bugs me about Seattle. When it's dry, I usually just walk the two blocks to my favorite little neighborhood restaurant. But when it's raining, and it was really coming down, I take the car and simply coast my way down the hill in neutral. It's that close.

I walked in and was seated at my regular table. It has the best light and you're mostly away from the noise where larger groups are seated. I've been going to the same place a few times a week since I moved into the neighborhood, so the restaurant staff knows me well. Even when they're busy, they keep a couple of tables open for regulars to make sure we don't have to wait. My favorite table is one of them. If you're not a regular at the restaurant, you might think I'm some kind of VIP the way I get to skip past those who are waiting and get escorted to a special table. That's one of the benefits of being a loyal customer so I don't feel bad. I also tip really well. I waited tables for a while in college and know how difficult that job can be.

The menu has something for everyone, so I guess you'd call it American cuisine. I have a couple favorites, but I mostly order something that pairs well with the bottle of wine I bring with me. That's another reason why I like the restaurant. They don't charge me a corkage fee when I bring my own bottle. It's not like I can't afford a few bucks to pay for someone else to open my wine, but charging me more than a buck or two to do it just seems kind of shady.

I ordered a medium rib-eye steak with extra broccoli instead of the giant baked potato that normally comes with it. I'm not a big eater, and oversized baked potatoes are the worst for people like me. Here's a little weirdness of mine I'll admit to. I rarely finish what's on my plate and always have my leftovers boxed up to take home, even though I almost never eat it later. I do it because I feel like, if I was a chef and customers weren't finishing the meals I prepared for them, I'd be a little insulted and wonder why.

I also feel guilty about throwing away good food when other people consider it a treat just to be able to take their family out once a month for pancakes at Denny's. So what do I do? I take my leftovers home with me so anyone paying attention doesn't think I'm ungrateful. Or that I'm some wealthy asshole who thinks it's impressive to walk into a restaurant with my own wine and then only take a few bites of my food because it isn't good enough for my royal palate. That's really the root of my problem, which is actually probably a phobia of some kind. I subconsciously feel guilty about the amount of money I make.

It probably wouldn't be a big deal if I worked really hard and made some great life sacrifices to get it, but I didn't. All I did was be lucky enough to have college friends who turned out to be technological geniuses. And I just happened to be the only guy they knew who spoke in 'Dude,' and also happened to understand the Federal Tax Code.

Now I know what you're thinking- *Poor little rich boy has too much money. Woe is me.* Well hold on a minute because it's much more complicated than that. First of all, I don't have millions of dollars. Second of all, here's how it affects me. When I enrolled in college, we weren't at war. The economy was wide open and there was no big crisis going on that compelled me to join the military, or Peace Corp, or some other kind of public service career. There certainly was no shortage of cops and teachers, that's for sure.

Fast forward six or seven years, and I'm still making ridiculous amounts of money sitting safely behind a desk in Seattle, but now the economy is in the gutter and Americans my same age and younger are dying in Iraq and Afghanistan. When the Sunday paper started printing short bios of all the soldiers killed during the previous week my heart ached, and I felt tremendously guilty about what I had. Suddenly my prosperity became a curse, and in one way or another, it seems like it's been that way ever since.

I tried to appease my guilt by getting involved in some philanthropy. That's when I learned how important our money was to my wife. You see, it killed me to have so much, but it killed her to see me give any of it away. Eventually, she figured out the only way to keep all that cash would be to trade me in for a new model, yet have a judge order me to put her on my payroll. It's amazing how divorce works. I'm not bitter and never really was, if you can believe that. I think I went from absolute shock to...I don't know...I guess you could call it being emotionally numb. That's all over with, though.

I had a nice quiet dinner while reading the material in my genealogy notebook. After a slice of chocolate cake for dessert, I told my waitress I was going to hang around and keep reading for a while if she didn't mind. You could seat four customers at my table so I asked her what the typical bill was for a party that size. When she told me, I calculated what their tip would be and added it to my bill. I also paid it with cash so her tip wouldn't be taxed, as long as she was smart enough not to claim it. I didn't want her to lose money just because I wanted to stick around and hog up her table.

The owner came by once and asked me how dinner was and I shared a glass of wine with him. I say 'share', but he recognized I was busy so he took his glass back to the kitchen. The next thing I knew it was closing time. I asked for a large black coffee to go and then drove home.

Reading in bed puts me to sleep within an hour, no matter how interested I am in whatever I'm reading. Smoking pot in college used to really knock me out, but I quit smoking that stuff when I got married. I never liked the idea of taking pills to relax and never really could develop a taste for hard liquor. So when I started having some problems with insomnia a few years ago, I started to read before bedtime. My problem on this particular night was it was already past my bedtime, and I was good and drowsy from polishing off that bottle of wine almost all by myself. But I didn't want to go to bed yet. I hoped the large take-out coffee I brought home would help me keep my eyes open for just a little while longer before I passed out. Thankfully, that turned out to not be a problem.

I got home and unintentionally snuck up on Roger who was fast asleep on the couch where I left him. I am really afraid I'm going to give him a heart attack one day. Even when I make every effort not to scare the old guy, it's sometimes impossible if he doesn't happen to be looking in my direction when I walk up to him. Once again he was startled, but I quickly comforted him with an ear rub, and then sent him to the kitchen where he happily sauntered off with a big chunk of leftover rib-eye in his mouth.

I turned on every light in the living room to help keep me awake and put on some soft background music. I then sat down on the couch and opened the vinyl binder again. Just as I was getting back into a nice pace of reading, Roger came back and joined me on the couch. I put my arm around him and told him, "Rog, my friend, I think this changes everything."

The deeper I got into the tales of my ancestry, the greater my anticipation became to learn more. Hours passed, and I was still eagerly flipping each page like a desperate explorer who knew he had finally discovered the map that would direct him to some great discovery. The difference was that I already knew where this map was leading- it was leading right back to me. In this case, it was the pathway itself that was my discovery. And the more I read about my ancestors' travails and accomplishments, and studied their faces in the photographs, the more I became fascinated with them.

It turned out my mother's family had been much more successfully traced than my dad's. On my mother's side, I had been raised to believe I was mostly of English descent, but never had I imagined that a 17th century grandfather had actually been a knight. His name was Sir William Franklin, and he wasn't just some rich guy who was knighted because he threw great parties. He was a fighter who made quite a name for himself during the First English Civil War. Unfortunately, he was killed in battle during the Second English Civil War just a few years later.

From there, unfamiliar names with modest titles filled the branches of the family tree until they began to migrate to America in the early 1700s. That was also about the time my father's side of the family began to appear.

I was proud to learn an ancestor had fought and died during the Revolutionary War. And I was just as fascinated to learn that another had been jailed for refusing to pay taxes to Britain on his Virginia tobacco harvest. There were also several men in my family who fought during the American Civil War on both sides. One died during the Battle of Shiloh, and two were killed at Antietam. But all were not so patriotic.

Halfway through the notebook, I learned that probably my most famous ancestor was a great-great-uncle who was a rather ruthless outlaw cowboy in Arizona. A photocopy of a newspaper article explained how he was recognized while riding east through New Mexico, and was gunned down by a posse of Federal Marshals trying to take him into custody. My parents copied several pages from books where he was mentioned and they all portrayed him as quite an ornery character. Probably the coolest thing they found, though it wasn't much to be proud of a few generations ago, was a copy of a Wanted Dead or Alive poster with my renegade uncle's picture on it. I have to admit, he did look like a scumbag.

The rest of my family consisted of fairly unremarkable people for their day and age. For every man who joined the military and served the country in times of war, there were others who made a living selling moonshine whiskey, or involved themselves in some other unscrupulous activity. I wasn't bothered with the knowledge of the ancestor or two who had blemished the family name. As far as I was concerned, once a few generations passed, those questionable characters actually added a little flavor to one's gene pool, especially someone with a name like Jackson "Mad Jack" Noonan, the Arizona bank robber from my mother's side of the family.

Every page and chapter was a new revelation to me, and the supporting documents and photographs were almost unbelievable. But what wasn't a surprise was that everything supported the little I already knew of my heritage. I was basically the result of a blending of various Europeans who were all as white as snow except for one. And that single exception which I am first revealing to you now, stood out as one of our great family mysteries.

I relished playing the role of Indian as a child when my friends mostly preferred to be cowboys. Back then, reruns of old TV westerns were as common as crime dramas and reality shows are today. When I was a little kid, you didn't get home after school and plug in a video game. We sat in front of the television with an afternoon snack prepared by our mothers, and watched old reruns of Gunsmoke and The Lone Ranger. And when we played outside, we strapped on our cap guns and reenacted what we'd just watched on TV. When it came to choosing sides, I proudly assumed the role of Indian Brave because I was, in fact, part Native American.

I never cared to ask how this came to be. As I grew older and games of Cowboys and Indians grew less frequent, it became clearer just how far removed from being a real Indian I actually was. Much to my disappointment, the question of my Indian ancestry wasn't clarified in the otherwise thorough supporting documents in my genealogy notebook.

What I did discover, as had my parents after months of frustrating research, was that the main branch of my dad's side of the family tree began abruptly in Indiana in the 1800s. My father added a note to the first page of that chapter, stating my parents were unable to ever locate any census records or related documents to confirm actual birth dates, or places of residence for the first Sextons, which is, again, my last name. There had only been family stories passed on from generation to generation until, finally, names and places could be confirmed by birth and death certificates, or other miscellaneous government documents.

The family's conclusion, according to my parents' research, was that an early member of the family-the first John Sexton- had simply made up a new name for himself when he arrived in the United States. It was assumed that ancestor, whoever he really was, probably had run into a problem with the law back home, was escaping some kind of debt, or could have even been an AWOL soldier and had covered his tracks by simply changing his name. But when he wiped his slate clean, he'd inadvertently erased an entire family history up to that point.

The other significant problem my parents found in researching the history of the Sexton name, was that the woman the original John married was supposedly a Choctaw Indian. That was the point where a supposed Native American bloodline was introduced into my direct chain of descendants. How the first John Sexton managed to find his Indian bride was now anyone's guess.

As I continued reading and arrived in the twentieth century, I began to recognize the names and was familiar with a few of the stories. They were of the ancestors I did know about, and eventually those who had lived during my lifetime. I learned that my grandfather, John Sexton III, supported his brother's family and his in-laws during the Great Depression, all on a Texas oil driller's paycheck. I'd never known that before. I also had never heard that he was brought back from near certain death after a car crash in 1937. His lingering injuries were the reason he was unable to join the armed forces during the Second World War. I'd always wondered why he stayed at home while so many others joined that fight. It turned out he actually tried, but no one would take him.

The next thing I knew, it was after 3 a.m., and my eyes were burning so badly I couldn't continue. I put the notebook on the coffee table, rubbed the pain from my eyes, then leaned back into the couch and tried to take it all in.

I suddenly felt guilty for not doing anything with my life. So many in my past had endured truly significant struggles and had overcome them. So many had participated in selfless sacrifice and were rewarded with nothing more than dignity. Not a single one had accumulated great wealth, and no one other than a criminal had achieved notoriety beyond their doorstep. But in every generation, someone had left their mark on history in one way or another. It was my time now and I was pissing it away.

The next morning I stumbled into work late and half asleep, yet feeling pretty good. I called my parents as soon as I knew they were up and moving around, and thanked them again for the wonderful birthday gift. I also had a new list of questions that I anxiously needed answered, particularly about my original namesake, John Sexton I.

I could tell my father was thrilled that I was so interested in their project. Unfortunately, he repeated the same conclusion that he had written in the notebook. They had simply hit a wall in their investigation of the first John Sexton, and it was almost certain too much time had passed to find anyone still alive who might know something about him. The search to find his name on a document had also been exhausted. As far as my dad was concerned, there was nothing left to conclude other than the hypothesis that my namesake was most likely a man who had given himself a new identity. If that were the case, and my parents were both sure it was, the original John Sexton didn't want to have his history known. So far it looked like he'd done an excellent job of keeping it that way, even in death.

I then asked my dad about my great-great-grandfather's wife, and how far they'd gotten in determining who she was. Did anyone have an idea what her maiden name was? Did Indians even have maiden names back then?

The problem, my dad explained, was that they couldn't find any mention of her first or last name on anything. When she was mentioned, she was only referred to as the *Indian wife* or *The Indian*. It had been difficult enough just to confirm the still somewhat debatable fact that she was Choctaw. I was disappointed to hear that. Here I was an American with supposed Native American roots, and we weren't even sure what tribe my ancestor belonged to.

Everything else about my bloodline seemed straight out of a high school American history textbook. The only thing more perfect would be a confirmation of my Native American ancestry. I shared as much with my parents and they agreed, but they also insisted they had exhausted every avenue of research they could think of. The best they could do was form a conclusion on conjecture alone based on family hearsay and some educated guesswork. In their eyes, the case was now closed.

After the call I logged onto the internet and began to research the Choctaw Indian tribe. A list of several hundred hits appeared on my screen, so I spent the rest of the afternoon browsing through the various websites, ignoring the small stack of work files I was supposed to be reviewing on my desk. The only thing I already knew about the Choctaws was that they were from the southeastern part of the country. I also thought they were one of the tribes the government screwed over and forced onto reservations in Oklahoma back in the 1800s, but maybe I had them confused with Cherokee Indians. I wasn't sure. That shows you how much I knew about Native Americans.

I scribbled some notes on a yellow legal pad as I scanned the web-sites and occasionally printed a page to take home with me. Once I was satisfied I'd made an appropriate appearance of a few hours at work, I packed my notes into my briefcase, bought a couple of deli sandwiches for me and the dog, and raced home to get back to work trying to find out more about my mysterious ancestors.

Again the hours passed unnoticed while I glared into a laptop screen on my kitchen table. My brain absorbed every detail of Choctaw Indian history that I could find. I only paused when it became neces-sary to refill my coffee cup or go to the bathroom. A legal pad was filled and then another before I finally ran out of gas. It was around midnight, and I'd moved to the living room where Roger could sit next to me. My eyes finally betrayed me so I rolled over on the couch to take a break.

The next thing I knew there was daylight streaming through the window and drool was running down the side of my chin. I sat up, wiped the slobber from my face, and scratched my napped hair. It was Friday and going to be a short day anyway, so I cleared my throat and called my secretary. I was glad no one would be in the office to answer the phone for another hour. I'm much more comfortable lying to an answering machine than to a real person. I left a message describing how some bad Chinese food had kept me up all night and it was best I just take the day off. I'm my own boss and do a lot of work from home anyway, so it wasn't a big deal. I only called because I told everyone the day before to make sure and be available for a quick meeting the following afternoon. They would be happy to hear it wasn't going to happen. No one likes my meetings. I'm the boring numbers guy.

I then stripped down to my underwear and climbed into bed for a few more hours of sleep. When I awoke around ten, I ended my shower with a blast of cold water to help wake me up and then got dressed. It was another gloomy day outside, but the weather wasn't having its usual effect on me. I was on a mission and a few gray clouds weren't going to slow me down.

I piled my notes and the vinyl notebook into a leather briefcase that looks more like a saddle bag. I was dressed in loose faded jeans and a blue t-shirt I should have parted with years ago. I probably looked more like a middle-aged perpetual college student than a successful software company CFO. I'll certainly never win any fashion awards.

I stopped off for a late breakfast at another local favorite eatery of mine. It's a tiny place and they close right after their lunch rush. There's a cute waitress there named Janine who clearly believes in flirting her way to better tips. I find it kind of entertaining to watch. She's a good waitress, don't get me wrong. If it works to wear extra perfume and give a little extra smile to the older men dining alone, kudos for figuring that out. I only remember her name because, after I came in a few times, she asked me mine. Now she greets me with a big, "Hello John," so I thought it would only be polite to respond with a, "Hi, Janine." Our social banter rarely goes any further than that. I'm probably almost old enough to be her father.

By chance I was seated at one of Janine's tables. She was able to recite my breakfast order to me from memory- an egg white veggie omelet with tomato slices on the side instead of hash browns, and dry wheat toast. I told her she remembered it perfectly which resulted in one of the waitress's trademark winks. Then she headed off to get me a cup of coffee, while I removed a stack of notes from my briefcase and spread them out in chronological order. As I sat back and refreshed my memory as to what they contained, an idea began to materialize in my head.

Since my parents had done so much work on charting out my heritage, I could pick up the ball and try to uncover the answer to the one mystery they were unable to positively resolve. I mean, I was already kind of starting to get into it anyway. Why not go all the way and really commit myself to finding out who the first John Sexton really was? I was named after him after all, just as two other grandfathers were before me. I was also certainly more computer savvy than my parents, and I was sure I had access to better research material. I might even be able to get some help from someone down on the Berkeley campus if I asked.

I was quickly convinced it was a perfect idea and, to tell you the truth, I hadn't been so excited and motivated to...well, do anything in a long time. If I pulled this thing off, my parents would be beside themselves with pride. And I'd actually be contributing to the family tree, not just occupying a branch of it. I had become a professional bean counter and I knew there wasn't going to be any opportunities to be a hero in my lifetime. There wasn't really even a chance I would accomplish anything, other than handing off a nice inheritance to my daughter when I died. Yep, I was going to do this, and I wasn't going to stop looking until I found my Holy Grail.

I reviewed my notes over breakfast and flipped through the vinyl binder a few more times to figure out where I should start. I got an idea that I should begin with my great-great-grandmother, and not waste a lot of time trying to figure out who her husband was. I figured that if my parents couldn't find my namesake after all of the work they'd done, I probably wasn't going to fair much better. But one thing they had almost completely skipped-over, was making any real effort in identifying his Indian wife.

I then tried to backdate the lives of the three John Sextons before me. By referring to what *was* known about those men, I concluded that my mysterious Indian great-great-grandmother and the first John Sexton had met sometime in the mid-1800s. By referring to my notes about Choctaw history during that time frame, I began to put together a theory of where they might have met. I figured if I were close, there was a chance someone in that area might have some form of information that would help identify both of them. And if that came to fruition, and there was some kind of marriage license or land ownership document that had the name of my great-great-grandmother on it, and her husband was identified on the same document as someone other than John Sexton, then that might prove John Sexton was an alias after all. If that was the case as we suspected, it would reveal my namesake's true identity and I might then be able to trace my father's bloodline even further into history than my mother's. The thought of the whole thing coming together gave me a chill.

I finished breakfast and then went back home to get my laptop before heading off to Seattle's main Central Library. I'd never been there before, but I figured it was as good a place to start as anywhere else. I didn't expect to find much Choctaw Indian information there, but I thought I might get lucky and find some genealogy records or some reference information that might help point me in the right direction.

I was disappointed the library was so modern when I got there. It would have been much more dramatic to begin my quest in one of those classic old municipal echo chamber libraries, with the multiple levels of towering bookshelves, surrounded by row upon row of darkly-stained and scarred oak research tables. Seattle's main library is quite the opposite. A glass-ceilinged architectural wonder I'll admit, but I got the sense I was in an airport instead of a library.

I talked to a young guy at the information desk and told him what I was trying to do. He made some suggestions and told me where I could find the materials he recommended. I then spent the rest of the afternoon pouring over maps, literature, and websites trying to narrow down exactly where I should start. By the end of the day I was fairly convinced I might actually be on to something.

It seemed to me that most of the Choctaw Indians were scattered throughout Mississippi and Alabama during the middle of the 1800's, or they had been forced onto reservations in Oklahoma. Since an Indian reservation just didn't seem a likely place for a white man to find a bride, I thought it more reasonable that my namesake had met his future wife in some southern state where Choctaws were living freely. If that were the case, my great-great-grandfather may have been a wandering outdoorsman, or farmer who associated with the local Indians. Or perhaps he had some other kind of relationship with the free Choctaws who were still in the South.

It also seemed plausible that the first John Sexton may have actually traded for his Choctaw wife. Maybe she decided to marry a white man instead of being forced onto a reservation, and she was possibly just a subservient companion to him. I wasn't so naïve to not consider that might be the case. How would I feel if my great-great-grandmother was basically a concubine slave? Would it change anything? Would it make me less proud of my heritage? Those were questions I didn't want to think about, but I knew they might need to be answered one day.

I decided to start with Mississippi first because it was between Oklahoma and Alabama and, well...I had to start somewhere. I discovered a famous Indian trail, now a large highway called the Natchez Trace Parkway, ran from the southwest corner of the state all the way up through parts of Tennessee. If you looked at the parkway on a map, you could see that if you drew an imaginary line that continued northward at the same angle of the trail, you eventually ended up in Indiana. Since the first certifiable evidence of a John Sexton in our bloodline was records of his property in Indiana, I thought the Natchez Trace was a plausible link between the two locations. I know that's a stretch, but I had nothing else to go on.

On my way out, I joined the library and checked out the maximum number of books the staff would allow. One in particular entitled, The Choctaw Trail of Tears, particularly interested me. Now that I had plenty of reading to do, I was eager to return home and get started without worrying about the library's approaching closing time.

∽

I spent the next two weeks completely preoccupied with learning everything I could about Choctaw Indians. I eventually discovered there was a Choctaw Indian Nation Headquarters in Durant, Oklahoma, and even exchanged a few emails with a nice woman there. She wasn't able to tell me anything about who my great-great-grandmother might be. She did give me the email addresses of some tribe members who were deeply involved in tracing their own Choctaw ancestry. I contacted a couple of them, but they weren't able to do much for me other than confirm general information about the tribe I had learned myself.

With all due respect to the people of the Choctaw Nation- I say that because this is probably a borderline offensive generalization- the following is what I thought I knew going into the third week of my search. The Choctaw people weren't the kind of Indians that ran around in buffalo hides and slept in teepees. As a matter of fact, they were about as far from my vision of a Native American I had, prior to taking on my part of the family genealogy project. By the 1800s, the government considered them a civilized tribe. Many of them spoke English and dressed in the contemporary fashion of the day, which made it even more difficult for me to understand why they were removed from their homes in the southeast to government land in Oklahoma.

After reading the story of their infamous Trail of Tears relocation, not to be confused with a similar relocation by the Cherokees, I'm even more ashamed of what our government did to them, and I can't imagine how my white ancestors allowed it. Even though there was no indication in my family history that any of my white family members had been directly involved, I desperately wanted to learn at least one had tried to stop it. Wouldn't I have? Could I have sat by and tolerated such cruelty? To me it was like the German citizens in the 1940s accepting their government's treatment of Jews. That kind of thing is just unfathomable to me.

Anyway, a few more weeks passed and I found myself at a standstill. I'd go to my office, work hard for two hours, and then spend the rest of the day staring at my Thinker statue, both of us trying to figure out what to do next.

Then one day while staring blankly into my laptop screen, I decided to see if there were any Sextons in Mississippi. I knew there would be, assuming there are Sextons in every state in the country, just as there are Simpsons and Smiths everywhere- doesn't mean they're all related. According to my genealogy chart, none of my family members actually had ties to Mississippi, so I'd been overlooking that angle just as my parents certainly had. I concluded it would probably be the final avenue of research I would investigate. At that point, the project had become frustrating and tiresome, and there had been no progress to fuel even the faintest level of motivation. I decided I would make this one last effort and if it also resulted in a dead end, I was prepared to put the whole matter to rest. At least I could feel confident that I gave it my best shot. If nothing else, the quest had given me something to be excited about. But it turned out, I was only getting started.

The only way I can explain it is that God, or destiny, or karma, or whatever force it is that's in charge of the universe, finally recognized my hard work and effort and decided to cut me a break. Because that last ditch effort was like two giant castle double-doors opening up for me. I had no idea if my answers were hidden somewhere beyond those doors, but I was more than willing to spend a few days going inside and taking a good look around.

It turned out the Sexton name is not only everywhere in Mississippi, but a number of living family members are very serious historians. Letters became e-mails and e-mails became phone calls, and I thought I was really getting somewhere. During the next month, it was like I had my own research team brainstorming with me, desperately trying to find a connection between what they knew and what I didn't. Every theory was tested and discounted, and every name and place was thoroughly investigated until, once again, I finally had to resign myself to the fact that this whole deal was going nowhere. Almost every single Sexton had been accounted for and none were known to have ventured to Indiana. And it was made fairly clear during more than one conversation that the Sextons weren't the kind of people back in the 1800s who would have thought it acceptable to marry a "savage" Indian.

A week after deciding I'd had enough, I received a consolation prize for my months of following the possible family connection to Mississippi. A particular Sexton family still owned a great deal of land in Copiah County, and one of their original plantation homes had become a bed and breakfast. Abigail Sexton, the operator of the inn, had been one of the most helpful to me, and she called to say that she might have discovered something I would be interested in. Though I begged to hear the news over the phone, Abigail promised it was only a theory. Even her own siblings thought it was nonsense, which was not very reassuring.

Still, Abigail thought it was a good lead, so promising in fact that she preferred to share it with me in person. Her explanation was that there were some documents I needed to see, mostly antique, and a few other things not fit for shipping or copying. Those items, she believed, supported her theory.

To sweeten the deal and further convince me that the trip south would be worthwhile, she offered me three nights of free boarding at her Royal Oak Bed and Breakfast, and all the history of the state I could handle. Even if her theory proved to be incorrect, Abigail was sure I'd find springtime in Mississippi a great place to unwind and relax for a few days. It didn't hurt that I thought she was kind of charming when we spoke on the phone. At first our exchanges were all business, but the last few had ended on more social topics. I could see us actually becoming friends.

I asked Abigail if she would object to me bringing my daughter along. I figured I couldn't make the trip for another month, and by then Megan, my kid, would be out of school. We could use my visitation time doing something different and Megan might actually enjoy it. Abigail thought it was a great idea and only asked that I give her a few weeks of notice so she could leave two rooms open for us.

I then called my ex-wife, Samantha, and briefed her on the trip. She didn't think Megan would want to go, but she encouraged me to ask anyway so I did. It turned out that Megan had already decided summer music camp was a much more appealing prospect than spending time with me. For over a month she'd been procrastinating about how she was going to tell me she preferred going to camp, and then spending the rest of the summer at home in San Diego with her friends. I knew better than to insist she come along with me It would only result in an argument and the risk of being hung up on. The last thing I needed was to give my kid an excuse to be even more distant from me. And I already told you how I feel about drama. As far as I'm concerned, the terrible twos have nothing on the terrible fifteens.

There wasn't any use in asking Samantha to help me overrule our daughter's plans. She already knew what Megan wanted to do all summer, yet she decided to not tell me and let me get the bad news from our kid. It fit right in to this typical pattern of my ex-wife skirting around a child visitation order we had actually agreed on when our divorce was being finalized.

At first our daughter just went along with the program as if she had no choice. I'd go pick her up and then do everything I could to balance spoiling her and being a responsible parent. But that was when she was a shy little girl who often missed her daddy. Now she was a popular teenager with lots of friends, and dropping everything to visit me was a drag. Of course Samantha could have simply told Megan staying in San Diego wasn't an option and squashed the idea before I even called. But then that would have been a wasted chance to force me to be the mean parent instead of her.

That pretty much sums up my relationship with those two. One can't miss an opportunity to dig her knife into me a little deeper. The other has a new dad who is probably much cooler than I'll ever be. About the only connection left between us is the child support and alimony checks I put in the mail the first day of every month. You know, I was eventually able to pinpoint the time when my ex-wife stopped loving me. But when she started hating me, I haven't a clue.

After learning it would probably be Thanksgiving before I saw my daughter again, I stared at the phone for a few seconds and then called Abigail back. "How soon could I come out," I asked. Screw the last minute travel airfare.

"Anytime," was the answer.

I then explained that the trip with my daughter wouldn't work out after all, and since there was no other reason to wait, I'd like to make the trip by myself as soon as I was able to wrap up some commitments at work. Abigail promised to have a bed waiting.

Next, I called my neighbors and asked if they could watch Roger for a few days. They have a ten-year-old son who loves to dog-sit, and he even lets Roger sleep in his room at night. They said, "Sure," and I went straight to making travel arrangements after that. I found a flight that departed on the following Saturday and booked it. I left my return date open, because I had no idea how long I might want to stick around and check out the area. I told the guys at work that I would be gone for up to two weeks, but I'd keep in touch and take some work with me. They didn't care.

Mississippi was pretty much a mystery to me. I knew they had a big river there and the state was somewhere east of Texas and west of Georgia. Since I had a week to kill before the trip, I decided I might as well read up on the state so I would have an idea where I was when I got there. The only thing I found really interesting about Mississippi was their Civil War history. Everything else I learned made me kind of nervous. I had never been in the Deep South before, and quite frankly, I was expecting a very rural, time-forgotten place. Even so, by the time I boarded my flight to the capital in Jackson via Kansas City, I had a full itinerary of things I wanted to see while I was there.

Sitting here writing this, I smile at myself when I try to remember the man I was when I stepped on that plane. Though it was only a short time ago, I don't even know who that guy was. He certainly isn't me anymore.

CHAPTER 2

THE INNKEEPER

Abigail had warned me that summer sometimes comes early in South Mississippi, but I wasn't expecting the blast of humidity to nearly take my breath away when I stepped into the boarding tunnel leading into the Jackson airport. I was already wiping sweat from my brow by the time I completed the short walk to the airport gate. The unexpected heat immediately drained any semblance of energy I had left in me. I remember thinking as I weaved my way through other travelers into the terminal, *Why is my carry-on luggage suddenly so heavy? Why do I feel like I just gained a hundred pounds?* I guess jet lag and having to walk through a toaster oven can do that to you. If I could just stretch and walk around a little, I knew my body would recalibrate and get back to normal. That's what I was trying to do when I discovered the terminal was nearly empty. Though it was only a few minutes after 5 p.m., the gift shops were closed and there wasn't anywhere to grab a quick bite to eat other than a row of vending machines. *Crap.*

I started the morning with coffee and a croissant, and assumed I would be able to find something for a decent lunch later. Unfortunately, my stopover in Kansas City was brief and I didn't even change planes. By the time I arrived in Jackson, all I had to eat or drink was two rounds of cranberry juice cocktail and a couple of those little worthless bags of in-flight peanuts that only give you bad breath and make you thirsty. I was also tired and could feel a headache coming on. Put all that together and I'll admit it, I didn't exactly arrive in Mississippi with the same degree of enthusiasm that I left Seattle with.

I scouted out the rest of the terminal and confirmed there was nothing open. It wasn't difficult to figure out why. Other than the passengers on my flight and the people picking them up, the airport was eerily empty. If I wanted something to eat, I wasn't going to find anything there. I needed to get out on the road and into the city.

I was a little nervous when I first spotted the rental car counters across from the baggage claim area. With no one waiting in line or standing at the counters, I was afraid they were also closed. I was wondering to myself, *Have I just walked into the middle of a Twilight Zone episode?* when I finally saw an attendant step into view.

Airport travel had become a necessary nuisance for me in the early days of my career. When I got the job in Seattle, Samantha was already seven months pregnant and her parents lived only a few miles away from us in San Rafael, which is just outside of San Francisco. At that time the job in Washington was still a big gamble, and we didn't want to uproot our whole lives on something so risky. We were also depending on Samantha's mother to help us out with our new baby for a few months. It just seemed smart for me to get settled in Seattle first, and fly back and forth on my days off. Cost wasn't an issue. I did that commute for almost a year.

I don't think the arrangement was tough for Samantha because her mother practically moved in with us. Besides, we were way too busy to try to find a new house and relocate once the baby arrived. I was only gone four days a week, and when I was home I did everything I could to provide some relief for Samantha. I was happy to do it but all that flying around eventually became a big hassle.

I hate standing in long slow-moving lines. It makes me feel like I'm somebody's cow being herded from one place to another. I am also not very good at waiting around in big crowds, which is probably some low level of claustrophobia. With that in mind, it's probably obvious why I don't fly much anymore. I just got totally burned out on it. But arriving at the Jackson airport with its few signs of life turned out to be a pleasant distraction to my initial jet lag, even if it did mean having to go without a few standard airport conveniences like food service. The airport was actually peaceful. I decided it was better to take care of my car rental before picking up the rest of my bags. I was sure a line would eventually form if I waited any longer.

The young African American girl at the Hertz counter greeted me with a smile and asked for my last name. Her Southern drawl made me grin. There was no question about it now- I was very far from home. The routine paperwork was promptly completed and then I asked for a local map. I wasn't at all comfortable with the directions Abigail Sexton had given me to her inn. I was confident that I could manage the first portion of the drive to Port Gibson, but the idea of traveling on several different country roads to get to my final destination made me uneasy. Mississippi was not a place where I wanted to get lost.

I got my map, but didn't bother looking at it before retrieving my luggage from the baggage carousel only a few feet away. I then walked outside into a blanket of steamy hot air so thick and heavy you could reach out and touch it with your finger.

The rental car parking lot was within walking distance of the baggage claim area. I welcomed the opportunity to continue stretching my legs to get my blood flowing again before getting back into a car for what was supposed to be about an hour long drive. After the short stroll, I arrived at the gated lot shared by all of the airport's car rental companies. I couldn't help but notice all of the employees loitering about the area were black.

It's probably relevant at this point that I talk a little about how I feel about race. In college I had watched Affirmative Action programs provide benefits to other students that weren't offered to me because I was white. I get it and I got it then. I also wasn't blind to the fact that the African American students had their own fraternities, and the Hispanics and Asians had their own, too. Each even had their own cultural centers, semi-underground newsletters, and so-called cultural think tank groups. I didn't like it, and I was always confused how a college campus could endorse such separatism. Not that white kids couldn't form their own Caucasian only organizations-that's just the same B.S. I just thought of college as a perfect opportunity to have young intellectual thinking people blend their cultures together to find some common ground. Not spend their entire formal education reinforcing their differences.

When I was in school white guys like me were usually the target when a group of minority students decided to protest some injustice they felt had been cast upon them by "The Man." The crazy thing was, most of the time they were right, but it was too easy to equate corrupt authority and shyster politicians and even bad cops to white people. That was where the craziness stepped in, and somehow I became responsible for societal problems that I had nothing to do with. Most of the protesting and finger-pointing was just ignorant college kids who wanted to feel like they were part of a cause. I think a lot of kids go to Cal just to participate in that junk, or at least that's what it was like when I was there. I tried to stay out of it. College was hard enough without having to solve the rest of the world's problems.

That was probably the only thing that disappointed me about going to school in Berkeley. I thought it would be like stepping back in time during the hippie days when the campus was the hub of the West Coast peace movement. It wasn't anything like that. More than once I walked across campus and had to pass a gauntlet of students yelling at me for having some part in stealing California from Mexico. I even had a class with a professor who spent almost the entire semester shaming the white students for what our ancestors had done to his. I had never experienced being disliked or even hated for being white before I went to college. Or at least that's the first time I had ever been confronted with it.

I needed to mention those experiences to you, because they're probably why I was so suddenly aware of my skin color and the history of racism in the South. I couldn't help but think the black car rental employees were sizing me up and judging me for what my ancestors had done to theirs. I felt strangely out of place, and as ridiculous as

I knew the thought was, I wanted to announce to everyone that my ancestors had never owned slaves, though that wasn't particularly true. *I'm a tourist from California!* I wanted to shout. *I had nothing to do with any of it!* How crazy would that have been?

Much to my relief, the attendant greeting me at the driveway entrance was very professional. His accent and genuine smile deflated my anxiety as he welcomed me to "Missi'ppi." He then examined my rental contract, selected a set of keys from a rack inside his booth, and pointed me toward a white economy class Chevrolet Cavalier.

"That gal inside put you in a red car. Yon't want no red car," he told me. "Troopers got eyes for them red cars. You take that white one, you won't get no speedin' tickets."

"Is that going to mess things up with my paperwork?" I asked.

"Naw. I'll change it," he said. Then he warned me again, "Yon't wanna be driven no red ve-hicle 'round here. I'm tellin' yuh."

"I've never heard that before," I replied a little mystified. "Thanks for the heads up."

The inside of my rental was nice and clean, but it reeked of cigarette smoke and ammonia disinfectant. None of the regular features were automatic, surely the reason why the car was so inexpensive. I had decided to go with a cheap rental to blend in and not attract attention. In my research I'd learned that crime was a problem in Mississippi. I didn't want to get robbed just because some crook saw me in a nice car.

I plopped down into the driver's seat and held my breath, cranking open the window before gasping for some fresh air. I then started the engine and headed toward the exit, hoping the breeze would flush the staleness from inside the car. The foul cigarette odor awakened my nearly forgotten headache. I had some Advil in my toilet kit, but it was in the trunk and I was too tired and lazy to pull over once I started moving. Like an idiot, I preferred to be in pain. It was all I could do to force a smile for the waving attendant at the gate as I pulled onto the airport driveway and headed north toward Jackson.

A large airport sign that welcomed me to *The New South* distracted me momentarily, and I came within a few inches of crashing into another car. It didn't help that while reading the sign I was maneuvering without power steering through a circular intersection with no traffic control lights. I uttered a few profanities under my breath and thought, *How about purchasing some stop lights, and not wasting money on a giant sign meant to convince tourists you people have finally crawling out of the 20th century.* Like I said before, I was tired and hungry and that can make me a lot grumpy.

I started thinking about how Mississippi had been the home of some infamous evil during the Civil Rights Movement and Desegregation. I wondered if I might be driving through some of those places during my visit. If I did, I wondered if there would be historic monuments or would the locals prefer an ugly past be forgotten. Could I feel safe today in a small town where once three young civil rights workers, who were only trying to register black voters, were murdered by actual cops and some of their Klan buddies? As a white man, how would I feel standing in the same place where a black teenage boy had been dragged kicking and screaming from his parents' home in the middle of the night, and killed for supposedly whistling at a white woman? I had learned about those stories in high school and had seen movies about them. The idea that some of that hatred might still be around made me feel nervous. This was a different world, I reminded myself. It was best that no matter what I saw or heard while I was in Mississippi, I should keep my mouth shut and mind my own business.

There wasn't a whole lot more that I knew about Mississippi when I first arrived there. I expected a place still divided along color lines, where whites and blacks likely just tolerated each other between occasional culture clashes. After all, Mississippi is still the proud founder of the term *Redneck*, and the state flag still resembles the Confederate Battle Flag from the Civil War. Even the national news coming out of Mississippi seemed to revolve around its backwardness and its people's reluctance for change.

I found my way onto westbound Interstate Highway 20, wondering how much of that great divide between black and white still existed in the state. How comfortable would I be traveling alone through the Mississippi back country if I were black? I caught myself feeling grateful that I wasn't African American, and then had to scold myself for my political incorrectness. I was thinking too much and making my headache worse. I decided to turn on the radio and distract myself with some music.

The highway took me through the south side of Jackson, a city I found peculiarly small for a state capital. The Pearl River borders the eastern edge of downtown. Old brick buildings with faded advertisements just barely still visible on their walls were mixed among the more modern structures. Large, full trees were everywhere. I was just beginning to appreciate the view of the clean cityscape when it quickly passed into my rearview mirror. A few more miles down the road and then it was onto the Natchez Trace Parkway. It was the very same trail that had initially drawn my search to Mississippi.

The drive on the parkway was the first thing I looked forward to during the trip. Not only was it supposed to be a beautiful drive, but it also had a great deal of history behind it. And that's what the theme of the trip really was about, history. Even better, I was hoping it was going to be a trip about *my* history.

The highway was mentioned in every internet visitor's guide of the state that I'd seen so my expectations were high. I was smart enough to know that it wouldn't be the equivalent to some of the spectacular views from the Pacific Coast Highway on the West Coast, but I'd reserved enough space in my rather shallow expectations of Mississippi to let the scenic route speak for itself. Much to my delight, the parkway was all I had imagined and more.

There were no awesome views of ocean waves crashing against the coast, or snow-capped mountain shadows fixed ominously in the distance. There was only an empty two-lane roadway gently wandering through the countryside just a few yards from the towering walls of a peaceful forest of giant trees. The grass between the curb of the highway and the tree line was a bright Kelly green, covered with patches of dark red Crimson clover and violet-colored wild flowers.

The first image that popped into my head was that of the Technicolor meadow that surrounded the magical Emerald City in the *Wizard of Oz*. I guessed it was a strong possibility the filmmakers had used the Natchez Trace as a model for the last few miles of the also legendary Yellow Brick Road. I had certainly never seen anything like it before.

I fumbled to get my digital camera out of its case. Then I began taking photos with my left arm hanging out of the driver's side window with my right hand grasping the steering wheel. It wasn't like I was going to crash into anyone. There were no other vehicles in sight.

Occasionally, the forest would creep all the way to the side of the highway and the branches from the trees on each side would join together, turning the highway into a natural tunnel passage. Fifteen miles into my journey I caught my reflection in the rearview mirror. I was smiling like a kid on his way to Disneyland.

The drive from Jackson to Port Gibson was only forty miles and it passed quickly. I planned to spend some time in the tiny city because it had some Civil War history, but for now it was more important to find the Royal Oak Bed and Breakfast. I pulled off the parkway just outside of the town of just a few thousand, and steered onto State Highway 61.

A few more miles south came the lumber yard that Abigail Sexton described, and the rural road just past it that supposedly led to the inn. The land was now open with wide swaths of cleared fields and pastures. I assumed I would see plenty of cotton growing when I got to Mississippi, but there was none. To me it looked like the land was only being used for cattle grazing, or for no particular purpose at all. Occasionally, a lumber truck with a full load of fresh-cut timber would pass by in the opposite direction. There wasn't a single Mercedes or BMW on the road, I can tell you that much.

The next turn came exactly two miles later as expected. The gravel road didn't have any signs identifying it by name, but it did have a small billboard indicating visitors seeking the Royal Oak Plantation Bed & Breakfast should turn left. I was sure glad to see that sign. It meant I wasn't lost.

My car created a plume of dust as I continued toward the inn. A dense thicket of trees and brush created a wall of foliage on both sides of the road. I felt like I had just driven into a maze. This leg of the trip was making me nervous again. It was as if I was driving away from civilization, and the anxiety of not being sure what was at the end of the road created a very tense few moments.

Again, my anxious stomach grumbled a warning that it needed to be fed. The peaceful drive south on the Natchez Trace Parkway had distracted me, and I scolded myself for being so preoccupied with staring out the window that I hadn't stopped in Port Gibson for dinner.

The old plantation home soon appeared in the distance off of a long private driveway that intersected with the gravel road I was on. I turned onto the driveway and gazed at the beautiful structure before me as I slowly approached it. The house was a huge two-story antebellum mansion with those Greek columns you think of when you picture a big plantation home in the South.

At first sight you couldn't help but appreciate something so beautiful, though the columns were a little ostentatious for my personal taste. I couldn't help but think about how the house was built by a family that made their fortune from the labor of slaves. I've met plenty of multimillionaires in the tech world who built gaudy estate homes that reflect their egos. The history of this home was probably no different in its time, except it had a cursed history. I couldn't let that thought go.

As I approached the house, a woman stood up from a white garden chair on the porch and waved to me. I was right on schedule so I assumed it was Abigail. By the time I rolled up to the front of the inn, the woman was standing next to the circular driveway at the bottom of a wide wooden staircase. I pulled up next to her and stopped.

"You Mr. Sexton?" the woman asked with a smile.

"That's me," I answered. "You must be Abigail."

"Call me Abby, please," she said warmly, and stuck her hand through the opened car window. "Good to finally meet you." We shook hands and she continued, "Pull 'round the side and I'll help with your bags."

I followed her instructions and parked my dust covered rental car in a small empty unpaved parking area on the side of the house. It was starting to get dark and the rhythmic music of bullfrogs and crickets filled the air.

"This is really beautiful country," I said as we met at the trunk of the car.

"How was your flight?" Abby asked.

"Not bad. The drive here was very nice."

"You'll have to come back in the fall and take the Trace all the way up to Nashville. That's when it's most spectacular. Our hidden gem."

I couldn't help but smile at the sound of her Southern accent. It was friendly and actually quite comforting.

"Am I the only guest tonight?" I asked as I pulled the bags from the trunk.

"You have the whole place to yourself," Abby answered. "To be honest, I had someone call about a booking last week, but I told them we were full. I wanted to spend a couple days with you, without having to take care of other guests. That make me a bad girl?"

54

"I think you'll be okay," I playfully consoled her. "But you shouldn't have done it just for me. I don't want to be any trouble."

Abby reached down to take one of my bags as I slammed the trunk lid shut. "No you don't," I said, and took the bag away from her gently. "You just lead the way to my room. I need the exercise."

Abby smiled and waited for me to sling my laptop case over my shoulder and then fill my hands with luggage. My mother raised me to be a gentleman, and I was going to make sure my being a gentleman went into overdrive on the trip, particularly since Abby was treating me to free room and board. That being said, as I followed Abby up the stairs, it was unavoidable that I noticed she had a very nice figure.

"The guest rooms are upstairs," Abby said as she closed the double doors behind us. I followed her to a large stairwell in the center of the rather grandiose foyer and we began climbing stairs together.

"Are you sure you don't want some help with your bags?" she asked.

"I'm fine," I answered, even though the luggage straps were digging into my collarbones. "Is there someplace where I can get a bite to eat tonight?"

"I'll fix you something. The nearest restaurant is in Vicksburg about thirty minutes up highway sixty-one from here."

"Oh no, that's fine," I said. "I have a couple granola bars in my bag." That was a lie. "Dinner wasn't part of the deal, and I've already cost you money by you turning away guests. I should have stopped in Port Gibson on the way."

"Honey," Abby began, "the only thing you was gonna find to eat in that town was gonna be some old man selling buckets of crawfish and boiled peanuts from his camper on the side of the road. Now you're my special guest, and I'm about ready to make my supper anyway. It'd be a waste just cooking for one person."

I wasn't going to argue with that. I was starving. "I'll pay you, of course."

Abby turned around and frowned as we reached the top of the stairs. "How about we just think of it as two friends having supper together? How's that?"

"If you insist," I answered, nearly out of breath from the climb.

"I do," Abby answered and opened the door to one of the bedrooms.

Before I stepped inside I had expected something much more modest in size. But this bedroom was huge. "Is this the master bedroom?" I asked.

"This was originally a children's room," Abby answered while opening a window. "They had up to five boys sleeping in here at one time."

"Wow."

"There's another one just like it down the hall where the girls slept. They liked big families back then. It made more sense to pile all the kids in these big rooms, instead of a bunch of small ones."

"Not much privacy," I assumed aloud.

"They didn't expect it back in the old days."

"I guess you're right," I answered and scanned the old Victorian furniture in the room.

Everything inside appeared to be an authentic antique. There was no television or stereo, or anything even remotely contemporary. The décor looked like the kind you would find behind a roped-off museum display, and the room even smelled musty as if it hadn't been occupied for several years.

56

"Is the furniture original?" I asked.

"Depends on what you mean by original," Abby answered. "Most of it is over a hundred years old, but we have no idea when it actually got here. Don't be afraid to use any of it. If I was afraid of it breaking, I wouldn't put it out for guests to use." Abby then swatted the mattress gently and said, "The bed is new so you don't have to worry about that. Your bathroom is directly across the hall and it's completely remodeled. There's a little alarm clock radio in the dresser. I keep it hid' 'cause it kind of messes up the vibe in the room when you first walk in and see all this old neat stuff, and then there's a digital alarm clock sitting by the bed. If you need me, I stay out in the old servant's house in back. My number is right there next to the phone. Won't be anyone else in the big house, so if you hear something it's either me or the ghosts."

Ghosts!?

Abby smiled and assured me she was just kidding. "Actually, I could use a few extra noisy spirits around here," she added. "Word gets out your guests might get to see a ghost or two staying in an old place like this, I'd be booked solid all year."

"Well for my sake, I hope they take the night off," I said as my heart rate steadied. I'd never seen or heard an actual ghost before and was one hundred percent certain I would be perfectly happy forgoing that experience for the rest of my life. I decided to change the subject. "This is much more than I expected," I said as I continued to look around the room. "I don't know what to say. You are very gracious."

"Oh hush,' Abby answered. "I hardly ever stay inside the big house anyway. We converted the old servant quarters into a real nice place about ten years ago. When it was first built it was just a bunch of bedrooms and a kitchen. Then some remodeling was done in the fifties and the rooms were turned into four tiny studio apartments. We decided to basically gut the whole place a few years ago and remodel it, and now it's a real nice little house. All this old stuff in here is nice and some of it is really expensive, but I'm not comfortable living with it. Everything creaks. You don't really pay attention to it during the daytime, but at night, well...I guess I'm just one of those gals that don't like the dark all that much without a man around. Don't you dare tell my momma I said that. I'm trying to prove to her I can handle this place on my own."

"Is your mother here?"

"She'll be here tomorrow. She's been over at my brother's house for a few days. Gonna be eighty-seven next month. This property is hers. My dad died about fifteen years ago and I came back here to help her out. Ended up staying. We turned the house into a bed and breakfast a few years back after some more remodeling. Momma's not real thrilled about it. She doesn't know why you're here either, so let's keep that between me and you."

That was odd, I thought. Why couldn't her mother know why I was there? I decided the reason was none of my business. "Do I have time for a shower before dinner?" I asked.

"Oh sure," Abby answered and stepped to the door. "There's plenty of towels in the bathroom, and I have some travel-size shampoos and soaps in one of the drawers under the sink if you need them. We can eat out on the patio. I got this super-duper mosquito machine out there so we should be fine. Gonna be a real nice evening. Might as well take advantage of it."

"Sounds good to me," I replied.

The innkeeper turned and walked out of the room. I followed her to the door, shut it, then returned to the side of the bed and sat down. "What have I gotten myself into?" I whispered to myself. A stale-smelling room full of old stuff that I was too afraid to touch, and no television set for three days! And if that creaking late at night was enough to scare the homeowner into living somewhere else, was I expected to be brave enough to tolerate it just because I was a man? No TV, a room that smelled like a neglected basement, and the threat of ghosts walking around at night. I buried my face in my hands and shook my head.

I was completely out of my comfort zone, three thousand miles away from home, and there was no way out. Maybe tomorrow I could come up with some crazy excuse for why I couldn't stay, but for now I was stuck. I took a deep breath and sighed. At least Abby seemed nice, and she was going to feed me which was a huge plus. I decided that I was being a big wimp and had nothing to be afraid of until I actually broke something, or my bed started shaking all by itself in the middle of the night.

I got up from the bed, unpacked a clean change of clothes, and carried it with my toilet kit to the bathroom across the hall. The bathroom was very clean. All of the fixtures were new but were designed to appear old. The tub was one of those claw foot things you see in old westerns, but this one had a shower and a curtain ring attached to it. I hadn't taken an actual bath in years but that big deep tub, coupled with the knowledge that I had the whole house to myself, gave me the idea that a hot bath sometime during the trip might be nice. But for now there was only time for a brief shower and a shave. After a quick scrubbing and rinse, I dressed in the bathroom before stepping back out into the hall.

Cleaning up made me feel much better. The last thing to do was to slick my hair back with a little gel and then walk over to a mirror that was mounted on an old cherry wood dresser and give myself a final once-over. I never thought of myself as particularly handsome. That doesn't mean I'm not capable of trying to do something with what I do have to work with. Since I was on the road and ragged from a long day of travel, just being clean-shaven and wearing clean clothes was about the best I could do for my dinner with Abby.

Instead of finishing unpacking, I decided to go downstairs and find my host in case there was some way I could help prepare dinner. I wasn't a cook, but at least I could set the table and offer some conversation. It wasn't difficult to find her. I only needed to follow the sound of the Bonnie Raitt music blaring from the corner of a downstairs room. When I pushed open the swinging door, Abby, standing at a kitchen counter, quickly lowered a Bose stereo's volume with a remote control.

"Too loud?" she asked.

"Not at all," I answered as the kitchen door swung closed behind me. Blues with a rock and roll edge to it is my kind of music. I had expected something a little more along the lines of old school bluegrass or hillbilly country to be more Abby's style.

"That's a nice stereo," I said.

"I love it," Abby answered. "I won it from a car dealership up in Jackson last year. They had this thing going where if you took one of their cars on a test drive, you got entered in a lottery contest. I took this little Honda for a drive and decided it wasn't cut out for some of the giant pot holes I have out here. Still got my ticket put in the fish bowl. About a month later they called me up and said I won second prize, supposedly this real nice stereo." Abby smiled at the memory in her head. "I drove up and they gave me a box with this plain dinky thing in it and I was, well, disappointed to say the least. Didn't make any difference that it was free, I was just expecting one of those big things. You know, the kind you have to buy a whole separate cabinet for. I drove back home and turned it on and thought, *You know what, this is a pretty nice little deal I got here.* It has a remote control and everything.

"Then my brother sees it, and he tells me Bose is some big time stereo company. A few days later, I was just horsin' around one night on the internet and looked it up and, sure enough, this thing is worth about four hundred dollars. Four hundred dollars! Can you believe that? It has some kind of way of bouncing the sound around inside the box before it comes out. Sometimes I fire it up so loud it's like having a concert right here in my own kitchen."

"I've looked at those before," I said. "You're right, they're expensive." The kitchen smelled of something cooking that was familiar to me, but I couldn't tell what it was. "Whatever you're making, it sure smells good."

"That's Southern cooking," Abby answered as she wiped the top of a large wood-topped cook's table in the center of the kitchen.

"I hoped I'd get down here in time to help out," I said. "Can I at least do some dishes?"

"I'm all cleaned up until after we eat. Want something to drink?" Abby offered. "Some tea, a beer, glass of wine maybe?"

"What are you having?"

"Got a real nice bottle of wine I picked up in New Orleans last time I was down there. You like red wine? I've kind of been holding onto it until I had a chance to share it with someone. Momma can't drink anymore, and it's too nice a bottle to drink by myself."

"Sounds great," I answered, more than a little suspicious I might be served the type of wine you find on the bottom shelf in the local grocery store liquor aisle. "And really, whatever it is you have in the oven, it smells really good," I said again.

"It's my personal favorite," Abby told me. "We used to beg my momma to make this for all us kids when we were little."

"What is it?"

"I'm just gonna say it's some good Southern cooking. Here," Abby said as she handed me a bottle of wine and a corkscrew. She then reached into a cabinet and removed a large glass decanter. "Open this and pour it in the decanter so it can breathe a minute before we eat. It's much better that way. I'll go set the table outside."

I looked at the label on the bottle and saw it was a ten-year-old Chateau Margaux Bordeaux, probably worth a modest car payment. *Was she crazy?* This woman that I'd only spoken to on the phone and in emails, had cleared out her inn for me and was letting me stay for three days for free, and was now treating me to dinner and a bottle of wine that was even too expensive for me. Hell, I was afraid to even open the dang thing! Then the thought entered my mind that she might be one of those lonely women who find men on the internet, and lures them out to the middle of nowhere where they get seduced and then really bad things start to happen. *Oh shit*, I thought to myself. *Have I actually fallen for this?*

Abby stepped out a side door with tableware for two as my mind raced. *Should I just pretend to be suddenly ill and go upstairs and get my things and get the hell out of here?* I was planning my escape when Abby walked back inside the kitchen.

"You need any help with that?" she asked.

No, I got it," I answered nervously, and carefully began twisting the corkscrew into the top of the bottle.

"When you get that poured you can grab a couple glasses for us in the dining room. They're all in the hutch in the corner. Can't miss 'em." Abby then walked back outside with a handful of plates and silverware warning playfully, "And don't you dare peek in that oven!"

I nodded that I understood and gently, and I mean really gently, slid the cork from the top of the bottle. As I filled the decanter, I wondered what scheme Abby might be up to. On the other hand, was this what they meant by Southern hospitality? Had I become so jaded that I couldn't accept the fact that someone might actually want to treat me well, without some evil underlying agenda? I slowly convinced myself that nothing was going to happen that I didn't allow and Abby wasn't someone I should be afraid of. Maybe she was just a good person and I should allow her friendly disposition to make me comfortable, instead of scared to death. And since when was I so afraid of women? *Be a man, dammit*!

Besides, Abby certainly wasn't hard to look at. Actually, I was sometimes struggling *not* to look at her. I guessed by the tiny crow's feet forming beside her eyes she was somewhere around my age or a little younger. She wasn't wearing any noticeable makeup, and there was no particular style to her straight long auburn hair. But her soft brown eyes and perfect teeth drew me to her when she smiled, and even in her loose fitting summer dress I could tell she had the kind of feminine curves that make men look twice. And that accent. What was it about that accent that was so disarming?

Abby re-entered the kitchen with the slamming of a screen door behind her. "Okay, you go on outside and I'll finish up in here."

"You sure you don't want any help?" I asked.

"Positive. I'll be right out. You find us some glasses?"

I'm on it," I answered, and pushed my way through the kitchen door into the adjacent dining room.

In the corner was a tall colonial-style wooden hutch with a faded depiction of a fox hunt painted on the frame around the glass door. I didn't know anything about antiques, but I was sure that thing was worth a lot of money and was maybe even older than the house itself. I gingerly opened the door to make sure I didn't break it and removed two large wine glasses that clearly weren't antique, but were fine expensive crystal just the same. I closed the hutch door even more carefully than I had opened it, then returned to the kitchen and stepped outside.

The patio was a beautiful Spanish-tiled courtyard with a monstrous oak tree in the middle of it. Tiki lamp flames and strings of multicolored party lights gave the impression that some sort of festive occasion was about to take place. I stood before the mammoth tree trunk and imagined how old it must have been.

"Sit down and close your eyes," Abby said from the door.

I sat in a chair at the small café-sized table Abby had arranged for dinner.

"Are your eyes closed?"

"Yes," I answered. I envisioned I was going to open them again and find something like a baked catfish with its head still attached, or a plate of chicken and some vegetables, all so deep fried I'd wake up in the morning with the complexion of a zit-faced fourteen-year-old. It wouldn't matter. I would have eaten almost anything at that point.

"Here I come," Abby teased as she moved closer.

I heard her place something on the table and then heard a chair scooting against the patio tile.

"Before you open your eyes, I want you to know this is a real Southern treat. It may not be pretty but, before you judge, I think you should give it a try."

"It smells great," I said, though I was now certain it really was going to be something with its head still attached. Still, it didn't matter. My hunger was starting to hurt.

"Ready?" Abby asked. "Okay, open."

I cautiously opened my eyes, afraid that regardless of the pleasant aroma, the source might be so disturbing I would be unable to conceal my reaction.

"Pizza?" I said with both surprise and relief.

"Best pizza pie in South Mississippi," Abby added.

I felt like I had just dodged a cultural bullet. I spread a napkin on my lap and said, "This looks great, but even I know this isn't Southern cooking."

Abby sat down across from me and gestured for my plate. "Anything that gets cooked in Mississippi is Southern cooking, especially when a Southern woman cooks it. See, you just learned your first lesson."

"Whatever you say," I answered, eager to get the first bite into my cramping stomach. Abby returned my plate to me with two slices on it. Each piece was nearly an inch thick with sausage, chunks of ground beef, and various sliced or diced vegetables. "That's quite a pizza," I commented as I leaned into the plate and gently blew into it.

"Best you'll ever have. Even better cold," Abby said. Then she too began softly blowing onto her slices.

I filled our glasses and raised mine toward her. "Thank you for your hospitality. You have an amazing place, and this is all just kind of...overwhelming for me."

"My pleasure," Abby answered and gently tapped her wine glass to mine. She then lowered it to her chin and gracefully breathed in the aromas. I did the same. For a few moments we sat silently swirling our glasses, occasionally revisiting the evolving bouquet of roses and dark berry fruit emitting from our glasses.

"That's very nice," I said.

" Glad I bought two," Abby answered, and then took her first sip. "Oh, that's heaven."

I smiled and joined her. She was right. It was extraordinary.

We then took our first bite of pizza together. Abby choked with laughter when she saw my eyes uncontrollably roll back into my head.

"Honey, it's good, but it ain't *that* good," she said, marveling at how much I was enjoying her cooking. She sat back in her chair, took another sip of wine, and watched me go.

"Yes it is," I mumbled almost unintelligibly with my mouth full. My manners had temporarily been put on hold. "This is delicious."

"Well, I'm glad you like it."

I nodded that I did, realizing my lapse in etiquette. I would make sure to remember my table manners for the duration of the dinner.

"I promise to make something a little nicer for you tomorrow," Abby said. "I don't know what was in the air today. I just had pizza on my mind all afternoon, and figured I never met a man who didn't like it, so, well, there you go."

"That's a great call," I commended her. "Thank you. I really do appreciate it, but you don't have to feed me dinner while I'm here."

"Honey, I quit school to be a chef. Least you can do is humor me a little. My momma can't eat anything I like to cook. If it ain't her liver, it's her gallbladder or something else. There's no one else to cook for. I can't make supper part of the deal at this place for our regular guests. I'd have to pull separate permits for that, hire a couple staff. It'd just be a big mess right now. Maybe someday, but not now."

"Did you actually study cooking?" I asked, genuinely interested.

"Oh, sure," Abby answered. "I about gave my daddy a heart attack when I told him I was leaving Ole Miss over in Oxford to move to New Orleans. Me and a girlfriend just got bored with school. We'd both changed our majors about five times, and we thought it'd be neat to learn how to cook and then we could open our own restaurant together in a big city somewhere. We didn't really care which one as long as it was far away from here. She got homesick, though, and came back home. I stuck with it 'cause I loved it.

"I bounced around to a few different places just soaking up everything I could, and then I actually moved to Paris for a year to see what they could teach me. When I came back, I was twenty-five and thinking I was ready to move right into a nice job at a fancy restaurant, or maybe get a loan and open my own little pastry shop. Patisserie," she clarified with flawless French.

"What happened?"

"Well, it turned out I wasn't the only one with the same idea. Plus, I wanted to run things- kind of create my own dishes, stuff like that. I didn't know anyone, and not too many people around willing to hand the keys to their kitchen over to a gal in her twenties. I found work, don't get me wrong, but it wasn't the kind I wanted. Now I'm here."

I took that as a cue she was ready to talk about something else. "So tell me about this place."

"Well, this farm has been in my family since the French moved out back in the late seventeen hundreds. This wasn't the original house. It took a few years for the plantation to start making money, so they didn't have the wealth to build this big place until the eighteen thirties. Since then about every other generation's had different Sexton family living in it. My grandparents had the house and raised my father here. When my mom and dad got married, daddy moved out and they raised all us kids in a regular house over in Port Gibson.

"When my grandparents died, my parents moved back in. Few years later, my daddy died and my momma ended up with this place all to herself. My brothers and sisters have all moved on now. Hell, they're all over the place and they don't want anything to do with it. I married a man who had a little money, and to be honest, he's still paying for cheating on me. We never had any kids, thank God. During our divorce I discovered I'm pretty good at making people feel guilty when they should be, so he basically gave me everything I asked for. It didn't make me rich, but it's allowed me some time to help my momma try and manage the place without dad around."

"When did you decide to turn it into a bed and breakfast?" I asked.

"It just got to the point where we had to find a way to put it to some kind of use. We didn't want to sell it, but I needed to go find a job. There wasn't anyone else in the family who could drop everything and come out here and take care of the house and momma. I don't remember who came up with the idea, but we decided renting a few rooms might do the trick. That didn't work out because the only people looking to board were people you wouldn't be real comfortable with having in your house, if you know what I mean. We decided we'd get a better clientele with the bed and breakfast crowd."

"Potentially more money, too," I guessed out loud.

"Not yet, but we're hoping," Abby answered. "We have some remodeling yet to do. I close down in the winter and this place turns into a construction zone. Momma also has some dementia problems, and some days she flat out doesn't remember what we're trying to do with this place. It's just a lot of juggling going on right now, really too much to start advertising and getting this place filled-up. I guess you could say I'm just testing the place out for now. As much as I hate to be thinking this way, when momma passes on I'll start running this place like a real business."

"You're being realistic," I said, trying to offer some degree of empathy. "Nothing wrong with that. What about the rest of it? Do you still own all the land around here?"

"Almost every inch of the original twelve thousand acres," Abby answered. "It's all leased out, of course. Half to farmers and half to people needing a place to graze their cattle."

"So you're generating some income already."

"Very little," Abby admitted. "Between taxes and upkeep, I'm just barely breaking even."

"Well, I wish you luck," I said sincerely. "It's a beautiful home. You don't see many of these where I come from."

"Now how about you? Abby asked.

"Not much interesting about me," I confessed. "I just turned forty. Not quite sure how I feel about it yet. Being in that middle age category certainly sucks."

"Amen to that, brother," Abby concurred and raised her glass for another toast.

"I'm just a regular guy I guess," I continued. "Once divorced like you, except I have a daughter. Don't see her much, which is not my choice at all. My father was an Army officer so we moved around a lot when I was a kid. By the time I was in junior high school my dad was out of the service and got a job with a consulting firm in Los Angeles. We moved into a house in Pasadena, and that's where I lived until I moved out and went to school up in Northern California. I got married right after graduating, got my CPA license, and eventually was hired by some old college buddies to be their resident accountant up in Seattle. That's basically me in a nutshell."

"So you must be a smart man," Abby said.

"What makes you say that?" I wondered.

"Don't you have to be smart to be a CPA? Isn't accounting what stock brokers and big money people study in college?"

"Some do. I got into it because math just came easy to me in school. When I was eighteen I wasn't interested in spending the next four of five years in college frying my brain, trying to learn something that didn't come naturally to me. So I ended-up taking a bunch of accounting classes. By the time I graduated I was planning on opening up my own tax prep business after I interned with some other company for a while. That's what I was doing when these guys I knew called and hired me to run the finances for their company up in

Seattle. The pay is good, I work with friends, and I can come and go as I please as long as the work gets done. I really got lucky."

"And how's your research going?" Abby asked.

I was glad she was ready to change topics. Accounting and my personal life didn't exactly make riveting table conversation. "It's about as complete as it's ever going to be, except for this one couple," I replied. "I guess they'd be my great-great-grandparents or something close to that. It sure would be nice if you've found something that can jumpstart this project. I'm about done with it."

"I wouldn't have insisted you come all the way out here if I didn't think I had good news for you. I just hope you're not disappointed."

"If it's a real piece to my puzzle, at least it's going to be a step forward," I assured her. "Besides, my expectations are pretty low at this point."

"John, how much do you know about the Civil War?" Abby asked, her tone now business-like.

"I know what they taught us in school," I replied. "I've read some things over the years. When I was a kid, we visited some of the big battlefield parks like the one in Gettysburg. I found out a couple of my relatives fought in the war. Two died at that battlefield in Maryland that starts with an 'A.' What its na...?"

"Antietam."

"That's it," I confirmed. "Antietam. I can't believe I couldn't remember that. Anyway, I've never been to any around here, or anywhere really in the South."

"Know anything about Mississippi?" Abby asked.

"That, I can honestly say no to. To tell you the truth when I think of Mississippi, I think of slavery and the KKK and all that mess."

Abby smiled and said, "Well, sorry to say there's still some things we need to improve on. We don't own it all though."

"That's true," I answered. "How is the whole race thing going down here?"

"It's much better than it used to be," Abby answered.

"You know, I can still remember the first time I heard anything about white people hating black people," I told her. "I was probably ten or eleven and we lived in Fort Riley, Kansas, out in the middle of nowhere. My Little League baseball team was playing in a tournament off the fort in some little town I don't even remember. We only lived there a couple years. Anyway, there were a handful of black kids on the team and I had black friends in school, and it never occurred to me that those kids were any different from me other than they were a different color than I was.

"So at some point during a game, I realized there were a bunch of these big burly black guys sitting in the bleachers behind our dugout cheering for us. I'd never seen them before, and they definitely stuck out because these guys were some big boys and they were basically making a scene with their loud cheering. I asked this black kid named Tony, who was also a friend from my neighborhood, if he knew who the guys were. He said they were another kid on the team's big brothers, and the others were some cousins or something like that. A little while later I told that kid that it was pretty cool his brothers and the guys with him were making so much noise because it was really motivating our team, and definitely distracting the kids on the other side of the field. My teammate then explained to me that his brother and his friends were only there because they had the Klan in that city. I was like, *The Klan? What's the Klan?*

72

"The kid then told me they were a club of a bunch of white men who hate black people so much they chase them down and hang them. I don't know if they really had the KKK in that little town, but word definitely got out to the black families on our team that they might. Instead of telling the coach their kids weren't going to play, they showed up in force and brought some pretty big dudes with them just in case someone wanted to start any trouble. I remember that to this day."

"That's a sad story," Abby said.

"I never looked at it that way, but you're right," I agreed. "I always thought of it from the perspective of the black families. Good for them for teaching their kids not to fear racism. Hopefully those days are much closer to being gone for good."

Abby agreed with a nod and asked, "What do you know about slavery?"

"I know the South was almost totally reliant on slaves by the time the war started," I answered. "I know it was despicable and lots of people suffered. I also know some people down here still just don't get it."

"Get that slavery was wrong?" she asked.

"Mmmm," I stumbled to make sure I didn't say something offensive. "It's bigger than that, I think. I guess I mean I know there are still people down here who hate just because they think that's the way it is. That's the way they were raised, or that's what they were taught on the street, so it's okay. Forgive me if I sound like I'm insulting the culture down here." I needed to back off. "I'm just some fool from the West Coast who believes everything he reads."

"You're here now. What do you expect to find?"

"I don't really know" I answered. "So far it's humid as hell," I joked. "Didn't see that coming or I would have packed some shorts. But what do I expect to find...I don't know. You tell me, Ms. Sexton."

Abby finished her glass of wine and refilled both of our glasses. She then told me, "I'm going to show you some things tomorrow that are either going to change your life, or make you feel this entire trip has been all for nothing. I guess there's a chance you might even be very upset with me this time tomorrow evening. Either way, I'm fairly certain I've found the answer to your problem. But it won't make sense to you if you don't understand where you are, and what was happening here back around the time of the war. You want to get into it now, or wait until morning?"

"Are you kidding?" I exclaimed. "How am I supposed to get any sleep with that intro? Let's hear it." I pushed the pizza out of the way and took a big sip of wine. As Abby watched me, I could see a thought forming in her head.

"Are you familiar with the French concept of terroir?" she asked.

"For winemaking?"

"Yes."

"Sure," I answered confidently. "It's the idea that a vineyard's soil conditions and weather, and all the other things in the environment give the grapes their unique quality."

"So you know your stuff," Abby surmised.

"I went to college down the street from the Napa Valley," I pointed out to her. "I also know a little about French wine, and know the stuff we're drinking came from a Premier Grand Cru Chateau in Bordeaux. It probably cost you more than my round trip flight out here."

Abby smiled.

"Believe me," I continued. "I'd love to sit out here on this beautiful patio and talk about wine with you. You seem really knowledgeable and I like a..." I caught myself before I confessed to how much it really turned me on to talk wine with a pretty girl.

"You like what?" Abby prodded.

"I really enjoy sharing a nice bottle of wine with someone who can appreciate it."

"Is that what you were going to say?"

"Yes," I lied. "So let's get back to what we were talking about. How did we start talking about wine anyway?"

"I asked you if you understood the concept of terroir."

"I do, so...?"

"Apply that idea to trying to understand what Southern culture was like back in the mid-eighteen hundreds," Abby said. "Let's start right here with Mississippi. We were the third state to defect from the Union at the beginning of the war. Back then we were also the fifth wealthiest state in the whole country, and I suppose a little cocky about it. The cotton industry was almost completely responsible for the economy down here and for lots of different reasons. We weren't just providing the rest of the country with cotton. We were taking orders from all over the world. The Mississippi River borders the entire western edge of the state, and reliable river passages in those days were the same as highways are today. There weren't trains like up north, just old roads and trails cut through the wild. You can imagine how nice it was to have around three hundred miles of that natural shipping lane attached to our state, and that was a real advantage over other cotton states like Alabama and Georgia."

Abby continued, "By the time the war started the industry side of cotton-growing had become modernized with the cotton gin and all kinds of other new machines that spun the cotton into thread and yarn. The problem was that we were still using slaves to plant and harvest before bringing the cotton to market. They say about half the population in Mississippi in eighteen sixty-three was slaves. Can you believe that? That's almost half a million people.

"Anyway, the average price of a healthy adult slave around that time was between eight hundred and a thousand dollars. Considering a typical plantation might take a hundred or more slaves to run it, cotton had to be a pretty good business just to cover the costs of paying for workers."

"Slaves, you mean." I wanted to make sure she knew I understood the difference.

"Yes...slaves," she corrected herself. "See, lots of people think slave labor was free and that's how all these plantation owners made their money. But the fact is, owning slaves could get expensive 'cause you didn't just buy them, you also had to keep them fit enough for work. You had to put some kind of roof over their heads and you had to feed and clothe them. Maybe not nice clothes, but you had to put them in something and all that cost money. Then there was the harsh kind of living back then with all kinds of medical problems. Larger plantations would have a doctor on contract just to stop by and provide slaves with routine healthcare like teeth pulling, and treatment for common sickness. You'd go broke if you didn't provide some kind of maintenance care for your slaves. One case of smallpox or yellow fever, or any of those diseases that went around back then, and half your workers could simply die off. It could take years to recover from something like that."

Abby looked deeply into my eyes and said, "I'm telling you this because understanding that slaves were a financial investment in the South, and not just expensive pets that brought you your slippers at night, will also help you understand why the South was so insistent on keeping them around. That being said, I'm a proud Southern woman born and bred, but that doesn't make it any easier to figure out how a people so consumed with honor and supposed Christian values could have slaves at the same time. There are lots of us now who shake our heads and wonder how it could have lasted so long here. But it did, and it's a sad part of history to know an awful lot of men had to die just to end it."

Abby took another sip of wine before continuing. "I guess you understand my family used to own slaves. I don't know how they treated them, and it's probably something I'd rather not ever know. My daddy used to tell me that sometimes being in the dark about something wasn't so bad, as long as you weren't afraid of the darkness. At first I thought he was trying to tell me I shouldn't be afraid when the lights are turned off. I don't know when it was when I finally understood what he really meant, but now that I do, I agree with his wisdom.

"I don't think it's any secret some slaves were treated terribly. Then again, if you can look past what slavery actually was, you could say some owners down here were very kind and considerate to their workers. People around here don't like to talk about the way slaves were mistreated. Everyone knows there were some who were whipped near to death for doing things that you would only scold a white man for doing. As a woman, it terrifies me to think what female slaves had to go through. Women were already second-class citizens back then. Imagine being a female slave. Imagine having your child taken away and sold to someone else. Some slave women weren't treated like human beings at all. They were more like cattle used for breeding.

"So Lincoln gets elected and the war starts," Abby began with a change in subject. "The Confederacy is looking good at first, but we just couldn't keep up with all the soldiers and the money the Union side had. Eventually, the Yankees took New Orleans and that meant getting control of the Mississippi River was next. The Yankee Navy started going up and down the river, bombing all the Southern cities they could get close to. The only one that wouldn't fall was Vicksburg, about thirty-five miles up the road. Vicksburg had a Confederate garrison there, and it kind of sits up on top of this bluff overlooking the river. General Grant was in charge of the Yankees and he tried to come in from the north side of town through bayou country. When that didn't work, he came down south and crossed over from Louisiana at Bruinsburg, which is only about fifteen miles west of here. They say that crossing was the largest amphibious infantry landing before the D-Day invasion of France during World War II.

"Once they got across, and there was something like fifty thousand of them, they ran into Confederates in Port Gibson. They had a fight there that the Yankees won, and then they headed to Jackson where there was an even bigger fight. The Confederates in Jackson realized they were going to lose, so they retreated to Vicksburg to regroup. Basically, Grant had swooped down and come around the backside of Vicksburg pinning the city against the river, which by then was full of Yankee gunboats. Grant tried to storm the city a few times before he realized he was wasting men. So he decided to just sit back and pummeled the city with cannonballs for almost two months until my people gave up. They surrendered on the fourth day of July in eighteen sixty-three, a day after the Battle of Gettysburg ended.

"With the Yankees owning the Mississippi, and having finally put a good whipping on the Confederacy in Pennsylvania, all they had left to do was start pouring Yankees into the South from every direction. Mississippi had pretty much gotten away with watching the war from a distance until Vicksburg was taken. After that, we were right in the middle of it until the war ended in sixty-five."

I nodded my head, trying to take it all in. "So I gather you think my great-great-grandfather might have been a Union soldier fighting down here?"

"It's a possibility," Abby answered with a grin.

"I'm sure Union soldiers from Indiana fought here."

"Yankees from almost every Union state fought here at some point."

"So give me the Indian connection," I begged. "He met her here, didn't he? I was right," I congratulated myself. "I knew she was from Mississippi."

Abby smiled wryly. "Did you know that many Choctaw Indians fought for the Confederacy?"

"But my great-great-grandfather wasn't the Indian. His wife was."

"Are you sure?"

The question startled me. Had I missed something? *No*, I reassured myself. Abby was just messing with me. "There's no way *he* was the Indian," I told her firmly. "It was definitely my grandmother who was the Choctaw."

The twinkle in Abby's eye said she was just poking around trying to see how confident I was with my research. "What if I had information that your ancestors were slave owners just like mine?" she asked. "Would that freak you out?"

"It would be unexpected," I answered, "but I don't think it would affect me one way or the other. I'm not so gullible to think in the eighteen hundreds an Indian woman would marry a white man because he was so good looking."

"So if she was basically a slave, you would be fine with that? What if your great-great-grandfather actually immigrated down here and started his own farm with slaves? What if there was a small fortune that's been sitting around in a bank vault in Jackson waiting for you to claim it? Would it make any difference how that fortune came to be?"

I have enough money already, I thought to myself. *Is she about to tell me she discovered I've inherited even more?"*

"Just a hypothetical," Abby clarified.

"I'd be more careful about what I did with it," I answered. "I'd be more likely to put it back into the community somehow."

"Good answer. Is it the truth?"

I thought about the question again. "Yah. I'd feel obligated," I answered confidently.

"This house was built by slaves," Abby reminded me, "and it was my family who owned them when they built it. Do I owe someone an apology for that? Should I donate some of this property to a randomly selected African American family because their ancestors were slaves here?"

"That's not for me to say," I answered.

"Why not? You're entitled to an opinion. I won't hold it against you."

"You're really putting me on the spot," I said. "Can I answer that question tomorrow?"

Abby sighed. "I'm just getting your wheels spinning, John. I fight with that question all the time, believe me. I can't expect you to answer it at the snap of a finger, when I've been searching for the answer just about all my adult life."

"So, are you trying to tell me my Indian grandmother was a slave to my grandfather?" The possibility had always been in the back of my mind.

"What would you think about that?" Abby asked. "Some Indian women were bought and sold just like black slaves."

"I guess I'd try not to dwell on the kind of relationship they had. I mean, once I knew the truth, if it was bad I'd try not to think about it."

"Just kind of push that part of your history aside? Sugarcoat it a little when it comes up in conversation?"

"This is getting really heavy," I said and took a big sip of wine. "I wish I thought better on my feet."

"Should we talk about something else?" Abby asked.

"No...I mean, I just haven't really thought about this kind of stuff before."

"Well, you and I are going to be sitting here again tomorrow night and everything is going to be different. Everything you thought you knew about yourself up to now, your family and where you came from, it's all going to change. If I'm right, and I really think I am, you, Mr. John Sexton the Fourth, will return home a different man. I'm just trying to prepare you."

"There's no way I'm sleeping tonight," I said rubbing my palms together with anticipation.

"Excited?"

"I think I'm more nervous now, thanks to you."

"Then I'll wait and start breakfast in the morning when you call," Abby said. "No sense in getting up too early. Call me when you get up, and I'll whip us up something nice in a jiffy. That doesn't mean sleeping in all morning. You have a busy day tomorrow."

"Then I'd probably better try and hit the sack," I said and stood from the table. "I won't leave you with these dishes, though."

"Oh, you go on and try to get some sleep," Abby insisted. "I'll take care of this. Won't take two minutes to get cleaned up."

"Can I at least help clear the table?"

"I appreciate the thought, but that's fine. I'm gonna sit out here and enjoy the rest of this glass of wine before I turn in. Might have another slice of that pizza while I'm at it."

I rubbed my full stomach and grinned. "That was very good. I'm afraid I may need to go for a short jog in the morning to work some of it off."

"Oh, hush. You'll be fine," Abby told me. "Now git, so I can have another piece and not feel like a pig in front of you."

I reached across the table and shook Abby's hand. "Thank you for a wonderful evening."

"My pleasure, sir."

I got this strange feeling there was something else I should say, but I didn't know what it was. She was a pretty woman, and I certainly could have given her my best attempt at a non-creepy compliment, but it just didn't seem like a good idea. She also had a look on her face as if she wanted to say something more and was having trouble finding the words. I decided my best option was to keep my mouth shut and run.

"Bonjour," I nervously said. For some reason it seemed appropriate after sharing the expensive bottle of French wine.

"You mean, bonne nuit," she answered. "Bonjour is day. Bonne nuit is night."

"I should have paid more attention in class," I admitted. *Man, I blew that one.* "Bonne nuit, mademoiselle," I corrected myself.

"Bonne nuit, Monsieur Sexton," Abby responded with a nod.

I then started toward the small porch that led to the kitchen when Abby said from behind me, "Wear your walking shoes tomorrow."

I turned around and nodded that I understood, and then entered the house.

I was too tired to snoop around the yet unexplored rooms inside the mansion. Instead, I warily made my way up the stairs, mildly embarrassed and somewhat concerned that I might have made a small fool of myself. *Did I really just try to speak French? Oh well, too late now.*

I stopped off in the bathroom and then returned to my bedroom. I peeled off my clothes and crawled between the sheets, then turned off the Tiffany-style lamp that was on the small mahogany bedside table next to me. In the darkness, I thought about Megan and wished she had taken the trip with me. I also thought about how I wasn't afraid of Abby's intentions anymore. She wasn't a crazy whack job looking to trap an unsuspecting man. Her knowledge of the region's history was impressive and I could tell she was a smart woman. I thought about how it would have been good for Megan to learn what I was learning, and to meet an intelligent lady like Abby Sexton.

The faint glow of moonlight seeping into the room cast just enough light to see the furniture and old landscape paintings on the walls. My thoughts turned to trying to envision what the Sexton Plantation must have been like in the days of slavery. Images of scenes from *Gone With the Wind* began to fill my head, and I replaced Vivian

Leigh with Abby in the starring role of Scarlett O'Hara. She certainly seemed independent enough to play the part. But Abby's beauty was simple, not the glamorous kind of a Hollywood starlet.

I'm always attracted to women who are naturally pretty. I'm even more impressed with a woman who can speak of history and politics, whether I agreed with their views or not. That's nothing new. I've always been like that. Unfortunately, I married a woman who possessed none of those qualities. No wonder it didn't last.

The combined long day of travel, along with my full belly and the peaceful setting surrounding me, made it impossible to hold a thought. My body slowly sank further into the mattress and my breathing began a steady deep rhythm. And as the old Mississippi plantation outside sparkled with the flashes of fireflies, I surrendered my consciousness to the night and drifted off to sleep.

CHAPTER 3

GHOSTS

I awoke the next morning to the sound of birds- hundreds of them squawking and chirping at each other in the trees near my bedroom windows. I scratched the stubble on my face and then checked my watch. Just like clockwork I had risen at my usual 6 a.m., 8 a.m. Mississippi time. I swung my feet to the floor and sat on the edge of the bed for a moment to get my bearings. I felt like I'd been sleeping for days, and needed to take a second to clear the fog and catch my brain up to where I was and what I was doing there.

I removed some clothes from my garment bag and then headed for the bathroom with my toilet kit. I was still having some trouble waking up, so I gave myself an extra shot of cold water in the shower just to get my body charged. I shaved again, even though I didn't really need it, brushed my teeth and got dressed. When I returned to my room, I found a glistening silver service tray with a pot full of coffee resting on the bed.

"God bless her," I whispered to myself as I poured steaming black coffee into a porcelain rose pattern cup. I raised the cup to my nose and filled my head with the rich scent of the fresh brew, then took a gentle sip. "Oh, that's good," I said and took another.

I then spent a few more minutes getting myself together, and then straightened up the room so Abby wouldn't think I was a total slob. She was obviously up so I wasn't going to bother trying to find a phone to call her. Instead, I gathered the tray setting with the coffee pot, and headed down the stairs to the kitchen where I was sure she was making breakfast.

"Good morning," I said as I carefully placed the silver setting on a clear space on the counter.

Abby was wearing tight faded jeans that highlighted her youthful figure. From behind, she looked like a twenty-year-old. I tried not to stare.

"Good morning to you, sir," Abby answered over her shoulder from the stove top. "You ready for a good Southern breakfast?"

"I'm not falling for that again," I said.

"Oh this is the real thing. How you like your eggs?"

"Scrambled." I didn't really care, but I knew scrambled was the easiest. "Want me to pour some coffee?"

"Nope," Abby answered. "Just have yourself a seat. This is a bed and breakfast and I need to get used to treating my guests like customers."

The cook's table in the center of the kitchen already had table settings for two on it, so I took a seat on one of the wood stools and waited for Abby to finish preparing our meal. "So what's on the agenda this morning?" I asked.

"We're going to take a little stroll out to the back of the property," Abby answered. "I got something I want to show you."

"What is it?"

"A surprise."

"Does it have anything to do with my family?"

"Maybe." Abby turned around with a skillet in one hand and a spatula in the other. As she scooped a pile of hot scrambled eggs onto both of our plates, she asked, "Are you still excited?"

"Sure," I answered. That was an understatement. I was rearing to go.

Abby returned to the table with a breadbasket full of biscuits and a gravy boat. "I hope you're a breakfast eater, and not one of those woosies who has a piece of toast in the morning and runs out the door."

"Woosie?" I smiled. I hadn't heard that term since high school. "No, I'm definitely a breakfast person."

"Good," Abby said and placed a large covered bowl between us. "You like grits?"

"Is that like Cream of Wheat?" I asked.

"Kind of," Abby answered and dropped four pieces of bacon next to the eggs on my plate. She then uncovered the large bowl, scooped a ladle full of grits out of it, and then emptied the ladle into a smaller bowl next to my plate. "These are real good with just a touch of butter," she said and filled her own bowl.

"Sounds good."

Abby took two biscuits out of the breadbasket and placed them in the middle of my plate.

"Holy smokes," I said as my plate filled with food.

"This is the best part right here," she said raising the gravy boat from the table. "You can't buy this in a store. My momma taught me how to make it. The recipe isn't even written down." Abby then smothered the biscuits and the eggs on my plate with the thick homemade gravy.

I gulped apprehensively at the sight of my seemingly average American breakfast being turned into an artery-clogging plate of slop. I could only stare into it and wonder how I was going to try to eat it. While Abby poured us fresh coffee and orange juice and then removed her apron, I analyzed my plate and tried to calculate the number of calories I was about to consume.

When I surrendered and looked up, I saw that the apron Abby was wearing had been covering a tight sleeveless t-shirt that read, *Ole Miss* across the front of it. As she sat down at the table she caught me reading her top.

"You like?" she asked.

Does she think I was looking at her chest? Jesus Christ, man, get a grip!

"I was just reading your shirt," I blurted out in my defense.

"What else would you have been doing," she said with a sheepish grin.

"I was reading your shirt," I said again, this time with some conviction.

"Okay, I believe you. Ever had a breakfast like this before?"

"Can't say I have," I answered, but I wasn't thinking about the breakfast. I was thinking about how I was going to have to look Abby straight in the eye or at her forehead whenever we talked from now on, just to make sure she didn't think I was some jerk who couldn't keep his eyes off of her breasts. And they were about perfect for my particular taste, so it wasn't going to be easy. *Shit!* Sometimes, it's a real curse being a man.

I looked down at my plate and took a deep breath, lifted my fork, but still hesitated.

Abby could see I was slow to get started. "Don't worry," she told me. "You'll have it all walked off by lunch time."

"I'm afraid to ask what you people eat for lunch," I said trying to lighten the moment.

"You people?" Abby questioned with a scowl.

"I didn't mean that in a bad way."

"I know," she smiled again. "Relax, John. C'mon, let's eat."

"You like teasing people, don't you," I observed.

"Not really."

"You've certainly been teasing me quite a bit," I pointed out to her. "I'm not complaining or anything. I've just noticed you definitely have a playful side."

"Isn't that strange?" Abby said as she looked up in self-reflection. "I'm not usually like that. I guess I've been cooped up with my momma too long. She's got the sense of humor of an angry bull."

"I think it's charming. You, I mean. Not your mother being like a bull." *What are you doing, man?! Shut your mouth!*

"Really?"

"Sure," I said, trying to recover like one of those tiny female gymnasts about to fall off a balance beam. I don't know what came over me then, but I just started talking- again, the man curse. "Look, I'll be honest with you. I was a little nervous about this trip. I don't know you, we obviously come from two different worlds and, I mean let's face it, there are some crazy people out there. But you've been so nice to me, I don't know..., it just kind of feels like we're a couple of old friends who haven't seen each other for a long time."

"I know," Abby agreed. "Isn't that strange?"

"Yeah, it's really strange, but it shouldn't be," I answered. "You're a nice person and I'm a pretty easy going guy. We have some things in common. There's no reason we shouldn't be comfortable with each other."

"What do we have in common?" Abby asked.

"I'm guessing we're about the same age," I answered tactfully. "We both think it's important to know our history. We're both good looking and we married people who didn't appreciate us."

"Amen to that, brother," Abby agreed and raised her glass of orange juice to toast.

I tapped her glass with mine and we both drank together.

"Did you like being married?" I asked as I started to eat.

"At first I did," Abby answered. "I was only married for two years, though. That's why we didn't have any kids. How about you?"

"I loved being married," I declared. "Actually, scratch that. I loved the companionship part of it. Once we entered into the binding contract part, it turned into a business and we were terrible business people."

"That's an interesting way of putting it."

"I've spent a lot of time trying to put my divorce into prospective. That's all I could come up with."

"And you only have one daughter, right?"

"Yes, Megan," I answered. "She'll be sixteen in a few months. She lives with her mother in San Diego. She also has a stepdad, who happens to be the same jerk that my wife was having an affair with when she left me."

"Do you see your daughter much?" Abby asked.

"Only during the summer and an occasional holiday here and there. She's at that age where it's cooler to hang out with your friends than with your dad."

"We've all been there."

"Yeah," I agreed, "but we went home at the end of the day. It was easier for our parents to sneak in a little time with us between school and sleep-overs and soccer practice. I'm supposed to see my daughter at least one weekend every other month, and two months during the summer. This year she chose music camp and a bunch of other little teenage girls over me."

"That's too bad," Abby said consolingly. "I'm sure you're a great father."

"We'll never know until she gives me a chance to try it out."

"Do you think you'll ever marry again?"

"Who knows," I answered with a sigh. "I'm not a member of the He Man Woman Haters Club or anything. Unlike most men, I think my fears about getting in another relationship are based on what I actually *do* know about women. Not what I don't."

"Got us all figured out, do you?" Abby asked with a smirk.

"Not in the least," I confessed. "That's the problem. You make absolutely no sense to me, and now I'm smart enough to know you never will."

We both laughed.

I'd swiped most of the pool of gravy to the side of my plate, but there was so much of it on my eggs and biscuits I couldn't avoid trying some. That's when I discovered how tasty the thick breakfast sauce actually was. Soon I was even dipping my bacon in it.

"We haven't talked about the Choctaws much," I said. "What do you know about them?"

"What do *you* know?" Abby countered.

"I know they were all over Mississippi and Alabama before we kicked them out and forced them to Oklahoma. That's about it."

91

"Well, you're right about this being Choctaw land," Abby confirmed. "By the time my family started this farm, the Choctaws had already become friends and neighbors with most the white folks around here. They even fought alongside Andrew Jackson against the British. The Choctaws were considered one of the civilized tribes like the Cherokees further over in Georgia. They had English-speaking schools and many were converting over to Christianity. Then one day the government decided they wanted this land down here all for white people. And just like what they did to about every other Native American tribe, the government stuck a self-serving treaty in their face, and convinced them they were either getting a good deal or didn't really have a choice."

"But I guess what I don't get is, if the Choctaws were basically integrating into white society, why did we kick them out?"

"Money and because we could, I suppose," Abby answered. "Isn't that terrible? By the early eighteen hundreds it was clear Mississippi was an agricultural goldmine, and the white people running the government weren't about to let it just sit here in the hands of Indians. Some fought back, but it was useless. They'd relocate a few hundred, sell the land to some wealthy white man, and then kick out some more when they needed more land to sell."

"That's just almost unbelievable to me," I said.

"It was a different time," Abby reminded me.

"Yeah, but don't you still have this sense of guilt when you think about it? I don't mean you as a person from Mississippi, I mean us as white people."

"I look at it this way," Abby started. "We all came from a bunch of hairy cavemen thousands and thousands of years ago, right? From

92

then to now our blood has passed through God only knows how many different cultures from around the world. Should we be expected to feel bad about what they've done? I mean, I see what you're saying, but you have to have some personal statute of limitations on guilt. Otherwise you're going to spend all day walking around apologizing."

"You're right," I said.

"Of course I am," Abby added with a broad smile. "But take that idea a little further in your case. You have this family tree your parents charted out for you and I'm sure you discovered you have blood from all kinds of different places. If it's true you got Choctaw in you, does the white side owe the Indian side an apology?"

"I think the Choctaw has been almost completely bred out of the family. Look at me. I'm white as a piece of paper."

"Interesting observation," Abby commented as if congratulating me.

"Well, it's true."

"I know."

"So what's so interesting about that?" I asked.

"Just tuck that thought away for a while. You might need it later."

I smiled. "More teasing. This is what I'm talking about."

"You like it?"

"I think I do."

Our eyes met for a moment and my heart started to race. With every word spoken between us I was growing more attracted to her.

"You said yesterday I'd get a chance to meet your mother," I said, trying to interrupt the connection that was turning awkward.

"There's been a change in plans," Abby answered nervously, breaking eye contact with me and looking down into her plate. "She doesn't drive anymore and I'd have to go pick her up. I called my brother this morning and she's going to stay with him one more night. I wanted to spend the day with you if that's alright?"

"Well...um...sure," I answered with a stutter.

"Did you want to be alone?" Abby asked. "I don't want to impose."

"No, no," I insisted. "I'd love to have your company. I just don't want to bore you."

"I'm sure that won't happen. I just thought I could be a better tour guide than a map, that's all."

"Great idea," I said. I finished the last bite of food from my plate and started to get up to clear the table.

"Nope, no you don't," Abby said and gestured for me to put my plate down. "You go get yourself ready for a walk and I'll clean up."

"I'm ready now," I replied. "How about I do the dishes and you get ready?"

"How about I charge an extra fifty dollars to your credit card because you're violating my kitchen policy," the stubborn innkeeper countered.

"And what policy is that?"

"It's the 'guest gets out of the kitchen when the cook says so' policy."

"Alright," I surrendered with a fake sigh. "Is there anything I should bring with us?"

"Got a camera?"

"Yep."

"You might want to bring that."

"Okay. Anything else?"

"Naw, that's it," Abby said. "Meet me at the bottom of the stairs in fifteen minutes and we'll take off."

"Sounds like a plan. Mind if I take a biscuit for the road?" My tummy may have felt like a swollen water balloon, but those biscuits were still calling my name.

"Just don't leave a trail of crumbs behind you."

I took a biscuit from the breadbasket and dipped it in the gravy boat. "That is really good stuff."

Abby smiled and gently pushed me out the door. Her touch made my body tingle. *What was that!? Did she just make a pass at me? Did I just enjoy that a little too much for my own good?" Uh, oh. This is starting to get kind of weird."*

I returned to my room, brushed my teeth, and returned a few minutes later with my digital camera in hand. The kitchen was empty so I decided to look around the lower floor of the mansion until Abby returned.

The first room on the east side of the house off of the main entrance gallery was the dining room. Instead of one long table in the middle of the room, there were two smaller tables preset for eight. Over the fireplace a large portrait of a gray-whiskered man glared back at me. Beneath it attached to the frame, a brass plate identified the subject of the painting as Bartholomew Sexton. The canvas showed signs of aging and attempted repair. A priceless family heirloom I surmised.

Across the hallway was another large room. This one's walls were lined with rich, walnut-stained cabinets full of books. Small tea tables with mismatching Victorian-era chairs were placed throughout the room, creating a beautiful reading parlor. Another large family portrait hung above the fireplace in this room- a painting of a woman in a regal navy-blue gown. I stepped over to the painting and looked for signs of resemblance to Abby. There were none. The woman in the painting looked unhappy and distant, her dark eyes appeared almost sorrowful.

"That's Lisette," a familiar voice told me from the entrance into the room.

"She was a beautiful woman," I replied respectfully. I figured she was probably one of Abby's ancestors.

"Think so?" Abby asked, crinkling her nose and turning her head to the side. "She looks kind of mean to me."

"I was trying to be polite."

"She's been dead a long time, sugar. I don't think you need to be worried about offending her."

"Did she live here?" I asked.

"Uh huh. Lived here during the war. The best we know, that painting was probably done right after the war ended. Look at those eyes. There's a lot going on there."

"I can only imagine," I said as I empathized with the woman in the painting.

"Did you see the one in the dining room?" Abby asked.

"Yeah. Who's that?"

"That's Great-Great-Great-Grandpa Bartholomew," Abby answered as she counted out the 'greats' with the fingers of her right hand. "He was Lisette's father. When I was a kid visiting my grandparents in this house, me and my brothers and sisters would sit around the supper table calling him Old Bart the Fart. We'd have contests to see who could say it the fastest ten times. Drove my momma crazy. My nieces and nephews still do it today."

"That's pretty funny." I could actually picture it in my head.

"Wanna try it?"

"Try what?" I asked.

"See who can say Old Bart the Fart the fastest ten times."

"I think I'll pass." Actually, I kind of did want to try it, but that wouldn't be cool.

"Okay, but you're really missing out. You ready to go?" Abby asked changing the subject.

"Ready if you are."

"Good."

I followed Abby to the front door and we stepped outside.

"I have to say I'm excited for you, John," Abby said as she locked the door behind us.

"I'm definitely excited," I assured her. "Even kind of nervous. Is this the part when you're finally going to tell me the big news?"

"In one way or another, yes."

"Sweet."

I followed Abby to the back of the house and through a cattle gate. On the other side, a dirt road led to the main body of the estate. I was glad to see a long line of trees would provide us shade from the sun. It was only mid-morning, yet the air was already thick with humidity. We were only a few minutes into our walk and I could already feel drops of sweat rolling down my sides beneath my shirt. I hoped my deodorant would hold out until I got back to my room.

After a few comments about the heat, Abby began to talk about the history of the estate. "This plantation doesn't look the same way as it did back before the war. There would have been slaves everywhere. Some would be out tending the fields. Others would be driving wagons full of cotton back and forth. They'd be everywhere. Only a few of these fields would have vegetables planted on 'em. The rest would be all full of cotton." Abby stopped for a moment.

"Listen to how quiet it is," she said. "Hear that? Just birds and bugs. Back in the day, you'd be hearing the foremen barking out orders and the racket of all kinds of laborers working this plantation." Abby moved up against me and held my arm. "Close your eyes for a second and listen."

I closed my eyes and turned to face the open field next to us.

"You can almost still hear it," I said.

"Isn't that incredible?" Abby agreed. "It's like the history is still trapped here."

"Kind of spooky, if you ask me," I admitted and opened my eyes.

"Depends on what you're afraid of."

"Ghosts, mainly."

"Plenty of those around here."

"Really?"

"Sure," Abby answered, and she wasn't using her playful tone, either. "Maybe not the flying around, jumping out of the closet kind, but this place is definitely full of ghosts."

"Have you ever seen one?" I asked as we continued on our walk.

"I don't believe in that stuff."

"But you said there were ghosts here."

"There are definitely ghosts here," Abby said. "I just don't think you can see them. All that nonsense about souls sticking around because they can't face the fact that they're really dead is a bunch of hooey. Makes a good story, but that's all it is. I think ghosts are spirits of people who have bonded somehow with a certain place. This plantation, for instance. You can't deny you just felt it."

"I felt something," I answered. "It's kind of like the same feeling I get when I'm in an old cemetery."

"That was nothing," Abby continued. "I'm gonna take you someplace where you're gonna be sure you felt a ghost. She's a good ghost, though."

"How do you know she's a she."

"Because I was named after her."

A chill suddenly jolted through me. "You were named after a ghost?"

"No, silly," Abby scolded me. "I was named after a woman whose spirit is still here on this plantation."

"You're not going to try to speak to her or anything are you? I'm not really into that kind of stuff." I was serious.

"I'm not, but you are."

"I don't think so," I said sternly. Was she serious?

"Then how are you going to find out who your lost relatives are?"

"I'm not going to find out by asking a ghost, I'll tell you that." Any attraction I had to Abby was quickly dissipating. Now I had to ask, "Are you serious?"

"As a heart attack."

"Okay, hold on a minute," I demanded and stopped walking. "I didn't fly all the way out here from Seattle to have a conversation with a ghost."

"That's too bad," Abby told me. "They have a lot to say." She continued walking without me.

I jogged up to her and said, "Look, enough already. What are we doing?" Abby suddenly wasn't very attractive to me at all.

"Oh, relax," she said. "You said you went to Gettysburg, right?"

"Yeah."

"Remember all those beautiful monuments where the different soldiers fought? Picture all those statues and plaques scattered all over the battlefield that talk about what went on in that particular area during the battle."

"Okay," I said as I refreshed the images in my mind.

"You know how you got that almost electric feeling that you were somehow in a place that was hallowed ground? Don't lie, everyone feels it," Abby said firmly.

"Sure," I agreed. "Like an old cemetery."

"That's the ghosts talking to you. If you take the time to listen, they might actually have something to say."

"Like...?"

"Like 'look how many of us died here and for what?' I imagine you could sit down beneath one of those monuments and have quite a conversation."

"With a dead soldier?"

"Who else?" Abby countered as if I should have known. "Not every conversation needs to be spoken you know. Ever pray?"

"All the time," I answered, but that wasn't true. Not anymore anyway.

"Does God talk back?"

"In one way or another," I supposed.

"Ah ha! How does he talk back?"

I pointed my finger at Abby and said, "Don't tell me you majored in philosophy before you took off for cooking school."

"What I majored in is irrelevant," Abby replied sternly. "I'm trying to get you to understand the concept of enlightenment through spirituality. If you ask God a question and you're satisfied he answers it in some way, then what's the difference between that, and seeking answers from some other spirit?"

"So you want me to pray to a ghost?" I needed some clarification.

"You're so cute. No, I don't want you to pray to a ghost," Abby said. "I want you to sit with her spirit and open yourself up to what she has to tell you. There's her old place now."

Abby pointed toward an area of untrimmed trees and overgrowth on the side of the road. Barely visible between the mangled branches was a decrepit old shack.

"Someone lived in that?" I asked as we stepped off the dirt path into the weeds and forest covering.

"We only have one or two of these things still standing," Abby said, brushing aside the vines and wild bushes.

"Was this a slave cabin or something?"

"For a while it was," she answered.

The tiny porch had rotted away and the front door was missing. Vines were slowly consuming the structure, and the white paint was almost completely chipped and faded away. I looked through the threshold and saw nothing but emptiness, highlighted by streams of sunlight breaking through the gaps between the wood plank walls.

"Watch out for spiders," Abby warned me.

"Are we going in?"

"After you."

I climbed up into the tiny outbuilding and then turned to offer my hand to Abby. She took it and I hoisted her up to my side.

"We aren't going to fall through the floor are we?" I asked before taking another step.

"Just be careful."

I took her advice and cautiously tested my weight against the dried-out floorboards before taking a full step. I didn't have to walk very far. The shack was just a small open room with a fireplace along one wall.

"We had a farmhand living in here all the way up through the sixties, if you can believe that," Abby said. "There used to be a separate room for a bed, but he took down the partition to make it bigger in here."

"Incredible."

"It was a different time," Abby reminded me.

"So this is what you brought me here to see?" I asked, more than a little confused. It was interesting, but what did it have to do with me?

"This is it," Abby answered. "Feel anything?"

"I feel sorry for whoever had to live here," I answered.

"I'm not talking about that. Do you feel any connection to this place?"

"Should I?" I asked.

Abby paused and let her eyes circle the room as if she were absorbing its history. Then she said, "I'm going to tell you a family story about this old cabin, probably the only reason no one ever tore it down. I have my own special feelings about this place. When momma's gone, I'm gonna fix it up. Not so anyone can live in it of course, but enough to keep it standing."

I was kind of spooked and preparing for her to break into some freaky séance or ancient Choctaw Indian spiritual ceremony. A few minutes passed with us just quietly looking around the room, and then Abby turned to me and smiled.

She said, "I think it'll help if you close your eyes and clear your mind, and imagine this place as it was around a hundred and fifty years ago."

I stepped backward and sat on a windowless windowsill and closed my eyes. Only the birds in the trees outside interrupted the silence.

Abby let me fill my senses for a moment and then continued. "You're going to hear me tell you a story, but there's a ghost here who I'm hoping is going to jump in and tell it even better than I can."

"Should I keep my eyes closed?" I asked as another chill ran up the back of my neck.

"If it'll help you focus."

"I got to tell you this is kind of freaking me out, Abby."

"Don't be afraid," she said warmly. "Just listen to the spirit. She's a very kind woman who's been waiting a long time to talk to you John, but you have to let her."

If I hadn't been frozen in place with such complete fear, I would have high-tailed it out of there and ran all the way back to Seattle. "And who is this ghost again?" I wanted to know.

"I like to think of her as my guardian angel."

Abby stepped backward to another open windowsill across the room from me and sat down. She was about to share with me the tale of her legendary namesake, and it wasn't going to be a short one.

"Okay," she began after a deep breath. "It's late November eighteen sixty-four, and believe it or not, the only person on this plantation is the woman living in this very room. She is a slave, probably a few years younger than us...and her name is Abigail."

CHAPTER 4

THE BEGINNING

November 25, 1864, began as a day of rest for the men of the 9th Indiana Volunteer Infantry Regiment. The Union men had made camp in a clearing of tall wild grass, littered with a scattering of dried manure piles. The livestock that once roamed the vast pasture was long gone, appropriated to the Union cause by a much larger force of soldiers that occupied the area a year before. The 9th had just finished ten days of monotonous marches from the capital in Jackson, Mississippi, south to Natchez, and then back again. Their mission was to secure an old Indian trail that was being used as a Union supply line between the two cities. An enemy presence, assumed to be nothing more than a small band of Confederate marauders, was making safe travel impossible on the well beaten path inland from the Mississippi River. The 9th's assignment was to spread out along the trail and either engage the enemy, or give the impression there was an overwhelming Federal force still there guarding it.

The veteran regiment hadn't met much resistance along the way. An occasional skirmish would break out when a small group of Rebel pickets would snipe at them, but there were rarely more than a few volleys exchanged before the enemy's riflemen disappeared into the countryside. This was their land and they knew it well.

The Confederate's mission was clearly to harass and monitor the position of the larger Union patrol. Though their numbers were assumed to be too small now for a large scale attack, the Rebels seemed increasingly desperate and more violent. That very presence of enemy soldiers still willing to fight was an obvious sign to the Federal command staff still stationed in the war's western theater that the Confederacy wasn't yet ready to surrender Mississippi.

By now, three years into the war, even the lowest of rank understood the system of the two great armies poking and prodding each other until one side determined they had an advantage and attacked. The seesaw results had finally fallen in favor of the much larger and better-equipped Union Army. Strategies had changed as casualties became more acceptable, and Federal commanders were now pushing forward when, before, they were more likely to stand fast and regroup. The new war plan, though costly in both lives and supply, created more opportunities for Union victories. And the result of those victories was the fighting had moved much deeper into Southern soil.

Morale was also improving, even though the men were exhausted and battle-fatigued. The war had begun with a spirit of chivalry between the two armies. After all, they were fellow countrymen. But after years marching in the bitter cold winters and smoldering hot summers, only interrupted long enough to occasionally square off and slay each other until a bugle sounded retreat, there was no more room for a gentleman's war. Both armies had come to terms with the idea that there was no polite way to kill. It was better to fight with the absolute resolve for victory, than the old codes of acceptable military conduct that often resulted in fruitless outcomes. If an enemy force barricaded itself among the civilians in town, then cut their supply lines and starve them out. If an outnumbered force refused to surrender on the terms of the aggressor, then battle would rage until the last of the enemy fell. This was the new code of war.

The nation's growing turmoil left Union President and Commander in Chief, Abraham Lincoln, tired of entrusting command to uniformed politicians trying to fight a civilized war. The Southern rebellion was supposed to have ended within months of its formal declaration, not continue for three years. Six different generals had commanded Lincoln's army, and none had been able to soundly defeat the Confederates into a final submission. Battles had been won, but no one had been willing to step forth and finish the enemy.

Lincoln, though it troubled him greatly to have to do so, finally succumbed to the fact that he would have to set aside his ideals of Christian and patriotic mercy, and show no quarter to the Southerners who continued to fight against the Union. If it meant destroying the South to save the country, then so be it.

The new battle plan was to invade and leave nothing but ash and destruction in the wake of the United States Army. After his successful taking of the last Confederate stronghold guarding the Mississippi River at Vicksburg, the man chosen to lead that task was future President, Ulysses Simpson Grant. The officer Grant entrusted to slice through the heart of the South was his highly favored General,

William Tecumseh Sherman. This new alignment of leadership would not fail, no matter the costs.

It was only coincidence that the 9th Indiana was given three days of rest, one of them falling on the eve of a new Federal holiday. Thanksgiving had been celebrated by New Yorkers for several years, and was even briefly recognized by George Washington when he was President. But the celebration of a feast between the original colonists and the native Indians who helped them settle had never grown to popular national status. Lincoln had been looking for an opportunity to unite his countrymen in some patriotic manner, and he saw the idea of a Thanksgiving celebration as a perfect resolve. So in October of 1863, he declared the fourth Thursday of every November to be a Federal holiday, primarily designated to thank God for the Nation's blessings.

The infantrymen of the 9th Indiana didn't care what the holiday was actually for. They only knew it resulted in them being permitted to leave camp to forage for food. If the men were successful, they could pool their quarry together and prepare their own Thanksgiving feast of sorts, even if they didn't feel there was much to thank God for. Unfortunately, Port Gibson was the closest city and, though not laid to waste on Grant's orders, was still a day's walk away. And even if there had been extra horses for the infantrymen to borrow, they would find nothing to eat there. Port Gibson was almost completely abandoned.

The livestock that once grazed the Southwest Mississippi plain had long before been evacuated or taken by the invading Federal Army. The corn and potato fields had already been picked through. Some were even burned by Union troops after the crops were pilfered and their supply wagons re-stocked. But by chance, much of the area where the 9th Indiana had made camp had escaped the destruction being laid upon the rest of the state. There were still some small private vegetable fields to be found that had been left behind by their owners. Most were weed-covered and rotting away, yet others still yielded edible produce that had become a delicacy over the often stale and tasteless military rations.

There was also plentiful wildlife living in the thick wooded areas that separated the property lines between the various cotton plantations. Deer were often spotted by soldiers sent forward for picket duty, and squirrels and rabbits were everywhere. Even those with a hook and some fishing line would be assured a nice-size catfish if they chose to find their meal in one of the many nearby streams or cattle ponds. Most of the men from the 9th Indiana were farmers or cattlemen themselves, more used to living off the land than from the food the government provided them. A chance for the men to hunt and gather something fresh for supper was a real treat and welcomed morale boost.

Among those men was B Company Commander, Captain John Chesterfield Fraser. As a member of the regiment's officer staff, he knew what lay ahead of the men in the coming days. Union regiments scattered through Mississippi were being called north to Tennessee, where another massing of Federal troops was taking place. The latest orders from 3rd Brigade Headquarters were for the 9th Indiana to march in advance and secure the eastern flank of the Natchez Trace Road, the old Indian trail they'd been patrolling for the past month. But this time, they wouldn't turn around in Jackson and march south again.

Their new orders were to continue into Tennessee and join an entire corps that would then mercilessly pursue and attack, and try to finish what was left of the Confederate Army. The coming marches would be long, the nights in the cold without shelter would be longer, and the reward at the end of their new mission would mean death to many. Those unavoidable truths were why the 9th Indiana's officers were ordered to give their men the holiday in peace, without the worries of what lay before them. The foot soldiers' knowledge of the battle plan served no purpose on a day of rest.

Venturing away from camp while in enemy territory was always a hazard. The Union soldiers knew that the best defense against a Rebel encounter was to travel in small groups. It made the hunting more difficult, but by providing their own lookouts they could contain a small area and then let their best shots hunt, or the lowest in rank gather food within their containment, and still prevent "Johnny Reb" from sniping at them while they did it. Captain Fraser made sure his men understood the dangers they faced, and ordered them to stick together and designate at least two in their party to keep watch for anyone not in a blue uniform. After ordering all to be back for a roll call at dusk, he wished his men "good luck" and watched them gleefully dash into the trees.

Captain Fraser would not be joining them. As an officer, his meals were provided by the regiment's cook. Now that the Mississippi River was safe for Union supply lines, there was rarely a time when an officer went hungry. His men were also provided with plenty to sustain them, but their undisciplined gorging always left them short of food the few days before the anticipated rendezvous with supply wagons. It was a waste of time to reason with the men about their inability to budget their rations. The war had turned in their favor now, but the previous months of starving in the field, even in the lower ranks of the officers at the front, were too recent to have been forgotten. If there was food in their haversacks, it was going to be eaten.

Fraser returned to his small canvas tent, gathered his most recent company report, and then walked to a much larger tent where the other company commanders were preparing for the next few days. A coffee pot resting on a campfire grill just outside the tent's threshold was being manned by a young corporal. The officer's aide filled a tin cup from the pot and handed it to the captain without having to be asked for it. Fraser thanked him and stepped inside the tent. As he tested the heat of the bitter coffee against his lips, he eavesdropped on the other men's conversations. There was excitement in their voices- an eagerness to join the rest of the Army and engage the Rebels in a surely final and historically grand defeat. The captain dragged a small stool away from the corner of the tent and sat down, placing his tin cup on the trampled grass next to his boot heal.

He was acknowledged with nods, but no one asked for his input or opinion. Fraser was an outsider, still commanding only because of his fearlessness in battle and not because of his ability to strategize. To his peers, the thirty-seven-year-old seemed to be more concerned with finding a safe way to avoid the enemy, not striking him. But when it was time to fight, there was no question Captain John C. Fraser was prepared to kill. And with every new encounter with Confederates, his fighting grew angrier and more furious, so furious that many of the other officers in his regiment were beginning to question his sanity.

Fraser listened to the others and quietly agreed when the forum was occasionally opened to him. His inclusion was nothing more than a small token of respect by the other men to recognize one of their peers. He had learned long before that his input had little value.

There wasn't much to disagree with in this meeting anyway. Their orders were to distance themselves a few hundred feet from the east side of the Natchez Trace Road, and march parallel with it north in a flanking formation. The maneuver would be time consuming, but necessary in order to discover any enemy artillery that might be in a position to bombard the larger number of Union troops or supply wagons that would be using the Natchez Trace in the future. It was a simple search and destroy mission. The chances of being outnumbered were slim. The ability to call up reinforcements was great.

Captain Fraser was already thinking beyond the next mission. It was the massing of troops in Tennessee afterward that consumed his thoughts. He knew a great number of men were about to die, something the others in the modest command post seemed hardly concerned with. Those deaths wouldn't come during the casual maneuvering through the tree-lined cotton fields and pastures as his regiment secured the road to Nashville, Tennessee. They would come in the hail of lead being poured into them when that next great battle came at the end of their march. They would come when the men would stand in line, bayonets fixed and glistening, and would exchange fire with a much more determined and desperate enemy. And when it was over and the smoke was cleared, there would be no stopping to treat casualties or bury the dead as before. There would only be pursuit and another day of killing, and then another until the Rebels yielded and surrendered their swords.

The captain was daydreaming of the impending horror when the pop of distance musket fire awakened him. The other officers in the room fell silent, each staring toward the tent's opened flap. A few moments passed-no more shots- and the young corporal attending them stepped inside the tent to report, saying, "Sir, the shots came from the trees where most of the men entered the woods. There has been no alarm. Perhaps venison stew for some lucky privates."

"More likely some bottom-feeding Southern varmint for his stew pot," one of the officers answered. The others laughed and then returned to their planning.

The captain decided to stretch his legs and clear his lungs of the stale cigar smoke and body odor inside the tent. Even officers grew foul-smelling after several days in the field. He returned his stool to the corner and stepped outside. A long deep breath inflated his chest as he rolled his shoulders and loosened his tired bones. He released the refreshing cool air and scratched the stubble on his face. As good a time for a shave as any, he thought to himself.

The officers' cook always had hot water on the boil, so the captain drank what was left in his tin cup and headed for the mess wagon to retrieve enough water to shave. Along the way, another distant pop and then another echoed from the trees on the south side of camp. Fraser stopped and looked toward the sound, but nothing emerged in the distance and there were no signals from the pickets that something was amiss. He brushed aside his concerns and continued toward the mess wagon.

The near-toothless sergeant tending to lunch preparations saw him coming. He wiped his hands on his stained apron and prepared to meet the captain's request.

"Don't let me interrupt, Sergeant," the captain said. "I just need a cup of your water for a shave."

"Want me to fetch it fer yuh, sir?" the sergeant asked, already moving toward a smoldering pot of water on his fire.

"Don't let me disturb you, sir. By the sounds of it, you may be a busy man tonight."

"I ain't gonna be fixin' no supper for this entire regiment, jus' 'cause you all decided to let them wander off an' bring back their own grub. We's got plenty of country boys still in this outfit can show them city boys how to cook up whatever they shootin' at out there. I got my hands full enough as it is."

"And you're doing a fine job," Fraser commended him.

"Well, thank you, sir. I got some biscuits left from breakfast. Would you like some?"

"I appreciate the offer, but I'm fine. You may need those later," the captain added with a knowing grin. "Good as gold after the tack and bacon's all run out, I hear."

"I don't quite follow, sir," the old sergeant answered, his face suddenly pale.

"If I know, so do the others," the captain warned. "Discretion is a virtue you might want to consider, my friend. Tonight, your...side business will be excused. It would be unfair that you not be allowed to participate in whatever the men bring you for trade. But I would suggest that, in the future, you reconsider your...clandestine market from this wagon. You are a good man, but another officer might not be so quick to excuse you. Are we clear on this matter?"

"Yes, sir," the humbled cook answered.

"This issue was never discussed between us then, was it?"

"No, sir."

"Then I'll have my water and leave you to your work," Fraser told him.

"Thank you, sir."

The captain dipped his cup into the steaming pot and headed toward his tent. He hated disciplining his men for minor offenses and, as he walked away, he hoped the loyal cook would understand his wisdom and not misinterpret his warning. Fresh-baked biscuits had been mysteriously appearing in the men's hands, long after it was common knowledge that they'd already devoured their regular rations. The only place biscuits were being prepared was at the officers' mess wagon, and the only one preparing them was the officers' cook. If the sergeant was caught selling food from the supply reserved for the officers, he'd face a court martial.

This late in the war it had become more difficult to control the men. To combat the increased disorganization and lawlessness, examples were being made and punishment was often severe. The Army was sentencing men to prison based on principal, hardly considering the circumstances surrounding their individual crimes. The captain couldn't understand why his superiors would prefer to send a fighting man to a stockade rather than finding some more suitable punishment in the field. It was that lack of understanding that prevented the captain from reporting his men for violations they committed. He simply wanted no part in judging the men who were sacrificing their lives, not only for their country, but on his orders.

Pop! Pop! Again, musket fire sounded from beyond the tree line. There was a moment's break and then a sudden crackling of a volley of shots. Captain Fraser turned to the command post tent. There, the remaining company commanders were filing out to investigate the source of the commotion.

"Captain Fraser, do you see anything!?" one of the officers shouted across the camp.

"Nothing!" he answered. "Gather some men and I'll take a look!"

A series of orders were shouted and a small group of lieutenants scrambled to their horses. The captain dumped his hot water and ducked into his tent. Seconds later he reappeared in a gun belt with a saber at his side and brass field glasses in his hand. A private leading a saddled brown mare handed the reins to the captain in exchange for the field glasses. Fraser swung himself onto the horse's back as the young soldier placed the field glasses into the saddle bag. Once the captain was secure, he gently kicked at the horse's side and yanked her head toward the trees. "Follow me!" he shouted to the others, and they all galloped toward the sound of the rifle fire.

The dense underbrush and tangled jungle of tree limbs made it impossible to continue on horseback once they reached the end of the cleared pasture. Two men stayed with their mounts while the remaining group of six young officers began slashing their way through the low branches behind Captain Fraser. With each step forward the volume of musket fire increased. Though they could not yet see it, it was clear some form of skirmish was taking place.

Now slashing wildly to get to the aide of their comrades, the small band of men behind the captain wielded their sabers in a frantic fight with the natural defenses. Pressing on, the engagement somewhere before them fell suddenly silent.

The captain raised his hand for the men behind him to stop. The others lowered their swords and listened for the sounds of yelling or some other signal that friend or foe was somewhere near. But the woods were eerily quiet.

Fraser motioned for the men to spread out and then raised his field glasses to his eyes. As he struggled to focus on an open gap between the trees he imagined the worst. *Nearly the entire regiment is scattered out there somewhere. Only a few aides and a handful of sentries stayed behind in camp with the officers. If a Rebel force has come upon us there will be no order for the men to make a stand. And if those shots have come from Confederate rifles, particularly the snipers that constantly plague us, our ill-prepared men are probably pinned down in small numbers, afraid to call out for help or flee back to camp.*

Fraser waved a nearby lieutenant to his side and withdrew a note pad and pencil from his breast pocket. As the lieutenant anxiously kneeled next to him, the captain quickly scribbled a note that read:

We have reached some two hundred yards into the woods southeast of camp. Our horses are left with Lieutenant Randall and Lieutenant Adams. There is no sign of engagement and no sign of our men. I would have expected contact with some of our regiment at this distance if all were well. I fear a Rebel force of unknown size may have come between our men and this flank of our camp and they are, therefore, unable to return to our picket lines. I will hold this position until I receive orders.

Captain John C. Fraser
Commanding B Company
9th Indiana Volunteers

"Get this to Major Bradley," Fraser told the young lieutenant as he handed him the folded note. "Express my deepest concerns that our camp is in a gravely disadvantaged position, then return with my orders."

"Yes, sir," the lieutenant answered and began his sprint back to his horse.

The captain returned to his field glasses and scanned the woods around him. Long minutes passed while he impatiently waited for the distant bugle calls that would certainly result from his message. A flock of sparrows swooped through the trees, and a scattering of gray squirrels began frolicking among the fallen leaves that blanketed the red South Mississippi dirt beneath them. The captain was momentarily distracted by the bushy-tailed creatures and lowered his guard to watch their playful antics. But just as soon as the wildlife appeared it was gone, passing by the small group of men concealed among the trees without even stopping to notice them. Then the woods fell silent again.

"Get back!" the captain commanded suddenly, his order urgent yet hushed to avoid detection. "Retreat to the horses!"

The confused lieutenants stood and began jogging back toward their camp. The captain raised his field glasses to his eyes for one last look as the peaceful silence was disrupted by clanging swords and cracking tree limbs. It had taken a few seconds to realize the telltale signs of an advancing battle line. Fraser wasn't yet able to see what was approaching, but the fleeing of wildlife and the growing cacophony of troops at double-time behind it was a sure sign the enemy was in full advance.

Once again the small group of junior officers from the 9th Indiana were slashing their way through the overgrowth. The expected bugle call finally sounded from the direction of camp- the all too familiar melody of *To Arms*. But another bugle answered from the right, and then another horn from even further beyond the camp. And then, as if an angry monster had been disturbed from its slumber, a violent roar filled the countryside. The Rebel yell!

In an instant, the pounding of cannonade joined the haunting sound of attacking Confederate infantry. The 9th was without artillery support, leaving no question as to who was behind the large guns as they launched their iron missiles into the small Union camp. This was no attack by a simple band of renegade Southern loyalists, and there would be no way for the regiment to defend itself. The only thing to do was retreat, and gather as much of the scattered Federal troops together as possible until the attacking Rebels abandoned their pursuit.

Captain Fraser and the others reached the tree line together, their view of the open pasture before them revealing a horrific site. Two lines of Confederate soldiers were firing into the camp from the east and northern flanks. Small groups of Union rifleman were trying to make a stand with only their tents and supply crates for cover. As the enemy's muskets and deadly cannon fire poured into them, the desperate Indianans began to fall.

"Has anyone a carbine!" the captain asked frantically.

"We have four, sir," one of the lieutenants answered.

"We will form a line fifteen paces between each man along these trees, horses to the rear," Fraser commanded. "We cannot lose a horse, gentlemen. They're our only way out of here. Spread the carbines along the line so those Rebels think there's a lot more of us in these trees. You with the carbines, I want you to aim for their officers. Those of us with sidearms will do our best with what we have. The objective is to distract the enemy so our men have a chance to retreat. Any questions?"

The men nodded that they understood their instructions.

"Quickly then," the captain ordered. "Get those horses far out of range and find yourself a good thick tree for cover."

Each man grabbed the reins of his horse and turned back toward the woods to find a safe place to secure his mount. They then scrambled back to the edge of the forest and concealed themselves in a deceptive battle line nearly fifty yards long, yet only consisting of nine men. On the captain's command they took aim and began their meager counter offensive.

The first volley from the relatively new Spencer carbine rifles was true- two Confederate Majors collapsed to the ground and a lieutenant fell to a knee, his femur shattered by the 52-caliber round. More Rebels fell with the second and third volleys, but none of the soldiers being fired upon turned to notice that the deadly rounds were coming from behind them. Frantically, the captain and his men emptied their guns and reloaded. More Rebels became casualties, but their lines continued almost undaunted toward the camp. The plan wasn't working.

Fraser's mind raced for some other strategy that might lure the enemy line toward him. As he struggled for an alternative, the first Confederate battle flag entered the Union camp. The attack was becoming a massacre.

"God damn you," he mumbled in frustration. Then, glaring up into the sky, "God damn you!"

The captain shoved his Colt revolver into his holster and ran back to his horse. He climbed into the stirrups and wheeled around toward his certain death. When he reached the front of the tree line, he ordered one of the men with a carbine to fill it with cartridges and then give it to him. "I'll need this for a moment and then it is yours again," he told him.

With the newly issued cavalry rifle fully loaded, the captain trotted into the open field and turned toward his men. "Hold your fire!" he yelled. "Save your ammunition! If they won't come to us, I'll go get the bastards!"

Before anyone could object, the captain chambered a round into firing position and dashed toward the rear of the Confederate line at full gallop.

Half the distance to the enemy's position, Fraser yanked at the reins of his horse and stopped to survey the battlefield. To his left a group of Rebel officers also on horseback were monitoring their troops through field glasses, completely unaware of the presence of a single Union officer nearby. The captain yanked the butt of the carbine into his shoulder and took aim at the most senior-looking commander.

Boom!

Beyond the rifle blast, an enemy officer slumped in his saddle. Only a few second's delay for the captain's horse to settle and then another- Boom! A second Confederate officer slumped and then fell as his startled horse reared.

Fraser chambered another round and glared down the barrel of the carbine for his next victim. Clearly now, the rest of the enemy officers were looking toward him as they tried to steady their horses. The captain pulled his rifle's trigger again. This time a Rebel commander grasped at his shoulder, blood seeping through his fingers and soaking his dirty, gray wool coat.

A bugler stationed next to the Confederates on horseback called for reinforcements, and a mob of enemy soldiers turned away from the Union camp. The Rebel officers pointed toward their lone Federal counterpart and signaled for their men to advance. The captain answered by raising his carbine into the air and taunted his enemy, "Come and get me, you filthy Rebel sons of bitches!"

The Confederates had attacked with infantry and cannons, but with no sign of cavalry to support them, the captain had to give the Rebel foot soldiers time to be drawn into the open before he returned to his own line. "Come on, you slave mongers!" he shouted. "There's still plenty to die today!"

A Confederate officer ordered his company to stop their advance and to take aim on the enemy soldier, but Fraser, steering his horse back and forth, was a nearly impossible moving target for the Confederate muskets. A billow of smoke enveloped the flash of sparks from the Rebel guns as their errant rounds sailed wildly around the captain. Fraser quickly pulled the butt of his carbine into his shoulder before the Confederates could reload and shot dead the Rebel officer who ordered the volley.

"Who else will die today, lads!" he shouted. "Who will join me tonight for supper at Beelzebub's table!"

Before they finished reloading their muskets, the enraged Confederates broke from their ranks and began a mad dash toward the captain. Fraser let them advance a few yards closer and then yanked his horse back toward the tree line. All chaos broke loose on the field as a mass of undisciplined Confederate troops sprinted toward the woods, some completely unaware of the reason for their pursuit. Rebel officers shouted in frustration to regain order as even the greenest of commanders could see what was happening. The only question was how large a Union force was waiting to spring itself in counterattack from the concealment of the forest line.

Fraser stopped his horse just before disappearing into the trees and wheeled around again to face the approaching Rebels. "Fire!"

The rapid muzzle flashes of Union guns hidden in the trees stunned the first of the enemy soldiers. The few who fell writhed in the tall dead grass while their brothers stopped and struggled to load their empty muskets in a frenzy. As they slammed new cartridges into position, more Confederates fell before given a chance to return fire. When they were finally prepared to answer the Union guns, few of the Rebels could locate a target and simply fired blindly into the trees.

The captain secured his horse and ran back to one of his lieutenants.

"Sir, we have been joined by some of our infantry," the young officer reported.

"Good, but we're not going to put up a fight here," the captain told him. "I want you to start at the far end of our line and tell the others they are to retreat one at a time. Two to a horse if need be. Hopefully those poor fools out there will continue to stand in the open until we escape. If they advance we're in trouble. Make haste, lieutenant."

"And where shall we rally, sir?" the visibly shaken lieutenant asked.

"Have the men make their way to the Natchez Trace Road and follow it south to the city," Fraser ordered. "We will regroup there. Anyone not present in three days will be assumed a casualty."

"Yes, sir."

The captain took his notepad and pencil from his breast pocket and scribbled another note. When he was finished he handed it to the lieutenant. "In my absence, you are in command, sir. Present this to anyone who questions it."

"But..."

Fraser interrupted, "Lieutenant, you have orders."

"Yes, sir."

The lieutenant backed away from the line and ran toward the end of the column of Union soldiers as the captain raised his carbine and fired toward another enemy soldier.

More of the Rebel infantry had turned their backs on the Union camp and were now targeting the Federals in the woods. Confederate officers were gaining control of their men and organized firing lines began to assemble. Then the enemy turned their heavy guns to the woods and began bombarding the scant Union position.

Dirt and splintered pieces of wood rained down with each explosion among the trees. The captain dropped his rifle and curled into a fetal position to avoid the lethal mixture of flying debris and shards of lead. The shelling continued for several minutes, a missile exploding so close to the captain that his senses were jarred from him.

When the barrage ended, the dazed officer uncurled himself and lay on his back. For a moment the woods were peaceful, the silence only broken by the faint ringing in his ears. His cares were oddly missing. Gone were the ghoulish memories of war that haunted him even in his waking hours. There was no sensation in his arms or legs, no struggle to gain his breathe. *Finally, I am killed.*

Fraser remained motionless and waited for the great light to come upon him. There was hope of seeing his family again, hope that they would receive him warmly and allow all of the past to be forgiven. No thoughts of heaven or hell, only relief that he was finally being delivered from the killing and death, and horror of war.

But the peace of death began slowly fading, replaced by the increasing volume of muffled pops and the whizzing of musket balls sailing over him. And as life returned, so did the violent sounds of an attacking enemy.

The captain rolled onto his stomach and grasped for his carbine, only to discover the wooden stock had been blown to bits. Now with no rifle, he drew his sidearm and faced his impending doom.

Beyond what was left of the ravaged tree line stood hundreds of Confederate soldiers poised to finish what was left of the 9th Indiana Volunteers. To stand and fight was no longer an alternative. Death was the card always dealt to someone else, no matter how many times he gambled with his own life in battle. It was more the captain's fortune that he would only be wounded and then captured, and have to spend the rest of the war maimed and starving in a Confederate stockade. Surrender was no option, either. If nothing else, he still had his dignity and he would never offer his sword to a Rebel.

Fraser looked to his right for remaining members of his regiment but didn't see any. They were all dead or dying, or had fled when the shelling began. To his rear nothing but his horse, un-tethered, but still waiting loyally for her rider. Too far a distance to crawl, the captain filled his lungs twice and then darted in full sprint deeper into the woods.

Enemy soldiers yelled and cheered as the lone Union soldier to survive their artillery assault was now running away like a coward. The only thing chasing him were a few wasted musket balls fired in sport. The cavalier attitude of the victorious Rebels allowed Fraser to reach his horse safely and, though he would have preferred to have died there and finally gotten the inevitable over with, Captain John Chesterfield Fraser would continue his flight to safety very much alive.

With no maps and no compass for guidance, there were only recognizable landmarks to help the captain find his way. Unfortunately, he was certain that between safety and his current position there were several hundred Confederate soldiers. To get back to Natchez he would have to make a wide circle to his right, which would eventually lead him back to the Natchez Trace Road. He could then follow it south to the Mississippi River port city and rejoin what was left of his unit there. He could only hope that the surviving members of the regiment were smart enough to do the same.

The captain rode out of the woods and into another series of unharvested cotton fields. Comfortable that he wasn't being followed, but cautious enough to stay close to cover, he followed the nearest tree line and avoided the open dirt roads. He was surprised that he didn't come upon any other members of the regiment. *Surely, they hadn't all been killed,* he thought to himself. *A few may have deserted. There are certainly plenty of places to hide until the war is over. But even with those expected to go missing, there should be plenty of stragglers wandering this same route. Pitty on those who have surrendered.*

Darkness began to dull the color in the countryside and the early evening air grew crisp. Fraser was glad to see that at least a blanket had been left strapped to his saddle. Nothing else had been packed in his saddlebag. The horses had been taken quickly with no expectation of being away from camp for long. He draped the blanket over his shoulders and continued until the daylight completely disappeared.

Once darkness fell, he lost all sense of direction and decided to find a clearing among the trees where he could try to sleep.

He found a spot near a shallow rainwater stream where he and his horse drank. He then dug a small dirt pit to sleep in a few yards away. Pecan tree leaves were used as bedding, and once snuggled beneath the blanket, more leaves were swept over him for insulation and camouflage.

Many of the regiment would lay themselves down on this night and pray for their safety. Others would only sleep after exhaustion overcame their fear of being captured or killed. For Captain John C. Fraser, commanding B Company of the 9th Indiana Volunteers, prayers were useless and his fate already sealed. His only fear was that he might survive.

CHAPTER 5

THE CARETAKER

Autumn's peace had finally settled into Southwest Mississippi. The summer locust and crickets were silent now, their chorus replaced by the gentle rustling of what was left of the brightly-colored oak and pecan tree leaves in their last dance before winter. The giant magnolias on the Sexton Plantation would remain green with the cedars throughout the cold season. The rest would turn to tall bony skeletons until spring gave them new life.

The vegetable fields were empty, stripped naked shortly after the plantation was abandoned with word that Union General Ulysses S. Grant and his horde of Yankee invaders were crossing the Mississippi River nearby from Louisiana. The fields used for growing cotton still had a season's harvest to pick, but there was no one left to do the job. It was as if a mysterious plague had swept through the countryside and all signs of life had vanished.

There was one soul remaining on the property, though, and she didn't know exactly when it was that she'd been left behind. She didn't have a watch or calendar, and there were no neighbors or occasional guests to reference the passing of time. The unique sounds of each season and the changing colors in the landscape around her tiny corner of the world were all she had. The twelve thousand fertile acres of the Sexton Plantation were her home and she was its caretaker. Mostly cotton fields, there were a few extra acres reserved for corn and various other vegetable-growing to support the landowner and his laborers. The south end of the property ended abruptly at the Wilson Hole Creek, a place to cool off and catch crawfish at the same time. The other three sides were bordered by a variety of moss-covered indigenous trees left standing when the property was cleared for farming two generations earlier.

In the middle of the north property line, two square brick columns stood on either side of the main entrance road into the plantation. One column displayed an iron plaque. It read: *Sexton House established 1785.* Beyond the columns, a quarter-mile long stretch of red dirt road shaded by a canopy of tangled vines and tree limbs disappeared into the distance. At the end of that private road, far beyond view from its entrance, six towering Greek pillars stood majestically at the front of a white antebellum-style mansion.

The caretaker had only been welcome inside the house once and that was as a child some twenty years before. Now, from her simple quarters far across the plantation, she couldn't even see the landowner's luxurious home. There was never anything there but potential trouble, so she stayed away and let the others tend to chores there. That was until the day after a night of commotion coming from the direction of her owner's home, and after the other slaves began to flee, that she was compelled to present herself to her master, fearing it might be worse to stay away. And that is when she discovered she was all alone.

Even before she stepped onto the porch beneath the massive columns that stood guard at the front of the mansion, she knew something was terribly wrong. The parlor furniture had been removed from inside and strewn about the front lawn. Empty wine and whiskey bottles lay scattered around the expensive French furniture that had been purchased and delivered from the port in New Orleans. Miscellaneous items of discarded clothing and some of the Sextons' smaller valuables were strewn from the front door all the way to the entrance gate of the property. Too fearful to open the door and step inside after her unanswered knocks, the frightened slave woman backed away and prayed that there was no one dead inside.

Mr. Sexton's cherished Confederate battle flag, awarded to him from the local volunteer regiment after he made a significant financial donation to their cause, still flew atop its pole in the front yard. The Yankees would have never left it behind had they been the culprits of the ransacking the woman reasoned. And Rebel soldiers wouldn't have disrespected the Sexton property in such a way had the family been home, or would they? Then again, she'd come across some of the ragged Rebel strays passing through. They all looked half dead and nearly starving. It was probably those men who found the house empty after the Sextons left. The war was getting close after all. She could feel it.

Relieved that her logic meant no one was dead inside, the plantation's new temporary caretaker spent the morning after she discovered it empty gathering the Sextons' property and placing it carefully on their porch beneath the shelter of the second floor colonnade. She still didn't dare go inside. There was no reason to believe the Sextons weren't coming back. And when they did, a misunderstanding might result in punishment and a great deal of punishment was coming, that was certain.

Of the nearly one hundred slaves owned by the Sextons, she was the only one that stayed behind. The rest had scattered into the woods when one of the housemaids overheard that the Yankees were headed their way and the Sextons were leaving. It was seen as a great opportunity for the slaves to escape and find their liberators who had finally arrived to free them. Some even spoke of trying to join the Federal Army so they could return and fight those who had enslaved them. It made sense to all but one, the caretaker.

She knew the chances of Rebel soldiers, or slave hunters she called *Pattyrollers,* finding the escapees first was a greater possibility. If they were caught, some would be hung in front of the others and the rest would be beaten. Stories of what was being done to fugitive slave women were even worse. Fleeing was simply not worth the risk, especially since no one had yet even seen a Yankee soldier. With such little contact with anyone outside of the plantation, news was never more than just a rumor anyway.

For the past three years it had been at least once a week that someone would hear the Yankees were getting closer. Hopes would be high until someone would tell what all the fuss was about, and Master Sexton would come out to the field and set the story straight. Then all would be depressed for a few days until someone else made up a story about how a slave from another plantation made it to freedom, or how they heard the Yanks were getting closer. But nothing ever changed.

In the passing months the caretaker decided to do her best to maintain the plantation as best she could. It was the only thing she knew, and it would surely put her in favor with her owners when they returned. If the Yankees came first, she hoped they might take some of the land away from the Sextons and grant her a few acres along with her freedom. She wouldn't mind being a neighbor to her previous owners as long as they gave her respect. God would see to it that she found the strength to forgive them for what they'd done to her once she was freed. The Sextons were Christians too, and there was no reason for them to not be able to find peace between them once the war was over. And if Jesus successfully brokered that arrangement, the caretaker was already prepared to stay on as a plantation worker, as long as she received a salary. In the meantime, she would remain a slave, rising at dawn to spend her days tending to a garden and some animals and preparing for winter.

The captain's eyes fluttered and then focused on the dimly illuminated woods around him. Even when he was exhausted it had become impossible to sleep into morning. He hesitated to move beneath the small pile of dew-covered leaves until he was confident that he was alone. First, listen...nothing but birds. He then sat up slowly, scanning the forest around him for Rebel shadows in the new morning's mist. When all seemed safe he staggered to his feet and dusted the debris from his filthy uniform.

He had no time to acknowledge his hunger the night before. Soldiers were accustomed to ignoring the calls from an empty stomach in the heat of battle. But now that his escape had been successful, at least for the time being, there was no way to put aside the cramping in his belly. There was no food other than some fallen pecan nuts nearby.

The water from the nearby stream would help temporarily pacify the growls within him, but he couldn't stay. After eating some nuts and filling his pockets with extras, he drank himself full, rinsed his face, and led his horse to the open field only a few yards away to let her graze. There was no sense in them both going hungry and she would work harder than he on this day.

The sky turned orange and then blue as the captain waited for men from his unit to appear. Few of them had horses and there was a much greater chance of capture being on foot. As an officer he believed it was his duty to wait for those who may have walked all night scared to death and having no idea where to go. But there were none.

He impatiently checked his timepiece and wondered what he should do next. To arrive in Natchez, an officer, alone, would certainly result in others questioning his leadership. There would be whispers of cowardice and inquisitions as to why he had left his men behind. But the greater concern was *for* his men. They depended on him. The captain had come to place very little value on his own life, but his rank made him responsible for others, and that fact his heart would not let him forget. He decided to make one final effort and cautiously return to their overrun camp to see if any lost or wounded men were still there.

The idea proved to be one of desperation. Only dead comrades lay sprawled across the field of battle that began at the camp and ended where the last of those running for their lives were cut down among the trees. The enemy had finished the wounded with bayonets and pikes. Prisoners slowed them down and there was still revenge to pay for the burning of Atlanta.

The captain dared not enter the field where the remains of the ravaged camp lay smoldering. A small group of Confederates were still there salvaging anything useful that hadn't been destroyed during the bombardment. As Fraser watched them from the woods, his despair turned to anger. How was it that he would again survive when so many around him had fallen? The fair result would be to join his countrymen and die as they did, fighting.

He counted six Rebels and a handful of their Negroes sifting through the camp and stocking a tattered covered wagon. They could have the accouterments and the food. It was the thought that they might find the maps and instructions to move the regiment forward to Nashville that concerned him. Knowledge of the Union build-up in Tennessee could be a disaster if the Rebels found out about it in advance.

Cautiously, Fraser recovered six muskets and ammunition from the dead nearby and quietly loaded each weapon. The six standard issue Federal Army Springfield rifles were too heavy to carry all at once, so the captain leaned three against a nearby tree trunk and laid the others on the ground. He then removed a small brass case from his jacket, kissed it, and returned it to his breast pocket. Then lowering himself to the ground, he grabbed the first rifle and took aim at the first unsuspecting Confederate soldier.

Kaboom!

One of the scavengers lurched forward and dropped in a heap. The captain pushed the rifle aside and grabbed another. Kaboom! Another Rebel soldier grabbed his throat then stumbled and fell. The slaves ducked behind some toppled supply crates as the four remaining Rebels tried to find a target for their guns. But before they could locate the sniper, another blast came from the trees and another man crumbled to the dirt.

The captain climbed to his feet and slung two of the remaining Springfield rifles over his shoulder. He then stepped into the open and lowered the barrel of the third toward the panicked enemy soldiers. Kaboom!

A fourth spun to his side and stumbled to the ground.

The two remaining Confederates returned fire in desperation, their Enfield muskets less accurate than the Union Springfield. Both their rounds zipped harmlessly past their unprotected adversary.

The captain dropped his empty rifle and pulled another from over his shoulder. He lowered the barrel, acquired a target, and waited. The Confederates frantically reloaded their weapons and aimed. Pap! Pap!

Fraser leaned into the rounds sailing toward him, hoping one would find his chest. A sudden stinging and then the scalding heat of just being branded on his left shoulder caused him to flinch and wince with pain. An enemy bullet had grazed him while the other errantly struck a tree.

"Damn you!" the captain shouted and pulled his trigger.

Kaboom!

When the fifth Rebel soldier fell, the frightened man kneeling next to him had had enough. He ordered the slaves into the back of their covered wagon as he scrambled to gather the reins of his small team of horses. Fraser armed himself with his last rifle, but his target was concealed by the wagon's canvas. A blind shot aimed at the wagon driver's position would have to pass through the innocents he knew were concealed in the rear. The chance of it striking one of them was too great. He lowered his weapon and watched the wagon disappear to safety.

The captain scanned the field for remaining Confederate soldiers before checking his arm. When he was satisfied he was alone again, he removed his coat and examined his wound. A long gash was bleeding, the enemy round having sliced through the skin and exited out the back of his coat sleeve. It stung, but only enough to make him angry. The captain held his hand over the cut, occasionally blowing on it until the blood began to dry. It would need to be bandaged and he knew clean dressings might still be in the battered camp. He whistled for his horse and she slowly walked up to his side. He then led her into the camp to see if anyone was left alive and to treat his wound.

The first bodies he passed were those of the five Rebels he'd just slain. To his relief, they had all passed before he came upon them. There was nothing worse than watching a man die slowly, even if he was an enemy. If there was one thing the captain was good at, it was killing. A head shot at twenty yards or less. Any distance further than that, aim for the heart. A quick death was the only kind of mercy he had left for those who chose to take arms against him.

Within the camp there were more of the same but mostly dead comrades. Their boots had already been stripped off. Their pockets rummaged through. The captain pulled his paper and pencil from his jacket and wrote down their names. Someone would have to tell their loved ones back home what had happened.

Fraser then walked to his tent and found everything of usefulness taken except for some candles. All of the letters he'd saved, his extra uniform and blankets, gone. The main command post was still standing, but smoke was seeping from between the flaps at the corners of the large canvas tent. The captain threw open the flap covering the entrance and stood to the side to allow the smoke to clear.

The Rebels had piled together all of the maps and paper and set them ablaze with a small stack of wooden crates. There was nothing left but smoldering ash.

As he stomped on the few remaining embers, the captain suddenly realized something. While the other officers in the regiment had chatted away about their new orders before the Rebel attack, he had looked over some of the maps of the area. Most were Federal Army maps drawn in Washington that were based on various sources of intelligence gathered in the field. But there were also other maps that were published by local townships or businesses dealing with travel or property ownership. The deeper into the South the Union Army marched, the less accurate their issued maps became and the more dependable the civilian maps proved to be.

Fraser had understood part of their mission was to clear and then secure the Natchez Trace Road. And since they were about to travel that road north to Tennessee, he had decided to study some of those civilian maps to see if there was geography they might need to consider before they began their march. He remembered a particular map of the area that charted the local plantation property lines. One of the large parcels was close by, and he remembered it because he had silently wished his commander had chosen the estate for their camp. There, some of the officers would have been permitted to sleep indoors, or at least take turns bathing privately in a tub and not in a dirty river.

Fraser closed his eyes and envisioned the map again. It was still there in his head, clearly, each stream line, bridge and road. The plantation would be southwest approximately two miles. He could also picture the series of curved lines that depicted the small farm roads and waterways surrounding the estate. Now if he could only find those landmarks.

One of the other officers in the volunteer regiment, Major Thomas Wallace, was both a dentist and a surgeon in his hometown of Terre Haute. Fraser found him laying dead next to his open medical bag, another Union soldier dead next to him with his shirt ripped open. Wallace had clearly been rendering him aide when he was also killed.

Fraser knelt down next to the bag and pulled out an amber-colored bottle and a bandage wrap. He had seen the doctor pour the liquid over injured soldiers' wounds before. He had no idea what it was, but knew it was some kind of antiseptic. The captain pulled the cork out of the bottle and drenched the open gash on his arm. The excruciating pain that followed caused him to drop to his other knee and roll to his side. His body wanted to burst with a ferocious cry, but even in his agony he knew better. To call out in pain would only alert Rebels still nearby. He took a few moments to catch his breath and then it was back to his knees to wrap his wound.

The last thing to do before departing was to find any remaining food items among the ruins and try to locate a carbine rifle and all the cartridges he could carry. The musket had excellent range, but it took too long to reload and was cumbersome. The carbine had a built-in magazine that could carry seven cartridges. You could fire all of them before an adversary could reload his musket once. The regiment only had a few of the carbines, obtained during the misappropriation of Federal property from a temporarily left unattended supply wagon. The formal request for the rifles had been refused.

After a short search, Fraser found his weapon of choice. It had fallen in some tall grass and the Rebels had simply overlooked the prized implement of death. Cartridges were in a box that was also overlooked, probably because it had been toppled over and assumed to have already been checked. There was no food. The barrels of hard-tack were empty and on their sides. The mess wagons were completely stripped and there was no sign of any coffee left behind. Not even a pot to boil it in. Fraser had expected as much.

As the war continued the state of the average Rebel soldier had changed drastically. At first they were able-bodied, not particularly well dressed for war, but a force of strong determined men to be feared. Fraser had noticed a change in those men since Bull Run. They now appeared in their lines wearing tattered clothing, some in bare feet, with faces caked in dirt and sweat. From their battle lines they were still imposing, but when the killing was done and it was time to clear the field, it was not unusual to find enemy soldiers in the most pitiful of condition. It was clear now to Captain Fraser they were fighting a desperate foe.

Luckily, the Confederate attackers from the day before had given their next destination away by leaving a wake of matted grass and weeds behind them. They were headed north. The captain would be traveling southwest, an area unfamiliar to him but, if he continued in that direction, would eventually deliver him to the banks of the Mississippi River and Union lines. There he could make his reports and rejoin the Army. First though, he needed food and the greatest chance to find it was at the plantation only a few miles away.

Fraser's arrival in Mississippi had been during the Union's final conquest of the river at Vicksburg, and he would never forget it. When Vicksburg fell, so went the last of the Confederate garrisons watching over the Southern lifeline. But the captain didn't remember the victory for its monumental value to the Union Army. During the siege that eventually led to surrender, the captain's regiment had been placed next to an artillery battery, and the daily thundering of shells being fired into the city resulted in a significant loss of hearing in both of his ears. It began as a constant ringing that eventually faded with time. He assumed the residual effect of the cannons blasting away next to him would mean having to ask people to repeat themselves for the rest of his life.

Mounted again, the captain rode to the edge of the field's tree line and began following alongside it in search of a road or stream he had seen on the map. Riding in the open would have been faster, but also much more dangerous. Instead, he took full advantage of the cover provided by the tangled foliage to avoid exposing himself to enemy pickets. It meant often having to dismount and coax his horse through the thicket of brush. Such were the minor inconvenience of war, the kind of inconvenience to which soldiers grew accustomed. When the undergrowth grew too dense, the captain would carefully step into the open, shoulder to shoulder against his mare, and use her girth as a shield.

There was only one instance of alarm that occurred during his short journey. He had eventually become sedated by the slow rocking motion in the saddle and his sense of caution momentarily dulled. When he realized he could clearly hear the sounds in the woods in both ears, something he'd been unable to do since the bombardments at Vicksburg, he stopped to focus on the natural cacophony surrounding him. A grin crossed his face as he twisted from side to side, capturing the forgotten noises and relishing in the return of his hearing.

Then more of nature appeared as what looked like a large armor-plated possum ambled across the road in front of him. The captain and his men had never seen an armadillo until they arrived with the rest of their brigade in Louisiana. At the sight of it the Union soldiers joked that even the Rebel's critters were afraid of them, thus explaining the peculiar protective shell. To the captain the odd looking mammal looked very much like a giant rat, and he'd come to despise those vermin creatures that seemed to follow the Army everywhere they went. Fraser gently tapped his horse with his heels and moved on when the unsightly creature appeared, fearful it might actually attack them.

A short distance later he came upon a wooden fence line and followed it to a dirt road. Convinced that the path was what he'd been looking for, he steered his mare into the open and continued toward the estate he believed was at the other end. He hoped to find a house empty but only recently abandoned. It might result in a full unharvested garden having been left behind. A boiled potato with some corn and carrots would surely make a nice meal, he imagined. Fraser was also no stranger to slaughtering farm animals and had hunted deer back in Indiana. If he got lucky and found stray cattle or a pig left behind, he wouldn't hesitate to butcher a nice steak or a side of pork for supper.

The captain struggled with the idea that some of his men may have come upon the plantation home before him. His duty was to hope there would be a few of his men there, but his instinct to survive reminded him it was easier to take care of just himself than to have to deal with the responsibility of caring for others. If for only a day he would prefer to have the home to himself. It would allow him to find some momentary peace in abandoning his responsibilities before he returned to the path of death that was his certain destiny.

He assumed there was little chance any Rebels would be there. Estate homes didn't make good hiding places. If a civilian was present, he'd take a chance and offer to pay for a cooked meal, or at least barter for some items to take with him. If the house was empty he would see what was left that was still edible in the garden, and even hunt for his supper if he had to. Then he'd find the softest bed in the house for a nice long sleep.

ᢒᢅ

The chill of morning had broken as the sun continued its ascent toward its perch in the sky. The caretaker had already made her early morning rounds, greeting her two dairy cows and taking a half-bucket of milk from one of the bloated udders. When that was done, she spread some stale bread crumbs on the ground for her chickens and checked for eggs as the hens frantically pecked at their breakfast. Every morning began this way, and every party involved in the daily ritual cooperated as if they knew how much they depended on each other.

Inside her tiny quarters the caretaker boiled her milk and fried two fresh eggs in a skillet, added the last of the week's bread to her plate, and then walked back outside to sit in a chair on her porch with her morning meal in her lap. A full day was ahead, but it was best to reserve this time for enjoying the temporary solace the war had delivered to her. This was also the time each morning that she prayed and thanked God for her temporary fortune, and asked that he might find her worthy of permanent liberation. All were asked to be blessed, even the absent slave owners who thought nothing more of her than an item of farm machinery.

When her plate was clean and she was satisfied with her prayers she began her inside chores. The first task was the feeding of her oven fire so she would have sufficient coals to bake with. It was bread day and she planned to spend the rest of the morning preparing dough, and then baking enough biscuits and corn loaf to last her through the next week. There were no Mondays or Tuesdays, or any other day most people identified on a calendar. Here, each day was identified by a succession of chores. Tomorrow would be firewood-gathering day.

She began by placing a handful of log splinters into the fire. When the inside belly of her iron stove began to glow, she selected a large piece of oak from a small stack of wood nearby and dumped it into the growing fire. The caretaker then stood back, brushing her hands on her apron, then leaned forward again to feel the heat emitting from her stove. But instead of soothing warmth, a frightening chill came over her.

She spun around expecting to find an intruder, yet there was no one there. Something wasn't right. The sensation of another presence having entered the room was all around her. The frightened caretaker listened as her eyes darted around the room. Only silence. She took a moment to begin breathing again, then cautiously returned to her stove.

Wham! Wham! Wham!

The caretaker's door slammed against its frame, three violent pounds and the disturbance suddenly stopped. The caretaker snatched a single barrel shotgun from the side of her fireplace and quickly leveled it at the threshold of her front door.

"Is anyone there?" a man's voice called from outside.

The caretaker stood frozen, her finger sinking deeper into the trigger. Again, the door began to slam against its frame.

The cross board that the caretaker used to secure the door from the inside was propped up against the wall. She only used it at night, having lost her fear of a stranger appearing during the daytime. Even if the board was in place, the hinges on the doorframe were loose and could easily be dislodged with only a modest effort. She was trapped.

"I mean you no harm," the man's voice called out as his shadow passed the window adjacent to the front door. "I can see the smoke from your fire. I only want to pay or trade for some food."

"Go on now!" the caretaker demanded. "You on Sexton land. They don't take kindly tuh no trespassin'!"

"Ma'am, I'm a Federal Officer of the 9th Indiana Infantry. I have no quarrel with you or the owner of this property. I only wa..."

"You a Yank?" the caretaker interrupted.

"Yes I am, ma'am."

"Step on over to the fron'a that window an' let me take a look at yuh. I got a gun so bessn' do as I tells yuh."

The captain slowly raised his hands and sidestepped to the front of the window. The caretaker's and the Union officer's eyes met, both unprepared for the vision before them.

Fraser wasn't expecting to find a Negro woman alone on the other side of the door. And he was particularly surprised to see that she actually did have a rather large-barreled firearm pointed at him.

The caretaker was also taken aback by the figure she saw. Instead of the image of a tall, gallant soldier as she imagined the men of her noble liberating army would be, she saw a haggard and disheveled transient- a man who looked more as if he'd stolen the uniform from a corpse, than a knight who wore it proudly in the fight for her freedom.

"Y'ain't no Yank," the caretaker declared.

"I most certainly am, ma'am. This is the uniform of a Federal Officer."

"You coulda' got that anywhere. You go on now an' leave me be."

"I have papers. I can prove who I am."

"That won't do yuh no good here, suh. Now go on yo' way. "

The captain assumed by the slave woman's response that she couldn't read. He scrambled for another way to prove his credentials and then it came to him.

"I'm going to lower my hands to show you something," Fraser warned. "Don't shoot me."

The caretaker motioned with her shotgun for him to continue. Slowly, Fraser slid his hand between the lapels of his dirty coat and withdrew a small tin case from his breast pocket. He then carefully held it out to the Negro woman on the other side of the window and motioned that he would pass it under the door. The caretaker nodded her approval and moved away from the window to retrieve the silver case from the floor.

"Put yo'sef back in fron'a that window," she ordered, still leery of the stranger's intent.

When the two were again facing each other, the caretaker cradled her weapon over her left arm and opened the case. Inside was a tintype photograph of two soldiers. At their right was the flag of the United States. At their left, on the wall in the background behind them, was a framed portrait of a bearded man she recognized. It was Abraham Lincoln.

"That's me in the picture," the officer said. "I got that three years ago in Baltimore. You know where that is? It's up north in Maryland."

The caretaker had to study the images more closely to determine if one of the men in the photo was the same person standing outside her door. She could immediately discount one of the figures. She guessed he wasn't much more than a grown up boy. The other figure had a vague resemblance to the man outside, but that image also appeared to be much younger. "Come up closer," she said.

The captain carefully stepped toward the window and forced a cautious smile to his face. "You must consider I was clean-shaven and rested when that photograph was taken."

"Uh huh," the caretaker answered, discounting the excuse. "Where's the res' a you?"

"My regiment was camped about two miles northeast of here. We were attacked while most of our men were out looking for food. They got the better of us and I'm afraid not many are left. I'm trying to get back to Natchez by myself. I found this property on a map and thought someone might be here to trade with, or I might at least find an empty bed to sleep for a few hours."

"Is it almos' over?" the woman asked anxiously.

"The war? No, ma'am it isn't," Fraser answered glumly. "But that could change any day. Federal troops are marching through the South with very little resistance. Yesterday was the first real fight I've seen since early summer."

"But they whooped yuh, you said."

The captain hung his head for a moment and admitted, "Yes, they did."

"Well...," the caretaker began, and hesitated. She could see the shame and disappointment in the weary soldier as he confessed to defeat. "I ain't got much," she answered sternly, still holding her shotgun on him.

"I don't ask for anything you can't spare, ma'am. And I will pay."

147

The two locked eyes and studied each other silently. The caretaker weighed her options, knowing all too well the stranger would eventually get what he wanted. Even if she convinced him to leave, he'd only return later with more soldiers and they might take everything she had. If the war was over she would welcome him, and as many others as she could manage. But while the fighting continued, it might mean her life if she was caught feeding Yankees.

The reality of what he had stumbled upon was also seeping into the mind of the captain. This was a slave who probably struggled to feed herself every day. Accepting anything from the Negro woman would be taking advantage of her situation, even if she did volunteer what little she had. Fraser decided he would rather go hungry.

"I'm sorry, ma'am," he said finally breaking the tense moment. "I'll be on my way." The captain then turned and began walking back to his horse.

"No!" the caretaker shouted and pulled the front door open. "Don't go!"

Fraser stopped and slowly turned around.

"I'm sho' I can find somethin' fo' yuh," the caretaker said, her shotgun now lowered to her side. "Take yuh horse over in them trees an' tether 'em up so's no one knows I got a Yank in my house. Then come on inside."

The captain smiled. "Thank you."

He took the reins of his mount and led the thrice previously wounded warhorse to a patch of trees where he wrapped the leather straps around a trunk. He then unbuckled and removed the saddle from his horse's back, and laid it in the tall grass a few yards away. It had a large stamp in the leather identifying it as property of the U.S.

Army, so he covered it with some leaves to prevent his horse from being linked to a Union soldier. His saddle bags were also stamped with the Federal Army brand, but instead of hiding them he draped them over his shoulder and returned to the caretaker's house, this time gently knocking on the door.

"Come in," the caretaker said.

The captain removed his dusty sweat-stained kepi cap and walked inside. He quickly surveyed the tiny home, constructed of eight-inch wood planks with a tin ceiling. There was only one door and two windows. A fireplace was cut into the wall to his right and an iron box stove sat strangely positioned beneath the window on the wall to his left. Instead of glass in that window, the flue tube from the stove had been placed in the opening and then sealed in makeshift fashion with boards and sod.

A small table with a chair at each end was the centerpiece of the modest home. Two additional chairs for the table were stored in a corner. The only other furniture items in the room were two rocking chairs placed in front of the fireplace, each with a quilt draped over it. Across from the doorway on the east side of the house was a wooden partition that separated a bed from the main room.

"Sits where yuh like," the caretaker said. She then watched the captain nervously try to decide which chair was most appropriate. His confusion made her feel more comfortable with him. If he wasn't bold enough to go directly to a chair without it first being offered to him, he couldn't be that much of a threat.

"Why don't yuh go on over in fron'a that fireplace an' takes off them boots. I'll make yuh somethin' tuh drink."

"Thank you," the captain answered and stepped over to the fireplace. He stood for a moment between the two rocking chairs and rubbed his unshaven chin. He wanted to make sure he didn't select his host's preferred rocker.

"That one's fine," the caretaker said as she pointed to the chair on the right.

The captain thanked her again and lowered himself carefully into the creaky seat.

"My name is John Fraser," he said as he struggled to pull off his boots. "May I ask your name?"

"Abby," the slave answered. "Abigail, if'n yuh wanna say it the long ways. Call me either, don't matter nuthin' tuh me."

"Very pleased to meet you, Miss Abigail."

The caretaker walked over to the captain and handed him a cup. "Drink this slow an' easy or it gonna turn yo' stomach."

"What is it?"

The slave woman was too distracted by the sudden waft of foul odor to answer. "Suh, I's real sorry, but you stank somethin' awful," she blurted out. "When's the las' time yuh had a bath?"

"I'm so sorry," the captain apologized as he rose from his chair and gathered his boots. "I've forgotten my condition. Do you have a well with some water outside?"

"I got me a well, but that water's so cold it'll put yuh in a sick bed. You needs a good soak'n in some hot water an' soap is what you needs. Stickin' yo' head under my well ain't gonna do no good. An' I's thinkin' them clothes you got on is half of it. Shed 'em off an' I'll give 'em a good scrubbin'. There's some man britches out in the shed an' yuh can fetch the tub out there while you at it. I'll put some water in the kettle."

"You don't need to do all that for me, ma'am," the captain said, rather surprised at the sudden flurry of candid commentary regarding his odor.

"If'n you gonna be in my house smellin' like a five-day-dead 'coon I do, suh." The slave took hold of the captain's arm and walked him to the front door. "That shed's where yuh gonna find alls you need," she said, pointing to a tiny wooden outbuilding. "Pile them dirty clothes in a 'tatuh sack an' we'll give 'em a good soakin'."

The last time the captain had bathed was in a Mississippi River cove somewhere near Port Gibson two weeks earlier. The water had been so muddy that he'd only replaced the old dirt with river silt. The opportunity to take a real bath and wash the sweat and grime from his uniform was almost as appealing as the idea of a home cooked meal. Without argument, he headed for the small storage shack as directed.

Inside, he found a straw-covered dirt floor with an empty stable area and a variety of farm tools hanging from the walls. A dust-covered dresser with a shattered mirror frame on top of it was stored in one corner. The captain discovered a pair of folded cotton pants in one of the drawers, but couldn't find any men's undergarments. He debated for a moment whether he should change completely, or continue to wear his filthy underwear under the clean britches. To resolve the dilemma, he sat on a milking stool and lowered his head to his thighs to get a good whiff of himself. The stench made him shudder. After waving the residual stink from his face and confirming he was alone, he quickly stripped naked and then slid on the clean pants. Once the loose trousers were around his waist, he attached his uniform suspenders to them to keep them from dropping back to his ankles. As he stood and tested the fit he felt odd that he was dressed in another man's pants, and particularly strange that he'd dressed without underwear, something he'd never done before.

The rest of the clothing in the dresser was either too small or fit for a woman. In the name of modesty he tried to fit into a large lady's blouse, having the opinion it was better to temporarily dress in peculiar fashion than go bare-chested in the presence of a woman. But even the top's allowance for buxomness was too small in the shoulders for him. Reluctantly satisfied with having at least found clean britches, he wadded up his uniform and undergarments, and placed the bundle in an empty burlap potato sack. He then dropped the sack into a large washtub and dragged it to the house.

Abigail had left her front door open in an attempt to air out the lingering odor of her guest. When the captain returned he found her standing at her table shucking the husks from a small pile of corncobs. "Put it close to the fire as yuh can," she said as the captain maneuvered the tub through the doorway. "The water'll be done in a bit."

The captain positioned the tub in front of the fireplace, and removed the potato sack from inside. "Where can I wash these?"

"Firs' off, get them smelly thin's back outside. They don't needta be 'round here 'til we'z ready tuh wash 'em. An' that ain't a commin' 'til after you."

The captain stepped back out the front door and tossed the potato sack into the yard. When he returned he apologized again for his condition.

"I 'spose it ain't yo' fault," Abigail told him. "Them britches looks like they fit yuh fine."

The self-conscious officer folded his arms together to cover his bare chest. Not only was he uneasy with being half-naked, but he thought the battle scars on his pale skin might be too frightful for the slave woman to see.

"What's that you got on yuh arm, suh?" Abigail walked around the table and approached the captain. He looked at his shoulder and saw the blood-caked bandage that had caught the slave woman's eye. "It's only a scratch, ma'am."

"That's more'n a scratch, it be bleedin' like that. Le'me take a look at it."

The captain kept his arms folded, making sure his nipples were covered with his hands as the slave examined his wound.

"Lawdy, Lawd," she said. "Gonna have tuh clean that up before it gets infected. That ain't no scratch neither, suh. You done look likes you been shot." She looked into the captain's eyes and waited for a response.

He nervously glanced away and didn't speak.

"Well," she said returning to her examination, "whatever it was, I don't see anythin' left of it in there. You'a lucky man. Do it hurt?"

"I'd forgotten all about it."

Standing next to the captain, Abigail could see the many scars on his body. "Is all them from the fightin'?" she asked.

Fraser swallowed hard and tried to force a smile to his face, but his trembling lips betrayed him. He had once been a handsome man, prideful of his good looks and careful to keep his body the temple that God suggested it should be. There was nothing left of that John Fraser. Only a marred shell defaced by years of battle was left as the constant reminder of what he had become.

Abigail thought he was only being shy about his partial nakedness and changed the subject. "Go on back tuh yuh seat an' drink what I done made fo' yuh. It'll clean yuh up on the inside whilest we try to get yuh right on the outside."

The captain nodded that he understood and returned to his rocking chair, relieved the topic of his scars had concluded. He then took a sip from the cup he had left on the floor before he'd been ordered to change clothes outside. The liquid was sour on the back of his tongue and tasted of some kind of alcohol. He raised the cup again to his lips and took two big gulps. This time the homemade elixir spilled into his throat and left a burning trail all the way to his stomach. The captain gasped for air and clutched his chest.

"I tol' you tuh drink it slow," Abigail said.

"Yes, you did!" the captain admitted as he coughed and wiped the tears from his eyes. "What is this?"

"If'n I tol' yuh, you wouldn't drink it."

"Is this some kind of homemade whiskey you made yourself?"

"It ain't no whiskey, but I do make it myself, yes'm."

The burning in the captain's stomach began to rise up to his brain. "I fear you have poisoned me, madam," Fraser proclaimed as he shook his head and batted his eyes.

"The only poison in you is what that snake root is a cleanin' out of yuh."

"Snake root? This dreadful concoction has no resemblance to any herbal remedy I've ever tasted whatsoever."

"Well, you's prob'ly right about that. But yuh mix anythin' with sugar an' let it fester fo' a few days, it ain't gonna tas'e nothin' like what yuh started out with."

"Oh my God..."

"No, suh!" Abigail said sternly. "Yon't be usin' the Lawd's name like that in my house."

"I'm sorry, ma'am," the captain apologized. "I'm just fearful you've fed me something that may be the end of me."

Abigail drew a deep breath and calmed herself. The captain clearly thought he was in danger of being poisoned and wasn't simply whining over a beverage that didn't agree with him. "I shoulda reminded yuh tuh drink it slow," she said. "An' I would likes you tuh stop calling me ma'am. I ain't used tuh bein' called no ma'am, an' I knows you means well, but I keep thinkin' you is talkin' tuh someone else ever' time you say it."

"Then...Miss Abigail, I would be glad to call you by your name. And I would like you to call me John."

"I will try, suh," Abigail answered, suddenly very humble.

"Is something wrong?"

"Naw. I jus' never called no white man by his firs' name before."

The captain didn't know how to respond. He thought for a moment and then rose from his chair. He walked over to his host and extended his hand. The nervous slave woman placed her hand in his.

"Miss Abigail, my name is Captain John Chesterfield Fraser, commanding B Company of the Ninth Indiana Volunteers, United States Army. On behalf of myself and the United States Government, I am very honored to make your acquaintance." The captain then bowed and released the slave's hand.

"I am also honored tuh meet you, Captain Fraser," Abigail answered slowly with a curtsy and trying to use her best English. If the captain was going to treat her like a lady, she was going to act like one. "Please allow me tuh cook you my fines' suppuh."

"I would be forever grateful, Miss Abigail. And I will, of course, reimburse you for your generosity."

"I got no use fo' no Yankee money, suh. It ain't worth nothin' down here. B'sides, you fightin' fo' my freedom. How'm I s'posed tuh take money from you?"

"Then I will repay you with labor. I'm sure you have some repair or chore I can perform."

"You can fill that tub with the water boilin' over that fire an' get that dang stank off'ya, is what yuh can do. Yuh doin' that's gonna hep me enough an' give me time tuh get this cookin' started."

"It is as well as done."

The captain returned to the fireplace and emptied the first kettle of simmering hot water into the tub. He then refilled the kettle with well water from outside and returned the iron pot to the hanger over the open flames. "Is there anyone else on the property?" he asked as he stood feeling awkward with nothing to do but wait for another pot of water to heat up. He could sit and relax, but that would be rude, he thought to himself.

"They all done took off an' lef' me," Abigail answered. "All of 'em. Even the folks who owns this place." She knelt next to the captain and began carefully cleaning his wound with a wet cloth.

"Why did you stay?" he asked and winced at the stinging when Abigail dabbed at his cut.

"Where's I gonna go?" she answered, ignoring his display of pain. "I ain't never been nowhere but town once. An' that was when I was jus' a chile."

"You've never been anywhere except on this farm?"

"I'm a fiel' slave, suh. I got no business bein' anyplace but here."

"Abigail, call me John, please," the captain reminded her warmly. "Well, when this war is over, you can go anywhere you want. You can take a train to New York City and see the opera, and then you can scoot on down to Atlanta and have yourself the finest steak dinner you ever imagined."

"That will be nice. I 'spose you already done those things?"

"No, can't say I have," the captain answered. "I've been to the theater once, but that wasn't in New York City. As for Atlanta, well, it'll be a while before any fancy restaurants return to that city. Half the Union Army burned it all down a short while ago. That must have been an awful sight."

"Is the fightn' comin' this away?"

"I don't think so," the captain said. "All the Rebels seem to be headed to Georgia and Virginia to make one last try at holding us back. At least that's what I thought before yesterday. My regiment was on its way to Nashville, Tennessee. We assumed we were moving back north because this part of Mississippi was secure. It appears we were wrong. It won't go on forever," the captain tried to assure her. "We just need these people down here to come to their senses and give up."

"So Lincum's gonna win?" Abigail asked.

"It's pronounced *Lincoln*, and yes, I don't doubt we're going to win eventually. But there's going to be a lot more who are going to die before this mess gets settled."

"God's side will prevail," the slave woman declared. "It always do."

"I'm afraid God's not paying attention to this war," the captain responded. "He can't be."

"Oh yes'm he is. God an' Jesus is lookin' down on all you fightin' men, writin' down all the names a them who's layin' theyselves down to the Lawd's cause in this war. Each one of 'em's gonna get his place in heaven, right there with all the other angels who done what God says is right."

"Who taught you about Jesus?"

"We all know Jesus," Abigail answered as she wrapped a clean strip of cloth around the captain's cleaned wound. "Yuh cain't keep his word out, even from us Nigras out here in Missi'ppi. Way I sees it, ain't no Nigra got nothin' tuh live fo', 'cept the promise of God freein' us up someday."

"Do you have a Bible?" Fraser asked.

"Yessuh' I do. Cain't read a word of it, but I knows what it says jus' the same. I ain't 'sposed tuh have it neither. Sextons won't be havin' none a us Nigras doin' no readin'. I guess they 'fraid we get a book or two out here, next thing yuh know, we start learnin' tuh readin' an' writin' an' we gonna get too smart or somethin.' The Bible I got was gived tuh me by a gal friend of mine over on another farm down the road. We use tuh worship together before everyone done runned off an' lef' me. Sometimes we'd stay up all night jus' a prayin' for God tuh he'p you Yankees get this war done with."

"We appreciate your support, Miss Abigail."

Fraser didn't want to share his opinion that God had turned his back on the men fighting the war. He wasn't even sure there was a God anymore. Abigail needed something to believe in and he wasn't going to take that away from her, no matter how naive her ideas of Christianity were. To the captain, the truth was that tens of thousands of American men on both sides of the conflict were dying gruesome deaths at each other's hands. Both sides believed they were doing God's will, yet the Almighty refused to intercede and give a clear sign to who was morally right. In the end, Fraser knew it would be the larger and better equipped army that would win the war. God would have little say in it.

"What'll yuh do when it's over?" Abigail asked and returned to the kitchen. "Do yuh have a wife?"

"No," the captain answered.

"Why not? A man like you should be married with lots a chilluns."

"I just don't have anyone." The blunt tone in the captain's voice signaled he didn't care for the direction of the conversation. "How about you? Were you married?"

"I had a man once," Abigail answered. "But he took tuh runnin' one too many times an' he got hisself strung up. Firs' time he got caught they jus' took a pine switch to 'em an' whipped him everwhich-way 'til he had a faintin' spell. But that weren't good enough, so the Patties took some salt an' poured it on his back jus' tuh wake him up. Then he started makin' 'em mad 'cause he wouldn't holla out or beg. The only thing lef' was tuh kill 'em, but I guess Massa Sexton wouldn't have none of it. So they 'cided tuh leave 'em tied up all night an' let the bugs an' critters get to 'em."

"I'm sorry," the captain offered sympathetically.

"Oh, that was a long while ago an' I knew it was a comin'. I tol' that man he better stop thinkin' 'bout takin' off all the time, but he went an' done it anyhow. I 'spose I shouldn't say it, but I was real mad when he did it again an' got hung up fo' it. Keepin' that man alive after that firs' beatin' was a lot a work on me. Fo' him tuh go off an' try it again, well suh, Lawd forgive me, I jus' didn't have the sad feelin's I believe I shoulda' had the second time 'round."

"So you never had a chance to have any children yourself?" the captain assumed. There was no sign of children at the house.

"I had babies," Abigail answered. "One didn't make two seasons. The other got took from me."

"What do you mean, *took*?"

"My massa come 'round one day an' jus' took 'em. Never seen 'em again. That's another reason why my man done runned off. He got so boiled up mad he had tuh go before he kilt somethin'."

"I am very sorry to hear that."

"I'm sorry I got that story in my heart to tell."

The room fell quiet. The captain emptied another kettle of hot water into the tub and began heating another. As he watched the flames flickering in the fireplace he tried to imagine Abigail's world, a place where humanity was absent and evil reigned. The captain had seen freed Negroes before in Indiana. There weren't many, but occasionally a colored man would appear in his hometown, mostly to buy goods from the general store or visit the blacksmith. They never stayed and never caused any trouble so no one paid much attention to them. The more the captain thought about it, the more he realized Abigail didn't fit the mold of the typical Southern slave he'd imagined. He expected a less articulate and much more humbled woman. The slave, although she couldn't read, spoke almost just as well as the average Indiana farmer, and she had pointed a gun at him one moment and successfully talked him out of his trousers the next. That certainly wasn't the expected behavior of an enslaved woman. The captain grinned at himself when he realized the irony and decided to take another cautious sip of the snake root tea. This time, it slid easily down his throat like a smooth Carolina apple brandy.

"See there," Abigail said. "You takes jus' a li'l at a time, an' it ain't so bad."

"No, ma'am, it's not bad at all." The captain took another sip. As the fermented herbal tea flowed through his veins to his head he began to relax. "Do you know what today is?"

"I los' tracka' the days a long time ago, Mister John," Abigail answered.

"Today is called Thanksgiving," the captain told her. "President Lincoln made today a holiday just like Christmas."

"I ain't never heard a no Thanksgivin', but I sho' knows Christmas. That's the day our Lawd baby Jesus got born from Mary."

"That's right. Do you celebrate Christmas?"

"Oh my yes'suh. We get all gussied-up an' have us a wonderful time. Ain't much to do in the fiel's 'round then, an' the Sextons get in such high spirits they lets us butcha' up some pigs an' we haves us a gran' ol' time. There's singin' an' dancin' an' all kindsa' good feelin's goin' on."

"That does sound grand."

"It was," the slave added. "Don't know if it ever gonna happen 'round here no mo'. I ain't got nobody tuh have no Christmas with now. Without the Sextons here tuh tell me when it's time, don't really knows whats tuh do. I jus' takes a day after all the leaves done falled off the trees an' makes myself a li'l extra fo' suppuh, an' think all day on what Jesus done fo' me. That's how I have Christmas now. 'Spose that's good 'nough tuh get me in heaven?"

"I'm sure it is," Fraser answered, marveling at the slave woman's commitment to her faith.

"What's this Thanksgivin' fo'?" she asked.

"I'm not sure exactly," the captain replied. "I believe it's a day to give thanks for our country. Kind of odd to celebrate while we're split in two and killing each other, but I understand the President's intentions."

"Don't make no sense tuh me," Abigail said.

"And, with all due respect, I wouldn't expect it to, ma'am. What I know and think of this country is far different than what you know,

I'm sure. When I think of America, I think about a ship full of people who came over here from Europe to escape the rules of kings and queens. And I think about how those people had to fight off the British when they sailed over and tried to take away what was earned by the first settlers. Those first Americans fought hard to be free and they won. Because of what they did we have the right to think and live however we want, and it's something to be very proud of. I believe President Lincoln is just trying to remind us of that. And I think this is about the best time for it."

"Someday then, I hopes I have me a Thanksgivin' Day," Abigail proclaimed.

The captain understood her meaning. She wasn't free and had no rights. Her ancestors didn't come to America to be free. They were kidnapped and dragged here for enslavement. That was no reason to celebrate. He suddenly wished he hadn't mentioned the subject.

Abigail saw his remorse and knew he hadn't meant to offend her. "Don't mean we cain't have you yo' Thanksgivin'. I s'pose you 'n yo's is tryin' tuh make me free, jus' like them that came over in them boats an' had tuh fight fo' they own freedom. I'm guessn' the Lawd put yuh here t'day jus' so I could fix yuh up so you could get back to it."

Now the captain was overwhelmed with guilt. He'd long ago discarded his patriotic will to fight for the restoration of the Union and the subsequent abolishment of slavery. He didn't care anymore. Too many had died around him, slaughtered to resolve an argument that should have been settled in Congress, not at the ends of bayonets in the broken nation's countryside.

The captain was there at Antietam Creek just outside of Sharpsburg, Maryland, where 22,000 would fall dead or wounded in a single day. He was there at Fredericksburg, Virginia, where pomposity and stubbornness in the Federal command would result in three Union casualties to every single Confederate loss. And then there was the three-day battle in the fields south of Gettysburg, Pennsylvania. Over 50,000 men who called themselves Americans, regardless of which army they represented, would fall there. As that battle raged, the captain and his regiment were in Vicksburg, piling rotten corpses into carts and wagons as the humid July heat bore down upon them.

And as if the agony of watching men die day after day wasn't enough, there had been the torture of the losses in the captain's own personal life. All who he once lived for, all that he was willing to fight and die for, those things were gone.

A gentle tapping on his shoulder awakened him from his spell. It was Abigail with a piece of soap in her hand. "You better get in that water before it starts gettin' cold."

The captain took the soap and Abigail emptied another steaming kettle into the tub. After placing the kettle on the floor next to the fireplace, she turned just in time to see her guest climbing into the tub with his pants on.

"You jus' wait one minute, suh," she ordered. "Y'ain't gettin' in that bathin' tub with them britches on. Them's all I got. What yuh 'sposed tuh put on whens y'all cleaned up? That nassy ol' uniform ain't gonna be fit fo' wearin'."

The captain raised his foot back out of the water and stood nervously like a child who'd just been scolded. "I'm afraid I'm a bit too modest to remove all of my clothing in the presence of a lady," he said.

"I won't look at yuh," Abigail answered as if it should have been understood. "I got plenty to do other'n ganderin' all over a neked white man. B'sides, y'ain't got nothin' I ain't seen before."

The captain waited for Abigail to turn away and said, "Thank you." He then quickly wrestled the cotton pants off and climbed into the tub. Just as the soothing hot water began to absorb into his tired muscles, Abigail began walking toward him with linens in her hand. The captain frantically grabbed the pants that he'd left folded by the side of the tub and covered himself.

The slave woman shook her head and tossed the towel and wash-cloth to the bashful bather. "You sho' is somethin'," she said with a disapproving shake of her head and then returned to her meal preparations.

The captain didn't respond. He wasn't only concerned about his manhood being exposed. He also feared that the rash of infected chig-ger bites and sores covering his lower extremities would be grotesque to his host.

"How's that feel?" Abigail asked from the table with her back to the captain.

"I cannot describe it," Fraser answered. "I only hope the layer of dirt I'm washing off isn't what's been keeping me warm at night."

Abigail smiled. "Make sure an' get that head a yo's clean, too. No tellin' what's crawlin' 'round up there. I don't want nothin' jumpin' off a yuh whiles you at my suppuh table."

The captain did as directed and began scrubbing a handful of soap lather into his oily matted hair.

"I'm gonna go out yonder tuh get a few things," Abigail said as she crossed the room. "You keep on with that what yuh doin', an' put them nassy clothes in the soap water when y'done. I shouldn' be long."

The captain's eyes were closed to keep the soap out, so he didn't notice the slave woman retrieving the shotgun from the side of the door. "Is there anything else I can do?" he asked.

"Naw, I won't be long. You can he'p when I gets back."

The door then slammed shut and the captain was alone again with only the sound of water spilling over his body and the snapping of embers in the fireplace. He rinsed the soap from his hair and leaned back against the side of the tub. Soon, he was thinking about the journey he'd traveled and how it had changed from the adventure he thought it would be. His days as a small town banker were almost too far gone to recall. In the Army, he spent most of his time on the march and in camp trying to forget his life before the war. As for the few things he wanted to remember, constant exhaustion and fear had nearly erased those things from his mind. Now it would be impossible to return to the life he once knew- wearing a fresh suit every day, being established in the community, and attending church on Sunday with his family. He could never go back.

Fraser leaned over the side of the tub and rifled through the pants he had found in the shed outside. He found the small tin case that contained his photograph and opened it. At the sight of the image inside, his hands began to tremble and his throat tightened. Then, alone and desperate in a slave cabin a thousand miles from home, the captain began to weep.

CHAPTER 6

THE TRUTH

The echo of distant gunfire was well known to the captain, even when it came in a single shot. He jumped to his feet and ran to his saddle bag where, inside, he retrieved his Colt revolver. Wrapped only in a towel, he scrambled to the front window and peered cautiously outside.

There was no sign of disturbance and no sign of Abigail. The captain waited anxiously for another shot, but it never came. He hurried back to the center of the room and put back on the clean pair of britches he'd been loaned. A trail of wet footprints followed him back to the front door where he carefully stepped outside.

He closed his eyes for a moment to focus on the noises around him. Among the birds chatting in the trees was a woman's voice singing, her melody drifting faintly in the cool autumn air. He turned his head to point an ear toward the sound. It was clear to him now. Abigail was walking up a dirt path, singing a song about her love for Jesus. The captain tucked his revolver into the front of his pants and waited. The cold steel barrel against his skin made him shiver. A minute later, the dark-skinned slave woman appeared over the horizon with a rifle in one hand and a lifeless goose dangling in the other.

"Got us a good'un!" Abigail called out when she spotted her dinner guest standing on the porch. "Did yuh put them dirty clothes in the tub likes I tol' yuh?"

Fraser smiled and waved, and then scurried back into the house to throw his laundry into the dirty bath water. When Abigail finally got to her front door and opened it, she found the captain kneeling over the side of the large wash basin scrubbing his uniform.

"I got somethin' fo' that," she said as she returned her weapon to the side of the fireplace and plopped the flimsy bird onto the table. She then walked back outside and returned a few seconds later with a metal washboard. "Use this tuh scrub them clothes on."

The captain took the washboard and thanked her. "I heard the gunshot and thought there was trouble," he said.

"The only ones in trouble 'round here is this bird," Abigail answered with a chuckle.

"Where'd you find him?"

"We got us a pond down the road a ways. Ever' once-in-a-while these things lan' so thick in there yuh cain't hardly miss 'em."

"Well, that's a fine looking goose, I must say. I also must admit I feel a little foolish having a woman go out and hunt for supper while I'm doing the wash."

The slave smiled. "Oh, I jus' done the easy part. You the one gonna take all them feathers off. I gots corn biscuits tuh bake an' some okra tuh fry. Thinkin' also about a sweet 'tatuh pie. What's yo' thinkin' on that?"

"Miss Abigail, I believe you are teasing me now."

"Well y'ain't gonna get nothin' if'n you don't get started on pluckin' this here goose. There's a big ol' wood barrel of rainwater out back. Take them clothes out an' give 'em a good rinse an' then hang 'em up on the line. If'n you don't hurry up, yuh gonna lose a couple hours a sun tuh dry them clothes out."

"I'll get right to it." With that the captain squeezed the extra water out of his uniform and returned it to the potato sack. He then carried it outside to finish as directed.

Abigail followed him with a large pot in her hand. She went to the well and pumped it full of water and then returned to the house. She then placed the pot on top of the stove and dumped the goose inside.

The captain rinsed the dirty bathwater out of his uniform in the barrel of clean water, and then draped the various clothing items that made up his uniform over a thin hemp rope that was tied to two separate tree trunks. Once his laundry was hung to his satisfaction, he pulled each item to his nose and made sure the stench was gone. Much to his relief, his uniform smelled nearly as fresh as the day it was issued to him.

"I fear I'll have that uniform back in its previous condition in no time," the captain announced as he stepped back into the house. "I'm very surprised that soap has almost given it a certain pleasant fragrance." The captain placed the towel over his shoulders to cover as much of his naked chest as he could. "Where's the main house on this property?" he asked.

"'Bout half a mile or so aways," Abigail answered. "Cain't see it from here. Used tuh be a beautiful place 'til them Rebs got to it."

"And the owners just disappeared one day?"

"I 'spect they got scared when they heard y'all was a comin'. They only took what they could fit in a couple wagons. Jus' runned off. I'm guessin' they took a couple house Nigras with 'em an' that's it. Those a' us out in the fiel's din't know what tuh do. Then all the talkin' started an' next thing I knows I'm the only one lef'."

"Why didn't you go, too?" the captain asked.

"Go where?" Abigail countered. "Missi'ppi ain't no place fo' a slave tuh be out wanrin' 'round loose. They got folks here who all they do is hunts down stray Nigras. An' with this war goin' on, it 'specially ain't no time tuh be caught runnin' 'round loose in these parts, no suh."

"I'm sure you're right," the captain agreed. "Was this your home before?"

"No. This was where the white field bossman lived who watched over us. He's how we firs' heard a war was goin' on, 'cause he went to go be a Reb soldier. That's his gun he lef' behind. He took the good one with'm."

"So how long do you think you've been here all by yourself?"

"Least one harvest and a whole plantin' season."

"And you never thought about heading north?"

"I was kinda wishin' y'all up north would show up down here one day, tuh tell yuh the truth," Abigail answered with a smile. "I guess you is it. How's it feel tuh be someone's wish come true?"

"I'm sorry I'm not exactly what you hoped for," Fraser answered dejectedly.

"I was jus' prayin' f'more of yuh, that's all. I guess I have tuh take yuh word for it that they's more a comin'."

"There are, ma'am," the captain assured her. "I can promise you that."

"You' an officer right, Mister John?" Abigail asked. "You can take care a things other men cain't, ain't that so?"

"It depends," the captain replied.

"Well, suh, I was hopin' you Yankees might let me keep a li'l a this here farm for my own when the war is over. You' gonna have tuh do somethin' with all us Nigras. I was hopin' you might see fit tuh break me off jus' a li'l piece a this here farm so's I can make it my own. Long as we talkin', I'd likes tuh put my name in line for the house right here."

"I'm not in a position to do that, Miss Abigail, but I'm sure government land will be made available for you in the future. There's nothing but wide open space between the Mississippi River and the Pacific Ocean. Have you ever seen the ocean?"

"Cain't say I have."

"Well...," the captain began, trying to find the best words to explain. "Looking at the sea is like you're looking over the edge of the world. You look out and there is a giant plain of blue water and it goes on forever. It's so big it makes its own wind and rain. Below that plain is a whole world of different kinds of animals, some we've never even seen before. There's fish bigger than elephants living down below. And there are others as big as a wagon wheel and flat as a flapjack, just gliding among the ocean reeds like they're flying."

"You talkin' 'bout fish?" Abigail was confused. "I seen lots a fish in my day."

"Oh, you haven't seen these kinds of fish," the captain insisted. "They're every color of the rainbow and some even have wings that can fly. But there's a lot more than fish living in the ocean. There's giant crawdads called lobster, and there's a creature with eight different legs called an octopus. The scariest thing you ever saw."

"Eight legs? You talkin' like a crazy man now, Mister John."

"I've seen it myself. They have a big fish market right on the harbor in Baltimore, and everything they catch they sell right there off the net. You'll go someday. You'll get to see it, too."

"I do believe I will."

"So, were you born here, Abigail, on this farm?" the captain asked.

"Don't really know where I comes from," she answered. "Far back as I can recollect, I is jus' here one day. Didn't have no ma or pa. Got raised up by 'nother Nigra named Belle."

"I'm sorry to hear that," the Captain said sympathetically.

"Don't miss much what yuh ain't never had. An ol' Belle was always good tuh me. I think they done gave me to her 'cause they was always sellin' off her boy young'uns. Soon as they'd gets big 'nough tuh lif' a cotton bale they'd be gone." Abigail pulled the soaked goose out of the pot on the stove and dropped it on the table in front of the captain. "Them feathers should come out real easy now."

The captain wiped his hands on the side of his pants and then began yanking clumps of feathers out of the dead bird.

"You pretty good at that," Abigail told him.

"I was raised on a farm," the captain responded proudly. "I've probably cleaned a hundred chickens in my day. It's been a while, though."

"You doin' fine."

"Ma'am, if you don't mind the enquiry, how old might you be?"

"How ol' you reckon I be?"

"I'd say twenty-eight." The captain's answer was a graciously low estimate.

"Well, if that's what yuh think, then that's how ol' I am," Abigail answered.

"You don't know?"

"How many years yuh been sweatin' out in them fiel's don't mean nuthin' tuh folks like me. Ways I see it, yuh start keepin' count a how ol' you is, yuh jus' gonna start actin' ol' 'cause that's what yuh think you be."

The captain had to replay the slave's response in his head several times before he realized how much wisdom was in her words. "That's a wonderful observation. I'll have to remember that."

"How ol' are you?" Abigail asked.

"I'm thirty-seven."

"See?"

"See what?"

"Soon as you thought how ol' you is, yuh started feel_n' how ol' you is."

The captain laughed. "You are very wise, madam."

Abigail smiled sheepishly at the compliment and continued with her meal preparation. No one had ever told her she was smart before.

The captain finished plucking their main course and volunteered for another chore. Abigail told him he could use a bucket to empty some of the water out of the washtub, and then take the tub back outside when it was light enough to carry. He then got a stern warning not to slosh any of the dirty water on her wood plank floor. The captain said he understood and set out to accomplish his designated task. After several trips back and forth emptying pales of water onto the grass outside, the tub was finally light enough to drag back out to the side of the house. Once it was rinsed again and placed in a sunny spot on the grass to dry, the captain returned to Abigail's table and asked for another assignment.

"You jus' have yuh'sef a res' over there an' keep us a fire goin'," Abigail insisted.

"Mind if I go take a look around the property?"

"If that's what yuh want. But don't be gettin' in nothin' now that I got yuh smellin' halfway decent. If you wanna see the big house, follow the road yuh came in on 'til it forks into another road that'll be lined with a log-rail fence. If'n you takes that road lef' a ways, yuh gonna end up at some empty cow pens. From there, take a shortcut through the grazin' fiel' jus' north a them pens, an' you gonna see the house once yuh get pas' the trees on the other side. Take a good look before yuh walks up on the place. No tellin' who might be in there."

"I promise to be careful," the captain said and turned to leave.

"I'd take that gun a yo's with yuh, if I was you. Jeff Davis still runs these parts."

The captain nodded that he agreed and walked out of the house, gun in hand. Before setting out to find the main plantation home, he checked on his uniform only to find it was still damp and had hardly begun to dry.

The air outside was cool and the occasional gusts of wind gave him goose bumps. Fearful of catching cold, he walked into the trees and removed the wool blanket that was strapped to the back of the saddle he'd hidden there. He unrolled it and shook out the dust and then draped it over his shoulders. He hoped he might find some men's clothing left behind in the main house, particularly a shirt he could wear for supper. It was one thing to go bare-chested in the presence of a lady. It was totally unthinkable to do it at the supper table.

Fraser decided to ride instead of walk and climbed onto his horse bareback, leaving everything behind that would identify him as a

Union soldier. Unfortunately, there was no way to hide the Federal brand on his animal's hind quarter. He thought of a plan that, if discovered and unable to escape, he would do his best at a Southern accent and claim he'd stolen the horse, or better yet killed its Yankee owner. If his subterfuge wasn't believed, there were six lead balls in his revolver waiting.

The captain soon came upon the fence-lined road just as Abigail had described. He then headed east toward his next landmark. As he passed though the plantation, it looked as if each field had been subdivided into a 4 or 5 acre square plot. Each plot had at least one uncovered flatbed wagon parked on it and what appeared to be a water trough. A harvest of dirty white cotton bolls blanketed each field, from a distance appearing to be an early snow.

He soon arrived at the empty cattle pens and turned his horse north to cross a wide open pasture. Across from the field of tall wild grass, a forest line of cedars and underbrush obscured the landscape on the other side. Once he reached the barrier of pines he dismounted and searched for an opening to cross through. His search led him to a wooden gate that was attached to the trunks of two trees. He swung the gate open and left it unsecured in case he met trouble on the other side and needed a quick escape.

The captain then found himself on a small path surrounded by a jungle of moss and vine covered vegetation. Sure that he was on the right trail, he followed the path through the forest. His horse was less optimistic of their direction and frequently had to be convinced to proceed.

The square white building in the distance seemed oddly out of place when the captain first saw it. He had entered the property from a side entrance, and wasn't introduced to the grand estate from its dramatically landscaped face. But as he carefully ventured closer, strategically approaching from the rear to avoid detection, he could tell it was a marvelous home. He could also tell as he grew nearer that it had been surrendered to the elements. Large black crows were flying freely from opened and broken windows, and dried weeds covered the once plush lawn.

The captain tied his horse a safe distance away and continued his approach on foot. His pistol at the ready, he crept along the perimeter of the house searching for signs of life or recent inhabitation. A two-story outbuilding he assumed were servant's quarters had all of its four doors wide open. He carefully looked into each room and found all were ransacked and pilfered through. Between the outbuilding and the side of the house was a stone-tiled courtyard. Though it was now covered with fallen leaves and a coat of dirt, the strategically placed garden furniture beneath a massive live oak that served as its center-piece and natural umbrella from the sun meant the patio was probably once a beautiful outdoor veranda.

The captain then moved to a window and looked inside. Squirrels were darting back and forth in a long hallway, and sparrows swept freely through the air as if the home had become a giant bird sanctuary. He followed the side of the house looking into each window. Each result was the same. The house was certainly occupied, but its residents were nothing to fear.

Once he was convinced of some degree of safety, he turned the corner and discovered the majestic order of towering Corinthian pillars on the front porch. He walked to the brick steps and stood for a moment beneath the plaster columns, studying the grand guardians of the mansion. The architecture was so spectacular that he paid little attention to the household items strewn across the front lawn. Now eager to investigate inside, he raised his sidearm to the ready and stepped up to the double door entry.

The door to his right was ajar, and when he carefully pushed it open, it revealed a wide staircase in the center of a large carpeted foyer. Tracks of dried muddied footprints were everywhere, and the disheveled order of the furniture and personal belongings scattered about the house were certain signs of pillaging. The thick layer of dust and delicate sheets of cobwebs throughout told that the vandalism had occurred long before.

Fraser stalked from room to room, first assuring himself of his security and, at the same time, logging in his mind what he might return to and take for himself once all hazard had been diffused. When the first floor was secured, he carefully ascended a smaller stairwell next to the kitchen at the rear of the house and cleared a series of bed chambers and a lady's parlor on the second floor. After briefly examining every room, the captain was comfortable that he was alone. The massive house even fell empty of its frightened temporary occupants. The stillness and quiet sense of peace was that final sensation that gave him the confidence to secure his revolver in the waistband of his trousers and begin searching the bedrooms for a clean shirt.

The second floor of the house was as violated as the first. Every dresser drawer was either on the floor or three-quarters removed from its cabinet. Two of the upstairs bedrooms each contained four small canopy beds. One room was full of dolls and little girl's clothing, the other with items typically found in a privileged little boy's bedroom.

The master bedroom was significantly larger than the others, yet much more modestly decorated than what the captain expected to see. The floor was bare except for the clutter and the walls were painted a bright orange, not covered with the fancy imported wallpapers he'd seen in the raided mansions in Virginia. Several framed portraits had been pulled from their positions of display and discarded upside down on the floor. Each had an angry footprint on its back.

The captain rummaged through the mess and found several men's blouses that he thought might fit him. He settled on a still fresh-smelling linen shirt with ruffled sleeves, and even found a vest to complement it. Once he was satisfied with his new attire, he returned to the first floor via the more elegant main staircase.

His thoughts wandered to who must have lived in such extrava-gance. He imagined women dressed in the latest fashion, being waited upon at every turn by a slave whose only duty was to pamper them. He envisioned dandily-dressed men in custom tailored suits, with expensive gold watches in their pockets and the finest cigars hanging from their mouths. The home may have been in disarray now, but the owners or some wealthy buyer would surely be coming back eventu-ally to restore the grandeur of the estate.

Satisfied that anything of value had already been pillaged from the home, and not comfortable with the looting that had become com-monplace with both sides during the war, the captain decided to return to the kitchen and see if there was something he could find for Abigail to help with her meal preparations. He had no interest in a souvenir or an item to pawn. That was stealing, and he would have no part of it.

Anything that could have been eaten was gone. As he rifled through the drawers and cabinets looking for useful kitchen accessories, he realized Abigail might not be comfortable having kitchen items from her owner's house in hers. Besides, she had plenty of time and opportunity to take anything she needed from her owner's home if she truly needed it. Without being able to assure her freedom from her master, the captain didn't want to put her in a position where she would be even more fearful of the plantation owner.

Fraser then walked back toward the foyer and turned into a large library parlor across from the dining room. A grand piano with its lid still open was the centerpiece of the room. Here, the captain imagined guests were received and entertained before and after being served their gluttonous fill. All around the room were undisturbed bookcases, stacked neatly with classic volumes the mansion's vandals clearly found no value in either destroying or stealing. Other than the areas where furniture was clearly missing and a few letters were scattered on the carpeted floor, the parlor appeared to have been mostly overlooked by the trespassers.

As the captain stood in the threshold of the room, the piano began to lure him inside. The last time he'd played was his last effort to comfort his agonizing bride the night before going to war- the day before the beginning of his end. A near prodigy as a child, only to become a teacher to his own son, it was the music of the piano that centered him. It was the place where he learned about dedication, perseverance, and discipline. As a father, it was the place he taught his child patience, beauty, and love of the art of music.

Fraser stepped to the side of the grand instrument and gently stroked the smoothness of its glossy wood frame. A thick layer of dust covered the keys and the exposed strings, but there was no obvious damage. It was a beautiful piano, finer than any he had ever played.

After one last look over his shoulder, the captain sat and placed his revolver next to him, then carefully laid his fingertips on the keyboard. With a deep breath and four taps of his right foot, his favorite Beethoven sonata slowly awakened from his soul.

The second movement of Beethoven's Sonata #8 had always spoken to him. It was the first classic piece he had memorized, not so much because it was slow and methodic, but because the melody captivated him. To encourage his son's continued development, the captain promised that one day he would teach his son his favorite sonata, but only when he had earned that right by proving he had the appropriate skills. For the captain's son, that day would be a crowning achievement, and it came on his twelfth birthday.

The vision of that day was playing beneath the captain's closed eyes when his fingers suddenly froze. He pushed himself away from the keyboard and struggled to his feet. His heart was suddenly racing. The melody that was so dear to him had only reminded him of the horror that his life had become. Everything haunted him now. Everything was tied to a memory of what he'd lost. It was time to finally end it.

The captain grabbed the revolver from the piano bench and thrust the barrel to his right temple. As his finger pressed into the trigger, he thought about how his life was coming to an end. Was there honor in splattering his brains in someone else's home? Was it selfish to leave his grotesque form to be found by a slave who had done nothing but show him kindness? Would God shun him for taking his own life and cast him down to spend eternity in some prison dungeon in Satan's inferno?

The captain swung his firearm toward the piano. If he wasn't going to kill himself, then something else had to be sacrificed. His left eye began to narrow as he took aim. One perfectly placed shot and the source of his burden would be forever dispatched. Anger boiled within him, opening the door for all of the moment's madness to flood his head. He gritted his teeth and growled.

"Aaaah!" he roared and dropped the weapon to his side. Even in his temporary insanity he recognized that killing the piano was absurd. He began to laugh at the depth of how pitiful he had become and how his character simply wouldn't allow him to die.

After a few moments of clearing his head and composing his thoughts, the captain stepped up to the darkly-stained oak cabinetry and scanned the titles for something interesting or familiar. He recognized almost everything. Complete sets of works by Edgar Allan Poe and Charles Dickens were among the classic texts of Shakespeare and Dumas. The captain narrowed his search for something he might share with his slave host while she continued to toil with her meal preparations, or even read to her once their feast was consumed. He turned to a cabinet of individually colored bindings where there were books from various authors of poetry and fiction.

He was pleased to find a volume of _Leaves of Grass_ by Walt Whitman, a favorite of his wife's before he left for the war. He pulled the book from its shelf and flipped through the familiar pages. Several of the verses flowed through his head, and he decided that reading a few of the poems to Abigail would make pleasant fireside entertainment. He tucked the book under his arm and looked for another.

On the next shelf he was surprised to find a copy of Harriett Beecher Stowe's _Uncle Tom's Cabin_. He removed the copy and opened its cover. It was of the first printing and an odd choice for a slave owner's personal library, he thought. Fraser reasoned that the purchaser probably hadn't been aware of the true content of the popular novel and its details of slavery in the South. He decided to take it back with him also, not so much to read with Abigail, but to show her the significance and power of such a story.

As he turned and walked to the door to leave, his eyes were drawn to a large glass vase full of peacock feathers used by slave children to gently fan occupants of the library as they read on hot summer days. Next to the vase was an ornately decorated brass stand placed beneath a window. On top of the stand was an oversized book that had obviously been left open for display. The captain walked over to investigate, discovering the book was a Bible. He carefully sifted through the delicate pages and found that among the written verses there were pictures of the biblical stories being addressed in that particular chapter.

The captain had never seen such a dramatic presentation of the scriptures. He decided it must be shown to Abigail whether she elected to keep it or not. Yet, when he lifted it from its display, he realized its weight and size was too much to carry while riding back to the slave's home. After a short debate with himself as to whether it was worth the trouble of trying to lug the heavy text back with him, he decided to spread his blanket on the floor and placed all three of the books inside. He then folded and rolled the blanket into a bundle he could brace against his lap during the ride back. Much to his satisfaction the idea worked.

∽

The captain could smell baking corn cakes in the air when he crested the bluff just before Abigail's house. The sweet smell of real food caused his mouth to water with anticipation. There had been many days in the field when food rations were low or even nonexistent, often the result of corruption and bad planning and not lack of supply. When hunger pains became intolerable the men were reduced to their most primitive state, sometimes feeding on stew made of rats and drinking tea made from boiled tree bark. It was during those desperate days that the captain began to yearn for the dishes that, before the war, had been so common- meat free of maggots and bread free of mold.

In great anticipation, he gave his horse an extra nudge and trotted the rest of the way to the clump of trees where his horse would again be concealed. Before going back inside the captain filled a bucket with water from the well and placed it at the front hooves of his nameless chestnut-colored mare. Then, after a parting pat of endearment, the captain left her alone to graze and drink.

He had learned not to grow overly attached to the horses the Army supplied him. At the second battle at Bull Run Creek, he'd been reduced to firing a round into the head of his own horse so he could use the fallen carcass for cover in an open field.

His next horse had snapped its knee when it stumbled in the mud a few days after the battle at Fredericksburg, Virginia. Only moments after the injury, he was forced to dispatch that horse also, this time to prevent even further congestion in the thick red quagmire. The loss of that second horse, Cesar, particularly saddened him because he had taken the time to name him and had personally removed two pieces of shrapnel from the horse's neck just so he wouldn't have to be destroyed. But before the wound from the lifesaving gesture had even begun to heal, the captain found himself firing a bullet of mercy into Cesar's temple.

His mare though, she had befriended the captain. Like the loyalty of a man's favorite dog, she seemed to have an almost unwavering trust in him. Even dismounted in the chaos of battle with explosions and musket balls whizzing all around, the captain only needed to look in her direction and she would gallop to his side to continue the advance. But the bond wasn't reciprocated. He was too sure the day would come when his devoted companion would fall, and he wanted to be able to walk away without a second thought about it.

Fraser discovered corn cakes weren't the only things cooking in the house when he re-entered. The spiced and buttered goose was also browning in the oven, and a skillet of okra frying in a puddle of bacon grease was sizzling on the stove top. "It smells absolutely delicious, ma'am," he said as he laid the blanket of books on the floor next to the door.

"Ain't you a handsome thing," Abigail complimented at the sight of the shirt and vest the captain had commandeered. "I see yuh foun' the main house. Kinda surprised there's anythin' lef' in that place."

"It has been gone through," the captain replied. "Almost sad to see such a beautiful home in such terrible condition, regardless of its owner."

"Weren't nobody in there?" Abigail braced herself for the captain's answer. The idea that the bodies of murdered Sexton family members were possibly inside had haunted her ever since discovering the house was attacked by looters over a year earlier. She feared the captain was going to return with a tale of discovering a macabre scene of the family's gruesome demise.

"Only if you count the critters," the captain answered. "May I help you with something?"

"Naw, I'm fine as it is," Abigail answered with a sigh of relief. "Gonna have suppuh ready in no time. Guess you could stir up them beans on the fire ever once-in-a-while if'n yuh want." Abigail motioned to a pot simmering inside the fireplace.

"Be glad to." The captain walked over to the hearth and slowly stirred the beans with a wooden spoon left in the pot. "Mind if I have a taste?"

"'Spose yuh could. But then you'd jus' wan' another an' before I'd know it them beans be gone."

"If I give you my word as an officer of the United States Army, would you trust me to just one sample of this fine-smelling brew?"

The slave woman smiled. "Guess it wouldn't hurt none. But jus' one tas'e. That's all."

"On my honor," Fraser replied and drew a spoonful of beans from the pot. He gingerly blew on the small sampling, making sure the taste wouldn't be spoiled by a burned tongue. When the steam subsided and his growling stomach called out that it could no longer wait, the captain closed his eyes and filled his mouth with the modest morsel.

Abigail had mixed small pieces of salted pork and molasses into the pot of beans, making them much more appetizing than the bland and often stale sort the Union troops were usually issued. The captain sucked the flavor from the beans until they had turned to mush and then swallowed.

"Miss Abigail, I've never had any finer," he said. "You have certainly taken something without substance and turned it into a delicacy."

"I don't know nothin' 'bout no delicacy," the slave said with a smile.

"Oh you do," the captain insisted as he replaced the spoon to the pot. "You just haven't had anyone around to tell you so."

"I 'spect them's jus' the words of a fightin' man who's been away from home too long."

"I brought you something from the house," the captain said. He walked over to the blanket and unwrapped it, revealing the heavy Bible.

"I don't want none a' that property in this house," Abigail declared before she saw what the item was. "It don't belong to me an' I don't want nothin' tuh do with it. Massa Sexton catch me with somethin' a' his in here, he gonna tie me to a tree an take a switch tuh me."

"I already thought of that," the captain replied quickly. "But I think this is something the Sextons would want you to hold for them in case more looters take to that house." The captain cleared a section of the table and laid the book before the slave woman. "It's a Bible."

Abigail wiped her hands on her apron and stepped to the captain's side to get a better look. Her eyes widened. "That's the bigges' book I ever did see," she said.

"I don't think I've ever seen anything like it either," the captain added. "But that's not why I brought it. Look at this." He opened the thick leather cover and began turning pages until he found the first illustration. "Isn't that nice?"

Abby's eyes widened even further when she saw the full page re-creation of Eve handing Adam the apple from the Tree of Knowledge. "Ooh, I knows what's goin' on there," she said. "That there is Satan's doin'. There he is right there in that tree." Abby pointed to a snake wrapped around a tree branch in the background of the picture.

"Yes indeed, I believe that is the devil himself," Fraser confirmed. "This Bible is full of such depictions. When I saw it alone in a room of dust and exposed to possible thievery, I thought, surely it was better to be in your safe hands than none at all."

"Oh my Lawd, this'd get me in a heap-a-trouble if I'z caught with it."

"It may if you try to conceal it from its rightful owner. Yes, I believe it would be reasonable for anyone to have quarrel with you for liberating from them such a fine piece of literature. But what if you were to offer it back to its owner the moment you are reunited, stating how, out of concern for this precious scripture, you kept it for safekeeping? I'm sure the family would be grateful for such a gesture."

Abigail thought for a moment and said, "I 'spose they would be happy to see it after all the other belongin's they got been stoled."

"And who's to say what could happen to it if they never return," the captain added. "That house and this whole plantation could become United Sates Government property tomorrow. If that happens, this beautiful Bible is going to end up in the hands of some heathen who only wants it as a war souvenir."

"That won't be right," Abigail said with a frown.

"Of course not. *You* have the right to this good book if the Sextons don't come back to claim it."

"Then we'll have it that a way," she answered. "Why don't yuh read me somethin' while's I get this bird cooked."

"I'd be honored to," the captain replied. "Any favorite verses you'd like to hear?"

"It all sounds good tuh my ears."

"Then I suggest the New Testament, Book of Matthew," the captain said as he flipped through the oversized pages. He stopped when he found the title chapter page and scanned down to the 18th verse where the story of Jesus begins. "Now the birth of Jesus Christ was on the wise...," he began as he settled into a chair next to the table.

Abby returned to her cooking, careful not to miss a word of the private recital.

The captain read the words as if he knew them well, his voice rising to dramatize influential verse. Abigail never interrupted. She knew the story too, though she'd never actually read it herself. The captain only paused long enough to show her a picture and then he would return to the King James Version of the biblical text.

Once the story of Jesus' teachings on the mount began in chapter 5, the captain became uncomfortable reading the sermon of hope and forgiveness to the slave. If there was any strength left in his character after all he'd been through, it was the captain's conviction to honesty. The Bible's version of Christ's birth had easily read like an ancient bedtime story. But the supposed Son of God's later promises of faith's rewards were just plain and simple untruths in the captain's eyes.

If he had never believed in God, the misfortunes in his life could have been more easily accepted. Sickness and war were facts of life. But his faith that God would personally spare him such tragedy if he lived righteously gave him someone to blame. Now on some days he was convinced God didn't even exist. But on the days when the Christian faith that had been embedded in his soul was undeniable, the captain considered the Almighty a great betrayer and hated him for it. Why mislead a poor uneducated slave into the same trap he'd fallen into?

The captain knew nothing of Abigail's treatment in captivity, though there was no reason to believe her life had been any different than the lives of any other slaves in the South. She wasn't a house slave.

There, she might have received favorable living arrangements to remain presentable to her owners. But as a field slave, she must have been sentenced to a life of hard labor. Naively thinking prayer and faith would deliver her from that bondage wasn't something Fraser wanted to be a part of. God was a selfish bastard. Faith was for ignorant fools.

The distraction of his thoughts caused him to stumble on the words he was reading. He stopped for a moment and rubbed his eyes to help regain his focus.

"You read real fine, Mister John," Abigail said and placed a cup of water on the table next to him.

The captain emptied the cup and cleared his throat. He paused again and struggled with an appropriate way to ask his host about her life on the plantation.

"You got somethin' on yuh mind?" Abigail asked.

"I do, I'm just not quite sure it's any of my business," the captain answered.

"Go on."

"Well...I'm having trouble reading these rather fantastic words of hope and faith to a woman who has every reason to believe it is make-believe hogwash. I can't decide if this conundrum is caused by my guilt as a white man, or amazement in your spirit."

"God is my salvation, Mister John," Abby said confidently. "He gives me good feelin's when I'z down an' lonely. He lifted me up when I got so tired in them fiel's out yonder, I thought I was gonna drop right there an' die. When them Sextons was runnin' the place the good Lawd he'p me keep my mouth shut, an' he give me a good mine tuh do the things that keep trouble on some other Nigra's doorstep an' not mine."

"Can I ask what it was like when the Sextons were here?" the captain asked cautiously.

"You wanna know what this plantation was like? Or do you wanna know how a Nigra slave gets along in Missi'ppi?"

"I'd like to know more about you."

"Not much tuh tell, 'fraid tuh say. Life out here ain't nothin' tuh brag on. Ever' day the same ol' thing. Up before daylight come. In them fiel's all day 'til suppuh in the summer or dark come along in the winter time."

"How did the Sextons treat you?" Fraser asked.

"They's worser folks, I guess. Massa Sexton an' one a his boys was the only ones we Nigras out here saw day tuh day. They lef' mos' the orderin' 'round tuh Big Jim, the boss man. Jim had three or fo' Nigras he favored so he gave them the orderin' an' they passed it on tuh us. Didn't much need no tellin' what tuh do after a while. Seems nothin' ever changed. Some days you lay yuh head down an' couldn't remember the diff'rence 'tween the day you jus' done, an' the one yuh had the day before."

"Were you ever mistreated?" Fraser asked. "You don't have to tell me if you don't want to."

"Depends on how you looks at it, I guess," Abigail answered. "Bein' someone else owns yuh, well, suh, that ain't no way tuh treat nobody. So I reckon you can call ever' day mistreatment. But if'n yuh wanna knows if I'z ever been whipped on, or taken by a man 'ginst my will, I'd have tuh say yes, it done happen' tuh me."

The captain suddenly regretted his enquiry. "I'm very sorry, Miss Abigail. This is none of my business."

"Now that we talkin' on it, I think maybe it oughta be yuh business, Mister John. You fightin' men come down here tuh free us

190

Nigras, yuh oughta be knowin' what yuh fightin' for. We ain't jus' a bunch a folks stol' offa some boat from Africa an' dumped in these fiel's tuh raise cawn an' cotton. We's treated lesser'n dogs mos' the time. Whippin's for workin' too slow, whippin's for drinkin' too much water from the barrel, down right beatin's for lookin' like yuh jus' don't favor what the massa jus' done told yuh.

"The women folk is even treated worse, them Sextons lettin' us marry an' then sellin' off our husbands an' young'uns. That husband I had, he's jus' put on me one day. I'z hardly more than a chile when Massa Sexton told us we was gonna be together. Weren't no love 'tween us or nothin'. I'z too young tuh realize all we was put together for was just tuh make babies. He was kind tuh me, but I wouldn't never picked him if'n it was my choosin' tuh find me my own man.

"One's I feels real bad for is them house Nigras stuck in that house with them Sexton mens. They used tuh come 'round here all whiskey'd up after dark, lookin' for someone tuh lay down with. Got so bad we Nigra gals stopped cleanin' ourselves 'til mornin', hopin' them animals would pass us by. After a few weeks a nothin' out here but hard smellin' women, the Sextons decided it wern't worth the ride out. Hate tuh wonder on what they be doin' tuh those fair-skinded house Nigras."

"Mullatos?"

"Nigras who done got a lick'a white in 'em." Abigail clarified. "The Sextons done breed they own house Nigras, I been told. How them Sexton women puts up with it, I don't know. Ever so cf'n, one a them house Nigras turns out a li'l too wild so they sends 'em out here tuh the fiel's. That's how we gets all the house gossip. One gal named Ophelia got sent away 'cause she turnt ugly when she got growed up.

Ophelia said them Sextons got slaves in that house that be plain as day white. Got they brown skin bred right out of 'em. Ophelia said she heard the Missus Sexton havin' quite a row one night with her husband over how the house Nigras kept birthin' whiter an' whiter young'uns. Massa Sexton denied knowin' nothin' 'bout it, a course. 'Bout that time was when he an' his boy started comin' 'round here at night."

"Men are capable of such cruelty," the captain said at the disturbing revelation. "I'm sure there will be charges when the war is over."

"You gonna charge a man for layin' with one a his own Nigras?"

"Rape is a very serious offense, Miss Abigail." "When order is restored in the South, I can assure you it will be addressed."

The slave began clearing the table, the captain assisting her without being asked.

Abigail continued, "I 'spose I shouldn't e'spect you tuh know this, suh, but you up north folk don't know nothin' 'bout how things go down here. I'z born a slave jus' as same as the Nigra who bore me. An' the same goes on back tuh some poor soul who got chained up in Africa when they's nothin' but neked injins runnin' 'round these parts. After time goes by, things jus' get taken for what they is. Things that yuh don't like, but they nothin' you can do 'bout it 'cept pray someday somethin' better's gonna come along. You talkin' 'bout puttin' charges on a Southern man for layin' with his own slave, but that ain't breakin' no law in Missi'ppi. Leas' ain't no law I ever heard of."

"Taking a woman against her will is against the law in every state, north or south, ma'am," the captain said. "Whether you're a slave or not."

"You talkin' white man's law, Mister John. You don't know nothin' 'bout no Nigra law. Nigra law say when yo' massa come callin' you takes him in. Y'ain't gots'ta like it. You can try ever' trick a Nigra ever come up with tuh have him pass you by, but they's gonna be a time when they ain't nothin tuh do but accept you a piece a property an' try tuh put yo' mind somewheres else whiles he has yuh."

The captain struggled for an argument but he couldn't find one. He could only feel empathy for the women exposed to such a tragic culture of brutality. "My apologies for the topic of this discussion, ma'am. It isn't appropriate for me to ask you of such private matters. Even though I'd have no part of it, I feel ashamed of my race while I listen to your words."

"Weren't jus' white men violatin' us Nigra woman." Abigail added. "We got a lotta Nigra men on this here farm, an' they's always gonna be one or two who goes bad. Diff'rence is, we takes care of our own. You a'spected tuh court your woman jus' like dem white folks do. Start causin' trouble with a Nigra gal who ain't got no man yet, you gonna find yo'sef facin' Nigra law. And you don't want a bunch a riled up Nigras decidin' what's tuh do with yuh. An' you go mess'n with a gal who already gots a man, you gonna jus' be gone one day."

"Has that happened before here on this farm?" the captain asked.

"Yessuh, it has."

"Do the Sextons encourage you all to keep order amongst yourselves?"

"Some things they wants to know about. You be stealin' or gettin' into homemade likuh an' causin' a ruckus, the massa 'spects us tuh tell on yuh. The men'll have a talkin' to you the firs' time, but if yuh dumb enough Nigra tuh keep on with it, you gonna gets told on. Ain't no way out of a beatin' once that happens. But they other things that we jus' takes care of ourselves."

"Wouldn't the Sextons get angry if you harmed another slave to discipline them?" Fraser asked.

"Likes I said, you gets a talkin' to the first time. Then the beatin' gets left up tuh the massa if'n you gets caught again."

The captain was confused. "But you said sometimes there are offenses that result in a slave just being gone. Doesn't that upset the Sextons?"

"Oh sho' it do," Abigail answered. "But the Nigra jus' up an' runned off, is the story. They's even a picker or two who goes tuh Big Jim an' tells 'em some made up thing 'bout how the miss'n Nigra'd been talkin' 'bout runnin' off. Jim'll go get a few hound dogs an' then all the white mens takes tuh huntin' him down. Thing is, that los' Nigra ain't gone nowhere. He in a hole an' covered up right in the middle of one a Sexton's own cotton fields."

As Abigail told her story the captain couldn't help but be surprised at the cunning of the slaves on the plantation. He'd always believed they were incapable of such complex thought and reason. Their supposed lack of intelligence was his only explanation why they could allow themselves to be held captive by whites. Now that he was learning they were capable of reason and creating their own law, he only had more questions for Abigail. But before he could ask any of them his host changed the subject.

"I think we 'bout done here," she said as she pulled the goose from the oven. "Gonna need a spell to cool off. I'll put out some servin' bowls, an' you can fill 'em whilst I go clean up an' change my dress."

The captain rose from his chair and listened attentively for his instructions.

"Put the cakes on this one," Abigail directed as she handed the captain a blue and white tin plate. "That okra'll go in this one," she said handing him another. "All them cawn ears'll fit in the bowl on the table, but you gonna have tuh wash it out first. Leave that bird alone. I don't want yuh fingers in it before it's ready," she added in playful warning. "Them beans can go in this," she continued, handing the captain another large bowl. "I got some things for the table-dishes an' such in here," she said pointing to a drawer at the top of a small wood cabinet. "You think you can make us up a nice table?"

"Absolutely, ma'am," the captain answered.

"Then get on to it an' I'll be back after'n I change into my finest. If'n I'z gonna have me an officer of the Yankee Army in my house fo' suppuh, least I can do is put on my best."

"It's not necessary, Miss Abigail. I've done nothing but intrude on you today, and I fear you're giving me much more respect than I'm entitled."

"You got business tuh tend to, suh," she said as she walked away. "Worry on gettin' those dishes on the table before I come back, instead of worry'n so much 'bout what you 'titled to."

"Yes, ma'am," the captain answered.

Abby disappeared around the partition separating the bed from the rest of the house. The captain began preparing the table for their first Thanksgiving dinner.

CHAPTER 7

THANKSGIVING

The captain was standing several feet away from the table, surveying his work to make sure every dish and utensil was in perfect position, when Abigail entered the room behind him. He turned with an already-prepared compliment, but was caught off guard by her change in image. Gone were the tightly braided cornrows lining the top of her head. Now, she had a full body of dark shoulder-length hair, pulled together and tied with a single red ribbon behind her back. Her dress, though simple, was a white linen gown fitted perfectly to her waist and draped loosely over her hips to the floor.

The captain realized he'd spent a moment too long admiring the change in her appearance and diverted his eyes nervously back to the table.

"How I look?" the slave asked, pulling the sides of the dress away from her legs and slowly turning in a circle.

"You are a vision to behold, ma'am," the captain answered.

"I got this outa the cabin of a house Nigra who done runned off. I ain't never put it on in front of nobody else before."

"Well, it does compliment you. I fear it compliments you almost to the point of distraction."

Abigail laughed. "Oh, you a sweet man, suh." She stepped up to the table and made sure it was prepared to her specifications. "You done good on this settin'. Looks real fine."

"I must admit it's taken all of my strength to ignore the influence of the aroma of this magnificent feast you've prepared. If you'd taken a second longer I may have surrendered and begun without you."

"Then let's have at it," Abigail said as she moved toward a chair at one end of the table.

The captain hurried to her side, pulling the chair away from the table, and then motioned for her to sit. Abigail smiled and thanked him for his chivalrous gesture and sat down. The captain then stepped around the table and sat opposite his host.

"Bein's you the man, yuh want to thank the Lawd, or yuh want me tuh do it?" she asked.

"I submit to you, madam. Whatever you prefer."

"Well, I s'pose since it's a day we s'posed tuh be thankful fo' somethin', maybe we oughta both say some words."

"Yes, I do believe that would be the right thing to do," the captain agreed.

They both bowed their heads and closed their eyes, the captain with his hands in his lap, the slave woman with her palms pressed tightly together beneath her chin. The captain had nothing to say to God, but wanted to be respectful and quickly saw an opportunity to show his appreciation to his host.

"Dear Lord," he began, "thank you for this day and for this meal we are about to receive. Thank you for Miss Abigail, and thank you for giving her the kindness in her heart to take me in. And Lord, we pray that you find a way to end this terrible war soon, so Miss Abigail can have her freedom and live the rest of her life with the same rights afforded every white man in this country. Amen."

"Heavenly Father," Abigail followed with a clenched brow. "You a great God an' we praise yuh with all's we got. Glory tuh you an' Jesus an' all them angels yuh got watchin' over us. An' glory tuh Pres'dent Lincoln up in the north, an' all his fightin' men doin' your will. Bless these Yankee men, Lawd, an' give them the strength tuh keep on, even when things ain't goin' they way. Bless Mister John, an officer in yo' glorious army of salvation, an' give him the power tuh do what's right. I thank yuh Lawd for givin' us this day an' for lettin' me do somethin' personal for one a yo' Christian soldiers. Bless this suppuh jus' like the water yuh bless fo' babtisin', an' let Mister John go on back to his fightin' knowin' he's got you with 'em all the way. Thank yuh fo' givin' me this house an' this food. An' I pray yuh keepin' watch over those Nigras who's out wanderin', lookin' fo' they freedom. Thank yuh for Jesus an' his dyin' on the cross, an' then raisin' him up again tuh wash away all my sins. Glory an' praise to you, Almighty God. Amen."

They both raised their heads and opened their eyes. The captain was embarrassed with his role in the rather lopsided prayer offering. Even though his words were only a token courtesy and roundabout thanks to Abigail, he felt he should have said more. And after hearing her prayer he knew there was no chance he could produce enough evidence to discredit Abigail's faith, even though God had sentenced her to a life of slavery.

Fraser recalled how he had once spoken to God with the same conviction as Abigail. Yet he was also sure that would all change for her as it had for him, when that one day would inevitably come when she would realize God had shunned her also. He could only hope it came in something less devastating than the years of grisly battlefield horrors and personal tragedies the captain had endured. The kind and hopeful slave woman deserved better.

"You gonna eat some a this or you jus' gonna look on it?" Abigail asked, breaking the captain's spell.

"I'm sorry," Fraser answered. "I was just reflecting on your prayer. You are very eloquent."

"Eloquent. What's that?"

"Your words were very moving," Fraser clarified. "They caused me to daydream for a moment."

"You seem to know the Lawd pretty good," Abigail commented as they began serving themselves and passing the dishes to each other.

"I do know the Lord's word," the captain answered, careful not to disclose his contempt of religion. "My parents raised their children on the Bible and we attended church twice a week. I can honestly say I've read every page at least twice."

"Then you have to tell me some stories of Jesus. They's got to be some I ain't never heard tol' yet."

"Why don't we save that for after supper," the captain answered. "You can look through that Bible and if any of the pictures look interesting to you I'll read you the story about it."

"That'd be real fine."

Before taking his first bite the captain gazed down upon the full plate before him. He thought how lucky he was to have stumbled onto Abigail's cabin, and knew none of the rest of the men in his regiment could have found such fortune. For those still alive, a few might have been able to catch a rabbit or squirrel, or maybe even found an orchard with some remaining fruit to eat. Of those, few would have access to fire or would be afraid to create one for fear of being discovered by a Rebel patrol. The majority though, were more likely wandering southwest with empty stomachs, terrified at every step that the enemy was lurking nearby. The captain was very lucky.

Fraser raised his cup and held it toward the slave woman. "I salute you, madam. This is quite a feast."

Abigail also raised her glass and said, "Thank you, suh," and then they both drank together.

The captain began with a bite of a corn cake, one from the pile that had been taunting him for over an hour. The sweet yellow biscuit was as delicious as he'd imagined, and he struggled to keep from shoving the rest of it into his mouth whole. Abigail saw he was enjoying it and smiled. She'd always taken pleasure in feeding a hungry man.

"Take yuh time, Mister John," she warned. "There's plenty here, an' even some tuh take on back with you. Don't put it down so fast it makes yuh sick."

"I will keep that in mind," the captain answered and filled his fork with a piece of goose breast. He dipped it in some of the sauce from his beans and placed it in his mouth. Before he chewed he let the bite rest on his tongue to make sure he savored all of its flavors. Abigail had seasoned the bird with spices from her garden and had marinated it in some butter that she'd churned a few days before. The medley of added ingredients to the moist piece of white meat caused the captain to hum with delight. He finished the bite and began cutting another piece. "Miss Abigail, this is the most delicious fowl I've ever tasted."

"Thank you, suh," the slave answered proudly.

The captain was careful not to abandon his table manners, yet at first he was too pre-occupied with keeping his mouth full to indulge in conversation. His host didn't mind. She enjoyed watching him eat. Being able to feed a Union soldier made her feel she was actually playing a role in the quest for her freedom.

The captain cleaned his plate and served himself a second helping of everything on the table. "I'll empty my pockets to you, ma'am," he said, "and I'll still not have offered enough to repay you."

"If'n you don't slow down, it's all gonna come right back up an' won't be worth nothin'," Abigail warned playfully.

"I believe you're right," Fraser answered as he slowly massaged his bloated belly.

Abigail saw that her guest was taking a break from shoving food in his mouth and she wasn't going to pass up the opportunity to rekindle some conversation. "You asked a bunch about me, but what about yo' kin? Did yuh folks come over on one a them boats to get they freedom theyselves?"

The captain thought for a moment, sipping from his cup. "Yes, I guess they did in a way. My mother and father were from Scotland. They came here to escape famine mostly. I'm sure the government had something to do with their decision, but the way my father told the story to me, it was not being able to eat that brought them to this country."

"Never heard a no Scotland. They got slaves there?"

"A different kind of slavery, but yes, you could say they do." The captain knew a lesson in Scotland's complex history would be difficult to explain, particularly to an American slave. He would have to offer his lesson as if to a child pupil. He began patiently, "Scotland has been ruled for hundreds of years by royal families, both from Scotland and sometimes by the English. Scotland shares a border with England, and it was often that the English would invade Scotland to take land or force the people there to pay taxes. The majority of Scots don't want to be ruled by anyone, especially the English, so there was often war between the two countries. Whenever the English won, that's when Scottish people were often treated as slaves. It went on for years until the Scots could assemble an army large enough to defeat the English."

Abigail frowned. "So you doin' for the slave man down here, kinda like what yuh kin done back home in they country."

"It's much more complicated than that."

"Don't sound like it to me. You got's folks slavin' for some rich man, an' finally it comes down tuh some killin' tuh make things right. Don't matter if'n that fight is in Alabam', Missi'ppi, or way over in that place yo' kins come from."

"I admire your ability to find sense in that which the most highly educated scholars of this world cannot," the captain answered with subtle sarcasm. "The truth is that slavery was even less a concern to my forefathers during their wars with England, than this country's concern for slavery is in this war. I find your plight despicable, ma'am. But history is always the same in wars whose generals shout the enemy's bondage of others as a rally cry. At some point the leaders on both sides will tire of battle and terms will be agreed upon to end the carnage. Long after the field of fire is empty and the bloodstained soil is again rich with harvest, slavery of one man to another always remains."

"It don't have tuh be that way," Abigail insisted.

"I wish it didn't."

"Then ain't that what this war is for?"

"Your freedom will be the result if the Union is restored," Fraser assured her.

"Then what you say 'bout slavery always gonna be, that ain't gonna be so."

"Miss Abigail, I hope someday you have your own place where there'll be no man standing over you. I hope that your grandchildren can someday look upon these days and they will be so far beyond reason that your current circumstance will seem unimaginable."

"Do you reckon that's gonna happen?"

"I wish it for you," the captain answered.

"The Lawd's smilin' on me today," Abigail said as she rose from the table. "Got me a Yankee officer come outa nowhere an' says his boys is finally right outside my gates. Then I'z finds out it's a special holiday I ain't never heard of, an' I got me another Christian tuh share it with. Way things been goin' 'round here, I'd say today's almos' a miracle."

"I believe chance is more like it," Fraser replied, quick to dismiss undue credit to God. "Could it just be that today was bound to happen eventually? The Union Army has been in Mississippi for some time now. Is it unreasonable to think I just happened to be the one who first found you before someone else did?"

"Oh, no suh," Abigail answered. "I been prayin' 'bout this night an' day for a long time. I been askin' for the Lawd tuh deliver me from my chains, an' today's a sign he's 'bout tuh do jus' that."

The captain squirmed uneasily in his chair. He had grown to despise those who naively credited God with everything they perceived to be positive in their lives. Even he had once thanked God for even the most minor of blessings- food to eat, or pleasant weather. But that was before God betrayed him. That was before the Holy Spirit rewarded his loyal servant's faith with his wrath of death and despair. For the captain, he had vowed himself to separation from the ranks of those ignorantly faithful, unaware of what God was truly capable of. And now, sitting before him, a lowly slave was setting herself up for the same downfall, dedicating her life to some spiritual entity that either did not exist, or had already dismissed her to a life of lesser existence.

Careful not to upset the woman who had just fed him, but compelled to provide a lesson on misguided faith, the captain said, "Sometimes things just happen because of coincidence. And sometimes things happen because we decide we want them to. I'm not sure you or I can make God responsible for all that is good. Or all that is bad for that matter."

"The Lawd is responsible for all things," the slave answered confidently.

"Really? Is the Lord responsible for you being here on this plantation?" Fraser asked. "For the loss of your children?"

Abigail sneered at the captain. "God ain't got nothin' tuh do with that. That's the workin's of the devil an' they'll be a reckonin'."

"Then what about this war?" the captain pried. "A great many men are killing each other in this rebellion. Is that God's will? Why doesn't he simply draw on the waters of the Mississippi or the Potomac and sweep through this Rebel insurrection as he's done before in the

Holy Land? Why not open the sky and unleash his anger on them as they stand poised for battle in their lines? "

The captain filled his mouth with a biscuit and waited for the response to his baited question.

"The Lawd has always punished evil doin' in one way or another," Abigail answered. "An' sometimes he calls on the good ones like you an' me tuh make a sacrifice, jus' like he done with his own son."

"There are Christian men fighting for the Confederacy," Fraser pointed out. "They believe their sacrifice is just as worthy of a place in heaven as ours."

"Them are fools," Abigail proclaimed. "They done let the devil get in 'um. And God don't count no man a Christian who holds another man a slave to 'em. Ain't nobody that knows the Lawd's word don't know slavery 'bout the biggis' evil one man can put on another. God don't care how hard them Rebel boys got it. They ain't doin' God's sacrificin'in this war. It ain't the massa an' his peoples. It's the Nigra an' those fightin' to make things right. Which one of 'em's gonna get tuh heaven's door? Ain't no white man with a fiel' full a slaves, that's for sho'. It's the Nigra who, through it all, praises the Lawd for the li'l he do got, an' not what he don't. An' it's the Yank fightin' that evil, an' dyin' right along with them Rebs. But ain't no Reb gonna be standing at that gate to heaven after they fall, no suh. It jus' gonna be a long line a those in blue coats."

"And those Confederate soldiers who believe God is on their side of this war?" Fraser wanted to know.

"They's lost souls who been tricked by the devil. If'n they prayed like they should, God would show 'em the way."

Clearly Abigail had already come to her conclusions about God's role in the war and she would be steadfast in her beliefs. It was all she had. Instead of a debate, Fraser decided to appeal directly to her heart, no matter the painful memories it would bring back to him. He wiped his mouth with a napkin and then withdrew a small tin case from his pants pocket. He then passed it across the table to Abigail. "Open it," he told her.

Abigail recognized the case. The captain displayed it to her from the other side of the cabin window when he first appeared and used the photo inside to convince her he was a real Union Officer and not an imposter. She opened it and saw the familiar photograph of the captain and another much younger soldier.

"That handsome young man next to me was my son," the captain said. "We joined together thinking this would be...well, I'm not sure anymore what exactly we were thinking."

"He gone?" Abigail asked, afraid of the answer.

"Yes. He was killed right next to me during a big fight in Maryland."

"I'm very sorry, Mister John. That ain't no way to lose a chile."

"No, it isn't, ma'am," the captain answered. "No it isn't. That's my point. When my boy died I was very angry at God because I thought he let it happen. All my life I prayed every morning and before bed every night, and when I became a father I took that child to church every Sunday. He knew every word of the Bible and believed it. But it wasn't enough to keep a Confederate ball from going right through him. I actually heard the thud when it hit him. Suddenly all was quiet and I grabbed him in my arms just before he hit the grass. Panic was on the field and order was completely lost in the smoke.

Men from both sides running drenched in sweat and blood, chaos all around us as I sat alone with my boy, the life running out of him as I stroked his hair and prayed for God to save him."

The captain wiped his eyes and cleared his throat before continuing. "I was busy begging for his life when he died. Didn't even get a chance to tell him I loved him and was proud of him. Imagine that. My only child is dying in my arms and I'm looking up to the sky talking to God, instead of looking in my boy's eyes giving him comfort as he passes. The least God could have done was taken me too, but no, that wasn't enough."

The captain rose from the table and tried to gather his thoughts. He was about to tell a tale that he'd never spoken of before, though it was well-known to those around him. He walked over to Abigail and she returned the photograph case to him. She didn't speak. The captain walked back to his side of the table and studied the picture of his son.

"My wife wasn't happy with us when we enlisted," Fraser began again. "Of course she was particularly angry with me. The governor needed to raise troops to send to Washington, and the men in our town were all joining so we could fight together. I could read and write and was a successful businessman, so they made me a captain even though I didn't know anything about soldiering. I thought my wife was going to be proud of us, especially proud of my being an officer. But she didn't speak to me for days before we got on a train to our first camp in Ohio. When she finally did speak to me, it was only to tell me I'd better bring her son back to her the same way he left."

"She mus' be heartbroke," Abigail offered softly.

"They gave me leave and I took my boy back home on a train in a pine box. My wife wouldn't believe he was gone. She refused to even look at his body. I had to bury him without her. She just couldn't accept the fact that he was dead and didn't want it proved to her. The Army gave me two weeks of home-leave and she cried the whole time I was there. I tried to bring her comfort, but it was clear she blamed me for what had happened. She wouldn't speak about it, but I knew. I could have stayed longer, but I thought my presence was prolonging her mourning so I returned to our camp in Virginia when my leave was up. Three days after I got back to camp I received a wire that my wife was also gone. She'd hung herself from a rafter beam in our son's bedroom right after I left."

"Lawd, Jesus," Abigail mumbled.

"Those two were my whole life," the captain said as he sat again in his chair at the table. "I couldn't believe a loving God would let it happen to us. We weren't sinners, we were fighting a just cause. What else could we have done? I prayed and prayed for an answer and got nothing. No, I did get something," The captain corrected himself. "God kept putting that sword in one of my hands and a pistol in the other, and kept sending me out to that line to lead other young men to their graves. Every one of them another man's son. Every one of them, some mother's boy. I'm so weary from writing letters of apology to wives and parents for killing their kin. There's not a day that passes that I don't wish some Rebel would fix his sights on me and finally end this burden that holds me in its grasp. But it never comes."

"You don't mean that, Mister John."

"Oh I do, ma'am. It's time I've had my own blood on my hands, and not just the blood of all those around me."

"The Lawd has a plan for us all," Abigail said. "His workin's ain't for us tuh say."

"But I have to believe *my* God is one of mercy," the captain insisted.

"The Lawd *is* a God of mercy...an' fo'giveness."

"Then where is my mercy, Miss Abigail?" the captain pleaded. "How many more will fall at my doing before God shines his light upon me? Am I to believe he has placed his hand on my shoulder to act as his angel of death? Am I to be rewarded with his grace only after I've served in his black legion of destruction? I would rather there be no God than to serve one who would expect this of me."

"You have a troubled soul, suh," the slave said softly. "I see goodness in yo' eyes, but you been led astray by bad thoughts."

The captain answered with a sinister chuckle. "Of all people, a slave woman defends God."

"Don't yuh go throwin' no stones at me, suh."

"I apologize," Fraser said realizing his rudeness. "This discussion has taken a very ugly turn. It is not proper for me to discredit your faith."

"My faith," Abigail answered. "It ain't jus' my faith. You believe in God, too. You jus' want everthin' laid out nice for yuh. I feels real bad 'bout what happened to yo' family, really I do. But it ain't no secret the Lawd had his own son nailed right up there on that cross, an' let him hang 'til he died fo' all our soul's salvation. Jesus didn't do nothin' but spread the good word, an' God still had 'em kilt in the mos' terrible a ways. Your boy went tuh war an' he gave his life fightin' fo' what's right. I 'spect no man in his right mind gonna put a gun in his hand an' go tuh war an' not think he might get kilt. Jesus didn't have no reason tuh think them sinners was gonna be able to nail him up, but God went an' let 'em do it anyway. His own daddy. How you gonna say you a Christian an' go off tuh war with yo' boy thinkin' God gonna keep 'em from dyin' when God let his own boy get kilt? You got ever' right tuh be hurt an' angry, suh. But y'ain't got no place tuh blame God fo' that. Blame the dad gum Reb who shot yo' boy down.

"An' I may be a slave, but that don't mean God don't hear my prayers. Them fiel's been plowed an' picked by Nigras over a hundred years I been tol'. When you a slave, all's yuh do is think about what it be like tuh be free. When yuh know Jesus, that's all yuh pray about. Now it might jus' be it ain't a miracle to you, but havin' a Yankee finally show up at my door is sho' nuff a miracle tuh me. An' it sho' is tuh any other Nigra down here been prayin' for they freedom. Way I see it, Jesus done freed me from my sins an' gave me hope. You and yo' Yankee friends is all that hopin' finally comin' 'round down here in Missi'ppi."

The captain sat silently, thinking of a response. He didn't want to argue and he certainly didn't want to upset Abigail. He still had the wisdom in knowing there was no way to win a debate over the virtues, or lack thereof, of Christianity with a devote follower of the faith. The captain also knew there were no clear answers or resolutions to his own position. If there were, he would have certainly discovered them sometime during the endless sleepless nights he'd spent study-ing scripture and battling the demons in his head.

Abigail rose from her chair and walked over to the captain. She stood behind him and gently placed her hand on his shoulder. "You a good man, Mister John. You sho' been put through it, an' I feels fo' yuh, really I do. Go on over an' have that chair by the fire. I'll clean up this table. We'll have pie later."

The captain placed his hand over his host's. "I'm so sorry for my tone," he said. "I'm very tired and my exhaustion sometimes brings me to a state of near lunacy. Please accept my apologies."

Abigail gently squeezed his shoulder, touched his head, and then began clearing the table. Fraser rose and helped her.

"We get done here, I got a surprise fo' yuh," Abigail said with a forced smile to break the uncomfortable tension in the tiny cabin.

"I don't know if I need any surprises," the captain replied.

"You be likin' this," Abigail insisted. "It'll help settle you a little."

"If you're talking about more of your homemade liquor, I think I'll have to decline."

"Oh no. Last thing you put in a man with troubles on his mind is likuh'. Even I know that."

The captain grinned. "I wish I had something for you." Just after he said the words he remembered the other books he had taken from the Sexton Estate. "Actually, I do believe I might have something."

The atmosphere in the simple country home suddenly changed with the tidings of exchanging gifts, and the rest of the table was cleared with a renewed spirit of anticipation.

"I'z gonna put the pie in the oven soon as we get back," Abigail said as she crossed the room toward her bedroom. "I sugges' you take one a them blankets with yuh since y'ain't got no coat. It's gonna get fresh outside now that the sun's goin' down."

"Where are we going?" Fraser asked.

"If'n I told you it wouldn't be no surprise," the slave woman answered. She walked into her room and reappeared with a gray shawl wrapped around her waist. "Light one a' them lamps and we'll take it with us. Full moon jus' passed us by so it's gonna get real dark out tonight."

The captain retrieved a lamp from the dresser in the corner and lit the candle inside with one of the small dried twigs Abigail kept bundled next to her fireplace. He then took the copy of Walt Whitman poetry and secretly folded it into one of the quilts. Careful not to forget he was still in enemy territory, he then tucked his revolver into the front of his pants beneath his vest.

The occasional stirring of the cool afternoon breeze had been replaced by the evening's damp crisp air. The captain offered his horse to Abigail, but she preferred to walk. When he again questioned their destination, she playfully chastised him for acting like an immature child and told him to, "Jus' wait an' see."

They then headed away from the cabin down the well-traveled farm road that led to the rest of the plantation. A few hundred yards into their walk appeared a lesser worn path of two parallel wagon wheel ruts.

"We gonna follow this here trail a ways," Abigail said as she directed the captain onto the weed-covered path. "Don't stir the grass more'n yuh have to. I got a big secret at the other end an' I got this path nice an' growd over so's no one can find it."

Now the captain was even more eager to see what lay ahead of him, but he knew another enquiry would only be met with negative response. Instead he asked, "Miss Abigail, do you ever think what you'll do if the Sextons get to keep all this land when the war is over?"

"I do think 'bout it," she answered. "I ain't got no money tuh buy my own place. Like yuh said before, maybe someone in charge'll he'p me get started out west somewhere."

"Aren't you afraid there might still be people who don't like the idea of you being free?"

"I don't tend tuh bother nobody, so's nobody got no reason tuh bother me. Any white folks still got bad feelins' 'bout Nigras after this war is over is jus' gonna have tuh make do."

The captain smiled. "There are some states near the frontier that will welcome you. Have you heard of Kansas?"

"I do believe I have. Ain't some white man come from there who tried to free up some Nigras a few years before the war started?"

"You probably speak of John Brown and his sons."

"That's right," Abigail said. "They hung 'em up, didn't they?"

"Yes, they did," the captain confirmed. "And the officer in charge of his execution is now in command of the entire Rebel Army. How did you hear of John Brown?"

"House Nigras mostly. Then one day Massa Sexton come out all proud of his'self, talkin' 'bout how some preacher from Kansas done got caught tryin' tuh free a bunch a slaves up north a here. Way he put it, the gov'ment hangin' that poor man was a sign we better keep our minds on our fiel' tendin' an' not takin' off. I guess I remember it so well 'cause that was 'round the firs' time we was hearin' they's white folks that was gonna he'p us. We was startin' tuh think they was some hope comin' our way, but when the Pres'dent his'self went tuh stringin' men up fo' fightin' fo' slaves, it was a sad day."

"If it makes any difference, Mr. Brown wasn't executed for trying to free your people. He and some other men, including his sons, took over a Federal armory and some people were killed by Brown and his men. It is true he was trying to take the armory to supply weapons to freed slaves, but the charge against him was murder and treason."

"Was he really a man of God?" Abigail asked.

"Yes he was," the captain answered. "John Brown believed everything he did was at the direction of God."

"What you s'pose?"

"About what he did?" the captain asked.

"'Bout whether God tol' him tuh do the things he done," Abigail answered.

"I believe the Bible says that slavery is an abomination of mankind's doing. But I don't think it's wrong just because the Bible says so. There are some things we know are wrong like stealing, because it is our nature. There are rules of civility that are as natural to us as feeling love or feeling anger. It is those laws of humanity, like knowing it is wrong to kill and steal, that keeps the human race alive. As for John Brown, I think he was a very religious white man who was extremely disturbed that other white Americans were participating in something he found so dark and evil. He thought it was his duty as a Christian to do something about it. Even kill if he had to."

"Do you think that was right?"

"I didn't think so then. But now the same government that hanged him for killing in the name of abolition, is *paying* me to do it."

"Wanna know how I feel's 'bout it?" Abigail asked.

"I'd be most interested," the captain answered.

"I think the Lawd tol' Preacher Brown to do what he done. Maybe not in words, but he gave him the feelin's tuh go do what was right. I think the Lawd was watchin' how the res' a y'all white folks was gonna take tuh Preacher Brown an' what he was doin'. I'd say by hangin' that poor soul, you showed God only one Preacher Brown ain't good 'nough for all the sinnin' goin' on down here. Next thing you know, God got half y'all killin' the other half. You Yankees ain't nothin' but the sea that opened up an'

215

swallowed all them chariots chasin' Moses an' his peoples. You the same as the flood water that drownded all them sinners while Noah sat peaceful in his boat with all them critters. Someday these Rebs 'round here are gonna see all them blue Yankee coats a comin' down on 'em, an' they gonna figure out who y'all really is. Ain't no army from up north comin' down here tuh stir things up 'cause you white folks cain't agree on nothin'. You Yanks is marchin' in the name a God, an' his revenge will be terrible on them that keep on with slave ownin' an' mistreatin'."

"I can appreciate your analogy ma'am, especially after having witnessed for myself how awesome an entire Union division appears when assembled together before battle. But the truth is, within those ranks are men who care nothing about your plight here, I'm sorry to say. Some are nothing more than criminals serving their sentence by forced enlistment. Others were ordered by lottery to join in the fight. Some are fresh from countries across the ocean and only fight because they thought joining the Army would put food on their tables."

"Jus' more proof the Lawd works in ways we ain't never gonna understand."

Again, the captain had to yield to Abigail's unwavering faith. "If you had a choice, where would you first visit with your new freedom?" he asked.

The slave woman thought for a moment. "I don't know a many places other'n this farm. I only been off it once tuh go tuh town, an' that was a long time ago."

"That's hard for me to imagine," the captain replied.

"Wasn't much as I recall. 'Bout the only thing that sticks in my head is all the pretty dresses them white women had on. Ever' one of 'em carried one a them things that keeps the rain offa y'head, but there weren't a cloud in the sky. I remember gettin' a good wack from the missus when I asked why the tail sides of all them fancy-dressed ladies was so big. Didn't know it was 'cause a what they was wearin' underneath. I jus' thought that partic'lar town was full a white gals with big rumps on 'em."

The captain laughed at the story's image in his mind.

"Oh, it weren't so funny tuh Missus Sexton," Abigail added. "She always liked takin' one a us young'un gal Nigras with her tuh town, but she never took me no more. I didn't like her much fo' that."

The humor in the story was quickly shattered by its outcome. The captain gently grasped Abigail's arm and stopped her. She turned and looked back at him with puzzlement in her eyes.

The captain said, "Someday soon you'll be one of those ladies you saw in town. You'll wear a fine dress of colors so spectacular every man will have to stop and admire you. The other ladies on the street will look away as you pass by, not because they are ashamed that you were once a slave, but because they are jealous of your beauty."

"Oh, suh, you done gone off the end," Abigail said as she looked bashfully to her feet.

"I will pledge to you right now, with the honor of an officer of the Unites States Army, if I'm still alive when this war is over, I will personally return to this place and accompany you to the nearest city where the finest in women's apparel may be purchased. We will spend the day searching out the most perfect dress you ever saw, and then we'll walk together in full display from one end of town to the other showing it off. When we tire of those frivolous antics, we'll find the fanciest restaurant in town and we'll eat and drink until that dress no longer fits, and we'll talk of this day in drunken stupor until the proprietor has us removed."

"That do sound like a gran' time," Abigail answered.

"Why sure it does," the captain answered, pleased that his shallow promise had been believed and had drawn a smile to Abigail's face. He knew he would never see her again after that day. Though she was too naive to realize it, his vow was no more plausible than as if he'd promised to take her on a ship's tour around the world. Still, the objective wasn't to lie to her. It was to encourage her to believe there was something better in her future. A future the captain was sure he would never live to see.

They returned to their walk as the sun continued to fade before them. Abigail removed the shawl from her waist and wrapped it around her shoulders for warmth. They began to talk about the size of the plantation and how easy it would be to become lost on the property. Abigail told the captain she'd done her best to disguise some of the wagon routes between the different fields, hoping it might prevent wandering soldiers from discovering the vegetable gardens and cattle she'd hidden. During that conversation Abigail turned to the tree line and asked the captain to help her clear some heavy fallen branches. To a passerby not paying attention, the carefully-placed camouflage blended perfectly into the overgrowth around it. But to stop and stand before the pile of limbs, it was clearly blocking a large gap between the trees. The captain dragged away the barrier, exposing two parallel wagon wheel ruts that disappeared through a grassy meadow into another clump of trees in the distance.

"What's out yonder's my secret," Abigail said. "If'n I ever have tuh run from my place, this here is where I'm a comin'."

The captain smiled and the two headed southward, each following the narrow path cut by the plantation's farm wagons. Soon, the shadowy image of a tall narrow shack and a small pond next to it began to take form beneath a small grove of mature pecan and oak trees.

"They it is," Abigail announced.

She led the captain to the door of the shack and reminded him to be careful with the lamp flame before they entered. She didn't want him burning the place down. She then pulled the door open and stepped back from the threshold. The sweet odor of fresh tobacco suddenly filled the air and the captain's nostrils flared with excitement.

"I know'd you'd like that," Abigail said with a smile when she noticed the captain's expression. "I feels the same way ever' time I opens this door. Makes yuh jus' wanna stand here a spell an' breathe it in don't it?"

"It certainly does, ma'am."

"Ain't no time fo' it now, though. Come on in."

The captain raised the lantern to his eyes as they both stepped inside. The glow of the candle flame reflecting off the glass panels of the lamp illuminated eight long rafters, each with a row of drying tobacco leaves hanging from it. The power of the trapped fragrance was so strong the captain could feel it in his throat. "This is wonderful," he said.

"You ever had any Missi'ppi 'bacca, Mister John?"

"I don't believe I have, Miss Abigail," he answered with a broad grin.

"Then come on over," she said and scooted two chairs together at a dusty wooden table. "We gonna have us a smoke."

The captain placed the lamp in the center of the table and sat down.

"I'z not much one fo' a seegar," Abigail said as she reached up and began selecting leaves from a rafter. "But it's in me tuh have a hunger fo' a pipe or two at the end of the day. You ever roll one up?"

"A cigar?"

"What else we talkin' 'bout?"

"No, I've never rolled a cigar before," Fraser answered. "Where I come from, that's a job for a tobacconist."

"A who?"

"A tobacconist is a person who makes his trade with tobacco."

"Well I'ma gonna show you how them 'bacconis' roll up a seegar," Abigail said. "Then you can grow yo' own an' won't have tuh be foolin' 'round no more with some fella doin' it fo' yuh."

"I don't think I'll ever grow my own tobacco, but I am very interested to see how this is done," Fraser answered eagerly.

Abigail selected some samples from one of the rafters and then sat down next to the captain, laying several dry leaves on the table in front of him. "Secret to rollin' stogy is usin' two differ'nt kinds a leaves. The leaf you gonna be puffin' on needs tuh be dry like these." She handed the captain some of the leaves. "See how they dry but not cracklin' up. Roll 'em 'round in yuh fingers. See how they still got some a that sticky to 'em?"

The captain nodded that he understood and laid the leaves back on the table.

"Now these is fo' the outside," Abigail explained, and handed the remaining few leaves to her pupil. "I picked these a li'l later so they ain't so dried up. Still gonna smoke, but they gonna hold them inside leaves nice an' tight 'cause they stronger. So yuh gonna take a couple them inside leaves an' lay 'em out flat on top a each other."

Abigail watched as the captain followed her instructions and then she continued. "Now take the end next tuh yuh an' roll them leaves tight as yuh can 'bout three inches along."

Again, the captain followed her direction and paused.

"Now hold that what yuh got started nice an' tight with one hand," Abigail said, "an' lay another couple leaves out underneath with yuh other hand. You gonna roll them new leaves into what yuh already got done, but only go 'bout three inches an' then lay some mo' down. Use them outside leaves last."

The captain delicately rolled the new leaves into the cigar he was creating, careful to keep the wrap as tight as possible. Abigail watched over him, offering advice and encouragement like a seasoned schoolmarm. When the tobacco roll was completed, she cut both ends with a straight razor that had been hanging from a post nearby.

"That be a fine seegar," Abigail observed and handed it back to the captain.

"Not the prettiest I've ever seen," Fraser answered, "but I think it'll do." He ran it beneath his nose and sighed with delight.

Abigail reached into a pocket on the side of her dress and withdrew a small hand-carved pipe. She then took a piece of tobacco that had been cut from the cigar and began tearing it into smaller pieces. The captain stood up from the table, put his cigar in his mouth, and surveyed the previously ignored contents of the shack.

"What is this contraption?" he asked as he examined a large open wood box with some kind of spinning cylinder inside.

"That be a cotton gin," Abigail answered. "They ain't got none a them up north?"

"Not where I'm from," Fraser answered. "How does it work?"

"You put the cotton in the top an' turn this here wheel. All the seed jus' come right off."

"And what is this?" the captain asked of the smaller machine next to it.

"That's fo' spinnin' the ginned cotton into yarn," Abigail answered. "Both of'm is broke. That's why they all the way out here. This is the Nigra barn where the Sextons let us hang our own 'bacca an' store cawn an' such fo' winter. It ain't much, 'specially when they start pilin' things in here that ain't workin.' Bes' thing about out here is that water hole outside. It always be fulla' catfish. Seems like ever' time you pull one out, two more is growed right behind it. Some a us even be thinkin' the Lawd his'self done blessed that very fishin' hole. Jus' ain't no other reason how it could stay so fulla' fish. Great big'uns. You know the Bible tells a story 'bout Jesus doin' nearly the same thing."

"Yes, it does," the captain agreed.

"You know a lot 'bout the Bible don't yuh, Mister John? Sho' is nice tuh have another Christian tuh talk to. Why don't we take our smokes outside an' have us a fire. Maybe you can tell me somethin' 'bout Jesus I don't already know."

"I doubt I'll be able to do that," the captain answered as he took the lamp from the table and followed Abigail back out the door.

The orange glow of dusk they'd left behind when they first entered the tobacco barn was in its last stage of submission to the darkness of the night. With no moonbeam to replace the sun, only an infinite universe of white twinkling stars began to appear overhead. The captain followed Abigail to a small fire pit a few yards from the edge of the pond. Encompassing the pit were three pine logs used for seating.

"I'll clean this hole out some if'n you can fetch us some wood," Abigail said. "There should be plenty 'round here."

The captain handed the lantern to Abigail and spread his blanket on the ground. He then walked over to the tree line in search of fuel for their fire. Even in the darkness he was able to find adequate supply of both large and small tree limbs that had fallen and already dried. He made several trips back and forth with arms full of wood, sure to stock a reserve pile nearby. By the time he was convinced his task had been satisfactorily completed, Abigail had a small flame growing in the pit.

"I ain't done this in a long time," she said and moved away from the fire. She then wiped her hands clean and sat on the blanket with her back against one of the large pine logs. "Them flames get goin', you cain't see nothin' sneekin' up on yuh. Bein's I'm a woman out here all alone, jus' askin' fo' trouble y'aint able tuh see somethin' comin' out of them woods."

The captain brushed the dirt from his vest and trousers and then sat down beside her. "I'll protect you," he said.

The slave woman smiled. She did feel safe with him.

They then sat together quietly enjoying the peacefulness, Abigail occasionally poking at the fire to help it breathe. When the captain felt he should initiate some topic of conversation, all he could think of was to comment, "This is very nice."

Abigail suddenly slapped him gently on the shoulder. "I plum forgot 'bout that seegar. Let's have us a smoke."

The captain grinned with approval and placed the tip of a dried twig in the fire. When it began to flame he handed it to Abigail. She put her pipe in her mouth and tilted the small flame to its bowl.

With a few strong puffs, she released a billow of smoke into the air and handed the stick back to the captain. He then held it up to the end of the cigar between his lips and sucked at the flame until his mouth also filled with smoke.

"My compliments, Miss Abigail," the captain said and then buried his nose in the cloud of smoke he'd just dispatched. He drew a deep breath, recycling as much of the aromatic cloud back into his lungs as they would allow. "I've never had anything finer. This indulgence is beyond my vocabulary."

Abigail didn't know the word 'indulgence' but she knew what the captain was trying to say. "Beins' I ain't never smoked on nothin' else, I cain't rightly compare this Missi'ppi 'bacca tuh no one else's. But it's good, ain't it?"

They both leaned back into the log and stared into the warming fire.

"I brought along something else I found at the Sexton house," the captain said. He reached beneath the corner of the blanket and withdrew the book of poetry. "This was one of my favorite books back home. The man who wrote it speaks so eloquently it's as if he's painting beautiful portraits with his words." The captain saw the puzzled look on Abigail's face and realized he needed to explain further. "Close your eyes and imagine the most magnificent thing you could ever see." He watched her concentrate for a few moments until the corners of her mouth began to rise. "Now think of the words you could tell me to describe what you're seeing, but those words have to be as beautiful as the picture you have in your mind."

"They ain't no words that can rightly tell what I'm seein' right now," Abigail answered, her eyes still closed to capture the image in her head.

"The man who wrote this book speaks in those words that you and I are incapable of finding," the captain explained. "He uses them to paint portraits and emotions,and create a kind of music. Sometimes you have no idea what his words really mean, but he's a master at putting them together with other words that somehow make you feel what he is trying to say. Now keep your eyes closed and clear that picture out of your mind. I'm going to read you one of his poems and you'll see what I mean." The captain then began to read from Whitman's, *I Sing the Body Electric*.

As the verses flowed from the captain's dramatic recital, Abigail let their rhythm dance in her head. Most of the words she didn't understand, yet they were soothing to her like a calming melody. The captain paused for a moment and asked if he should continue. Abigail answered by tapping his leg and nodding.

Onward, the captain spoke the poetic prose until familiar verses began to bring back memories of home and the times he read those very lines to his wife as she drifted off to sleep. And as those memories grew more vivid, the captain had to stop and try to clear his head. Abigail gently placed her hand on his thigh, offering sympathy and encouragement. She knew he was thinking of home again, but the poem had turned to the topic of slavery and she wanted to hear the rest of it.

At the 8th chant, Whitman's words of the value of motherhood began to clutch at the captain's heart.

Have you ever loved a woman? Your mother...is she living? Have you been much to her? And has she been much with you?

The captain fought through Whitman's philosophical questions while the scene of his weeping wife, upon hearing her only son had

225

perished, played out in his head. His eyes began to well with tears and he had to clear his throat again before finishing the last two lines. When the final verse was completed, he laid the book on the blanket and rubbed his face in his hands.

"You alright?" Abby asked.

"This poem is always quite moving to me," the captain answered.

Abigail frowned. "I might notta understood all that, but I got 'nough sense tuh know that weren't no sad story. Them was words of strength an' good feelins'. What got you all stirred up?"

"While I was reading I was thinking of home."

"You done this with yo' own?"

"Yes," Fraser answered. "Almost every night, my wife and I would retire with a few verses of poetry. This book, _Leaves of Grass_, was our favorite. I didn't really like poetry before I met my sweet Mary Ann. It all started when I began reading bedtime stories to our son and I learned she enjoyed the readings as much as he did. Someone had given us a book of Emerson poems when we were first married, and I began to read it privately to her one night when she was ill, only because there was no other literature in the house. The effect so comforted her, I continued even after her recovery."

"I wish I had a man tuh read tuh me come time fo' sleepin'," Abigail said. " I'm sho' yuh was a good husband, Mister John."

"No," the captain answered softly. "I wasn't a good husband. I was selfish. I knew she wouldn't want me going to this war, and what did I do? I stuck my chest out like a drunken fool looking for a fight and dragged our child into harm's way right along with me. I wouldn't listen to her. She had it in her mind the minute we signed up that one of us wouldn't be coming home. If I'd only gone alone we'd all still be alive and I'd still have a son and a wife to go home to. We had a good marriage, but I really believe she hated me when I took her boy to war. It scared me. When I brought him back home in a coffin there wasn't any more hate left in her. There wasn't anything. He was my son, too." The captain's voice cracked and he began to weep.

Abigail moved closer and embraced him. "You go on now an' get it all out," she told him. "Ain't no one 'cept me fo' miles 'round so have yo'se'f a good hollerin' out if'n yuh want to."

The captain's body shook as the tears poured out of him. The slave woman gently rocked the tired soldier with tears of sympathy also filling her eyes. And as the flaming logs crackled and released orbs of glowing embers into the sky, Abigail began to softly hum the melody of a Negro gospel tune. At that moment, there was no one else in the world but the two nestled together on that Mississippi plantation. The captain was no more than a man finding comfort in the arms of a woman. The slave was no more than a woman comforting a troubled man.

Abigail was unprepared for the captain's sudden display of emotion. She'd always thought of white people as being hard and too privileged to have such tragedy in their lives. She was also surprised at herself for how natural it was for her to want to ease his pain. Never had she imagined welcoming a white man against her bosom. And regardless of the reason for him being there, his warm body against hers was soothing the pains of her own loneliness, a burden Abigail had been praying would someday be lifted.

The captain gave no thought to the color of Abigail's skin or her circumstance as he gathered himself and stared into the flames. Instead, his mind filled with the idea of how oddly his life was coming to an end. How strange it was that his last moments of peace would come in Mississippi, at the side of a kind woman he would only know for one day. He thought of how complete the moment was, coming to terms with the end of his own family and accepting the idea of his own inevitable demise. Abigail had given him one last chance to feel he still had a soul and, like seeing a dying wish come to fruition, he could now accept that his time on earth was nearly done.

"You gonna be better now," Abigail told him gently.

"I think I am," the captain answered confidently and sat up, clearing his throat. "I'm sorry for the loss of my faculties. It's not very manly of me to display such emotion."

"You jus' bein' human, that's all."

"But there's a time and a place."

"And there ain't no better place than right here," Abigail told him.

Fraser paused and then answered, "I think you're right."

"You gonna stay in the house tonight," Abigail said. "I'll fix a bed fo' yuh."

"Oh, no ma'am," Fraser answered. "I've taken too much time already. I need to find my way back to Natchez and help get this regiment back together. Night is the safest time for my travel."

"It's mighty dangerous fo' yuh Yankees wanderin' 'round out here in the dark. Why don't yuh take tuh bed at leas' a few hours an' then yuh can ride back at dawn? Yuh leave early you gonna get back in Natchez before them men a yo's who's still walkin' they way tuh town."

"I am very tired," the captain admitted. "But I wouldn't trouble you for a bed. One of those chairs in front of the fireplace will be fine."

"Then we bes' get on back," Abigail suggested. "Stay out here much longer, we ain't gonna feel like doin' no more walkin'."

They both rose and prepared to leave. Abigail relit the candle inside the lantern and the captain kicked dirt over the fire pit until the flames were extinguished. Before leaving Abigail pulled some more tobacco leaves from a rafter in the barn. They then headed back to her home beneath a sea of South Mississippi stars.

Fraser was quiet and to himself. The lack of conversation during the long walk back to the house concerned Abigail. She wanted to give the captain some privacy with his thoughts, but he seemed so troubled she was afraid of what he might be thinking about.

"What yuh gonna do when the war is over?" she asked, trying to interrupt him from his solitude.

The captain smiled warmly and debated with himself whether he should be honest, or humor Abigail with a fairytale answer. He decided she deserved the truth. "There's not going to be an 'after the war' for me, ma'am."

"Why you say that, suh?"

"Call me John, Miss Abigail," he answered calmly. "I want to be honest with you because you've been so kind to me and it would be disrespectful to tell you a lie. This war is far from over, and it's only going to get worse now that we're so far down here in the South. Those Rebel boys are just going to fight harder from here on out. I expect this coming winter is going to be worse than the last. We'll be on the march or fighting almost every day. There won't be any more retreating when the bodies start piling up. Those days ended when General Grant took over. And when this war is finally done, the thousands still to die in battle will hardly match the number of men who are still to die from disease and fever." Fraser stopped walking and faced Abigail. "Ma'am, I've been cheating death for three long years.

And the longer I live, I believe the more angry death becomes with me. I'm not going to win that fight. I'm no more capable of reversing my dark fortune than I am calling an end to this war tomorrow."

"You'll be jus' fine, suh."

"I am fine, ma'am," the captain assured her. "Something changed in me today, as if my heart has settled up with what's in store for me. I feel peace, really I do. After having my boy taken away and then losing my wife, all I've been doing is dying a slow miserable death. There were even times I'd take the front of the line, not to lead, but to make sure some Rebel had an easy shot at me just to get it over with. Every time we get in a fight I'm more angry about not getting killed myself, than I am about the men around me dying."

"Don't have them thoughts," Abigail scolded. "You an' yo' men is gonna live tuh whip them Rebs. Then we gonna have us a country that's free fo' all. Not jus'a bunch a white folk."

"You will have yourself a free county, I can promise you that."

"And you gonna be here tuh see it."

The captain took Abigail's hand and continued walking. "I'm so very glad I met you," he told her. "I rose today having completely lost sight of what this war is about. Because of you, I'll soon meet my final calling, there is no doubt whatever in my mind, but I'll now take my final breath having full understanding of what I'm fighting for."

"You ain't gonna die, Cap'n John. And it's upsetin' me somethin' terrible tuh hear yuh talkin' 'bout it like it's a done thing."

"Then you should take comfort in knowing there are thousands and thousands of men fighting for your freedom, maybe even right now while we walk together. Most have seen a slave before, but hardly any have ever shared a word with one. Union ranks are even filling with liberated Negro men who are coming back to fight for you. I'm going to leave here, but some of those men will surely march down your road one day. When you see their faces you won't recognize a single one of them, but I hope it reminds you of this day. It'd be my honor to know you'd do that for me."

Abigail wiped a tear from her cheek. "It ain't gonna take no column a Yankees to make me remember you, suh. I'll think back on this day 'til the day I die."

The captain gently squeezed the slave woman's hand and they continued to the house in silence.

CHAPTER 8

REVELATIONS

"So, he was here," I said, clinching my fists with excitement. The story of my ancestry was now falling into place and I could feel it. "This is just...unreal."

Abby was pleased that I appeared to believe John Fraser was actually the man who became my great-great-grandfather, John Sexton. "Glad you came?" she asked.

"This is great, Abby. You have no idea how grateful I am."

"There's more," she said from across the dusty slave cabin.

My mind raced. "He defected, right?" I couldn't wait for all the drawn out details. I needed short simple facts. "He probably stayed around here and hid out and pretended to be one of the Sexton family members until the war was over, didn't he? That's how he got the name."

Abby watched me continue to ramble without interruption.

I continued placing puzzle pieces together. "This definitely puts him in Mississippi and explains where the name Sexton came from. What about his wife? Do you know that part, too?"

"I believe so," Abby answered.

"Did he meet her here while he was hiding out?"

"In a way, yes."

"I should have brought something to write with. This is great!" I hadn't been that excited in years. "Okay, before you tell me, let me guess. He's out here with this slave woman all alone on this huge plantation. He decides to go AWOL and probably just moved into one of the other slave houses. He and this slave just hang out doing their thing, but every once-in-a-while some Indians come around to trade. They don't care who he is as long as he has something to sell, right? Ever see that movie *Dances with Wolves*, where Kevin Costner ends up falling in love with an Indian woman?"

"She wasn't actually an Indian," Abby corrected me. "She was a white woman who was raised by Indians, but she was white."

"But the reason they let her get married to Kevin Costner was because he was a good guy and the tribe liked him."

"I think you should let me finish the story," Abby said.

"Okay, so it wasn't that pretty. So, maybe he bought her, right? I guess I can understand that. Some Choctaw father could see the end was coming with the government forcing them onto reservations, so he tried to give her a better life and sold her to a white man. That still doesn't make my granddad a bad guy, does it? Like you said, it was a different time. Maybe they grew to love each other. Women didn't need to be in love with a guy to marry him back then, right? It was more important just to find a man who could put food on the table, and keep a roof over their heads."

"That's true," Abby agreed.

"So I'm right?"

"You're right about some women's priorities a hundred and fifty years ago."

"What about the other part?" I asked.

"I'd like to finish the story," Abby said. She clearly wasn't as excited as I was. Actually, she seemed a little disappointed. And that's when she said, "You know, since you've made an observation about women, I'd like to make one about men. Why is it y'all have to be in such a hurry all the time? I mean, everything has to be right to the point. Everything black and white. Short, simple, nothing complicated. *You* say you want to know who your great-grandparents were, but all you really want is the bottom line. What were their real names? Where'd they meet? That's not knowing someone. You came down here thinking you already had the answers, you just wanted someone to prove them for you and give you a couple names I think you better forget all that and listen to the rest of my story...your story. Otherwise, you may walk out of here with a name or two to fill in some blank space on a family tree, but you won't have any clue who those people really were."

I glared at Abby trying to figure out if I should be mad at her for lecturing me, or embarrassed that I'd made a fool of myself. I looked down at the floor and rubbed my chin nervously. I knew my next move was an important one. Abby had a point about wanting simple, uncomplicated answers. But I had also always taken the project seriously, and the whole reason I'd travelled halfway across the country was to get the story straight. Had I somewhere along the line become less concerned with knowing about my missing ancestors, and only truly cared about finding their missing identities? Had the project been reduced to nothing more than the quest for a few puzzle pieces missing from a box? She was right. I had become so narrow-minded in finding those missing pieces, I'd lost sight of the purpose of the puzzle in the first place- to understand who I really was and where I came from.

Abby could tell she had embarrassed me. "It's okay" she said. "You're just being a typical man."

I looked up and nodded she was right. "Guilty."

"Ready to hear the rest of the story?"

"Yes, please."

"Okay," Abby began again. "So at some point after they had supper together, he read her poetry. She thought that was just wonderful and always remembered it..."

CHAPTER 9

DELIVERANCE

The captain smelled the smoke from the chimney first and then, walking a few feet further, could see the soft amber light of the fireplace faintly reflecting off the trees outside the front window. The tiny slave cabin was a welcome sight. He was exhausted and the lack of conversation during the walk back had become uncomfortable. Both he and Abigail, joined at the hands, were alone with their thoughts of the captain's future- the slave woman trying to cope with a soul that needed saving and the captain thinking only of his inevitable demise.

Abigail hoped their return home would mean a chance to liven their fellowship. She had a pie ready for baking and some fermented elderberry juice that would go well with it. At first, she'd been afraid to offer alcohol to the captain, afraid of what it might do to him if he insisted on having too much. But now, she thought it might calm him and help him sleep through the night.

Though he was tired and still full from their Thanksgiving feast, the captain agreed that a glass of homemade wine would be the perfect conclusion to their evening together. He didn't have any room in his belly for dessert, but thought it rude to deny his interest in a slice of pie. While Abigail returned to work in the kitchen, the captain gathered his clean uniform from outside. It was still a little damp, but nothing a few hours stretched out before the fireplace couldn't fix.

Abigail saw him returning with the uniform and asked, "Is them clothes dried?"

"Almost," Fraser answered. "I think if I spread them in front of the fire they'll be fine."

"They'll be all puckered up an' wrinkled is what they'll be," Abigail told him. "Bring 'em on over an' I'll take an iron to 'em. Make 'em look good as new."

"That's not necessary, but I do appreciate the gesture," the captain said.

"Suh, you bring them clothes over here," Abigail snapped, "and let me press 'em fo' yuh."

The captain complied, surprised at his host's sudden burst of temper. Abigail locked eyes with him in frustration. This was about more than a wrinkled uniform. It was about what it represented to her and how the soldier who would walk out her door wearing it in the morning had convinced himself he would soon be killed in battle.

Abigail's every day was lived on a foundation of hope, and she couldn't bear to see the captain going back to war feeling he had nothing to live for. She tried to assemble words that would make him want to live, but she couldn't find them. As the iron heated on the stove top and the room began to fill with the scent of baking sweet potato pie, Abigail handed the captain a tin cup half-filled with fermented elderberry juice and sat down next to him in front of the fireplace.

"Aren't you going to have any?" the captain asked when he saw Abigail's hands were empty.

"Naw, I'm not much fo' drinkin'. I only use it for medicine."

The captain took a cautious sip. He wasn't much of a wine drinker either, but any tolerable alcohol was just another welcomed treat.

"Yuh like it?" Abigail asked.

"It's very good, ma'am. Thank you."

They both began to watch the fire quietly to themselves. It had been a long emotional day and the captain was too tired to attempt another round of small talk. But Abigail wanted to speak. For her, there was still very much more to say, yet the words wouldn't come to her. Finally, she nonchalantly covered her eyes with her left hand and prayed for God's help. When her short request was completed, she returned her hand to the arm of the rocking chair and waited for an answer. Awkward and long minutes passed, and still nothing came. She grew anxious with the lack of a heavenly response and, in frustration, got up to check on the pie and the iron.

The iron was ready so she began pressing the captain's uniform while standing next to the stove. As she ran the heated plate over his wool coat, she struggled again with the appropriate words of wisdom that would make him want to live.

"I'm sorry, Miss Abigail," the captain said and began to rise from his chair. "But I don't think I can keep my eyes open another minute. I think I'll have to pass on the pie tonight, though it does smell delightful."

Abigail panicked. "Now, you jus' sit back down, yuh here?"

"I'm very serious," Fraser insisted. "I'm nearly unable to keep my eyes open."

Abigail scrambled for a way to buy some more time. "You jus' sit back down an' let me make a bed fo' yuh then. Since you gonna be out sleepin' on the groun' fo' a while, I'm gonna insis' on yuh havin' my bed fo' the night. Jus' wouldn't be proper fo' me tuh put yuh all propped up in a rockin' chair."

"No, ma'am, that's completely unnecessary," the captain said. "I couldn't sleep for the guilt of putting you out of your own bed."

"Hush," Abigail demanded. "I ain't gonna hear 'nother word on it. I falls asleep all the time in front a that fire an' sometimes I prefers it. You have my bed an' I'll have a look at that fine Bible over there 'til I take tuh sleepin' myself. This way I can get some breakfast on fo' yuh before you go in the mornin'."

The captain began to continue his objections but was cut short again.

"You go on an' do what yuh need to tuh get ready tuh do some sleepin'. I'll go put a fresh sheet on the bed. Go on now," Abigail ordered.

The captain nodded his gratitude then walked outside to use the privy and rinse his hands and face under the well spigot. Abigail removed the dirty linen from her small bed and replaced it with clean sheets. She then found the freshest smelling quilt from a stack in the corner and draped it over the top of the bed. Before she left the tiny bedroom she lit another small candle and placed it on a wood vegetable crate that served as a nightstand.

When the captain returned to the cabin Abigail was back in front of the stove removing the pie from its belly. She asked the captain if he would reconsider trying some, but he said he'd be fast asleep before it had cooled enough to eat. Abigail then offered another glass of wine and it was also refused, but this time the captain noticed the sense of urgency in the slave woman's voice. "Is everything alright?" he asked.

"I'm jus' makin' sho' yuh done had yuh fill," Abigail answered and turned away nervously.

"Again, I'm so thankful for your hospitality, but you must stop."

"I'm jus' ..."

"What is it, Miss Abigail?" the captain now insisted.

She turned to him and defensively folded her arms across her chest. "I'm jus' not feelin' right about the way you leavin' my house."

"What do you mean?"

"It jus' ain't right you goin' off tuh fightin' thinkin' y'ain't got somethin' worth fightin' fo'."

The captain stepped up to Abigail and gently unfolded her arms. "I know what I'm fighting for," he told her. "Believe me, I know that more today than I've ever known it before."

"Then you gonna let go all that talk about dyin' from here on?"

The captain smiled warmly. "I've had a free life. I was married and had a family and was successful at business. I also got to serve my country. That's more than most men will ever have, even those who live to be old men. So it didn't go the way I expected. Was I owed something? No."

The captain looked deep into the slave woman's eyes and continued. "You don't know how many times I've put my own gun under my chin and tried to be man enough to pull the trigger. For the last two years I've only stayed a soldier hoping someone else would do it for me. People think men who are killed in battle are heroes, but a man

241

who fights wanting to die is only looking for a way out. He doesn't care who wins or loses. It's a different kind of coward, but a coward all the same and that was me. But you taught me something today, Miss Abigail, and I won't go with regrets when I lay down and give my last breath. I'll go fighting for a cause I'm willing to die for. The same cause I was fighting for when I first volunteered. I just needed to be reminded of it. And, again, I thank you for that."

"But why do yuh have tuh be so fixed on gettin' kilt?" Abigail pleaded.

"I don't expect you to understand," Fraser said consolingly. "I don't think I want you to understand the horror of this endless bloodshed. But you reminded me it is a just war, and now I'll go with dignity and honor."

"But y'ain't even close tuh bein' an ol' man," Abigail insisted. "You could have a whole new life all over again."

"Honestly, I don't think I'd want it."

"Yuh don't wannna have another family?"

"I already had one and they were everything to me. I could never replace them."

"Don't yuh have some holdins' back home, some property or somethin' tuh tend to once the war is over?"

"I don't see dirt and empty space the same way you do, ma'am," Fraser said. "When this war is over the government will surely give you some land and it will mean everything to you, as it should. You'll see freedom in every blade of grass because it is your own. If I were to return to my property, it would only remind me of the things I no longer have." The captain took both of Abigail's hands into his. "I'm fine. Don't worry about me."

"But I care fo' yuh, suh," Abigail pleaded. "You a good man, an' I hates tuh see a good man go tuh waste."

"I'm not going to waste," the captain answered.

"You know what I mean," the frustrated slave said. "I don't have the words tuh put it rightly, but you know what I means tuh say."

"I believe I do," the captain responded sincerely. "And I'll take that as a compliment and thank you for it." He moved to her for a final hug before bed.

As their arms enveloped each other, Abigail pulled him even closer to her. The prolonged embrace became more than a gesture of casual friendship. Both were suddenly aware of the other as man and woman. The captain slowly lowered his right hand to the bottom of Abigail's back and pressed her even closer to him. Abigail welcomed him with a faint sigh. The two then held each other as if they were lovers about to part, one venturing to some unknown place where danger awaited.

A few moments later the captain pulled away and smiled warmly. "Thank you," he said, and then turned and walked behind the partition to the bed behind it.

Abigail stood frozen in the middle of the room, desperate to sort her emotions. She wanted to go to him, but why? Was it something maternal inside her that made her want to comfort him? If this truly were his last days, should he not be shown more compassion? Or was it that she was about to be left alone again, with no one to talk to, to touch, or to share life with. Or was it simply pity that she felt for the captain.

She nervously straightened her hair and dress, and tried to gather herself as she paced anxiously. She prayed for spiritual guidance, but

God only answered with more confusing questions to fill her head. Did she actually want him? Was this wrenching pain in her bosom what love felt like? If she went to him, would it be a sin? Would she feel shame? Would God punish her?

Abigail cleared her thoughts and took a deep breath. *What am I doing? Why do I feel this way?*

She whispered another prayer and pleaded for an answer. "Lawd, I need you tuh give me somethin' tuh say that'll make that good man whole again. He's los' an' I cain't send him on his way with an empty heart. He knows you, but he's thinkin' yuh took him tuh some dark place where there ain't nothin' tuh live fo'. Give me the words, Lawd, like the words in that poem he read tuh me, that'll fix all the hurtin' that's been buildin' up inside him. Please Jesus, if'n you can only find me one thing I can do tuh he'p in this war, let it be savin' this man who yuh brung tuh me today. It ain't right that yuh sent him out tuh killin' in yo' name an' then took away all his hope. Tell me how tuh make him wanna live. Please, Jesus, tell me how tuh make him feel love in his heart again." She then clenched her hands together and waited for God to speak to her.

The response came slowly, not in some angelic sign from heaven, but in the form of a soothing calm falling over her body as the answer filled her head. The pain in her chest subsided, and for the moment Abigail felt truly free. She placed two more logs into the fireplace to make sure there would be plenty of coals in the morning, and then stepped quietly behind the partition into the dark bedroom.

❧

When Abigail awoke the next morning at the crowing of her rooster, she found herself alone. She scrambled into the dress she'd left on the floor the night before and ran outside to see if the captain had only risen before her and was tending to his horse. But his horse was gone. Abigail then solemnly returned to her home to confirm all signs of the captain having been there were vanished, but one.

On the kitchen table sat a book where she had left the pie the night before. She couldn't read the title on the cover, nor could she have read the short paragraph handwritten on the previously blank first page. She didn't even know the value of the small stack of currency tucked inside. She only knew it had been last touched by her captain, and she held it tightly to her heart to feel close to him one last time.

CHAPTER 10

PROVIDENCE

"Umm...you're kidding, right?" I asked in disbelief. Then the only other thing I could think of slipped out of my mouth, "Are we on candid camera or something?"

"No," Abby answered calmly, ignoring my ignoramus response. She gave me a moment and then asked, "What do you think about that?"

"What do I think about that? What *should* I think about that? Are you kidding me?" For some reason I was upset.

"No."

I rubbed my face and shook my head. "Let me get this straight. You're trying to tell me my great-great-grandfather and this slave...?" I couldn't even finish the question. It was too far out to even picture in my head.

"Yes," Abby answered confidently.

"This is just...not right," I said almost panicking. Abby was way off course, and I suddenly realized how big a waste of time it had been for me to travel so far from home.

"Not right, morally?" she asked. "Or not right, unbelievable?"

"Abby, do you have any idea what you're saying?" I asked. "No, wait a minute. Exactly what are you saying?" *Maybe I missed something.*

"There's more to the story," she answered.

Abby's calmness seemed patronizing. I told her, "You know what? I think we can skip the Harlequin Romance version from here. Just spit it out. What's the bottom line?"

"Abigail was your great-great-grandmother."

"A black woman!" I almost yelled. "Have you lost your mind?"

"Why is that so difficult for you? You should be relieved."

"Relieved? Oh yeah," I began sarcastically, "that's what I feel right now, relief."

"I know this isn't what you expected," Abby said, "but open your mind a little. It's not bad news."

"It isn't good news."

"Why not?"

"This just...I don't know." I don't think I'd ever been more confused in my life.

All of my research was spinning around in my head like a cyclone and I couldn't think clearly. When I finally got my bearings I simply couldn't find an opening for Abby's story to fit in. I told her, "First of all, I don't really buy this whole...thing. I'm not saying I don't believe you, I'm just saying you got the wrong people. My great-great-grandmother was a Choctaw Indian, not a black slave."

"Says who?" Abby replied.

"Says everybody in my family!" I answered in frustration.

"I think you need to go back and look over your notes."

"I don't need to go back over anything. My parents spent almost two years doing this research and they found absolutely nothing that shows my grandmother was anything other than an Indian."

"But did they ever find anything that actually proved she *was* an Indian?" Abby countered.

"That's why I'm here," I insisted.

"Really," Abby said. "Why are you here, John?"

"Because I thought you had some proof."

"Proof that your great-great-grandmother was Native American? I never told you that."

"So you have proof she wasn't?" I asked, assuming I was calling Abby's bluff.

"If I do have it, then what?"

"What do you mean?"

"If I can convince you that John Fraser and Abigail are your great-grandparents, then what? Are you going to tell your mom and dad, or are you going to tuck this away like someone else in your family apparently did?"

That sounded like an insult. "This is bullshit," I declared, only because I couldn't think of anything more articulate to say.

Abby shook her head with disgust. "I think we should go back to the house and let you cool off. I'll tell you the rest there if you want to hear it."

Abby was obviously disappointed in my reaction. At that point, we both knew I wasn't in any condition to have a meaningful debate until I got a chance to clear my head. We both stepped out of the shack frustrated with each other. I jumped down to the ground first and then helped Abby to my side.

As we began our long walk back to the house I tried to figure out what the hell had just happened. Unfortunately, Abby being beside me and the sweltering heat slow roasting me like a rotisserie chicken were insurmountable distractions. I began to fan myself and plot my escape back to Seattle.

"Different kind of hot down here in South Mississippi," Abby said, trying to change the mood between us.

"Feels like a hundred and ten," I agreed. I didn't want to be mad at her. I just thought she'd made a big mistake at my expense.

"Naw, it's only eighty-something," Abby pointed out. "It's the humidity that gets you."

"No wonder no one wants to live in this place." The instant the words escaped from my mouth I regretted them. Why I didn't apologize right then, I have no idea.

Abby bit her lip.

We wove our way through the weeds back to the dusty farm road without speaking and then headed back to the house.

"I'll pour us some lemonade if you want some then I'll get started on some lunch," Abby said as we stepped back inside the old mansion. Her tone sounded like she was cutting me some slack for my rudeness. Maybe she was smart enough to see I was just hot and very, very confused.

"Actually, I think I'll skip lunch if you don't mind," I said.

"Oh, okay," Abby answered. "Are you mad at me?"

"I'm just mixed up, that's all. Sorry if I got bent out of shape out there. I think I just need some time alone to put this all together. Do you mind?"

"No. That's fine."

I decided to go even further and extend an olive branch. I'm not a jerk and I hate it when I do something to make people think I am. "I'd like to take you to dinner, if that's okay." I said. "Maybe you can tell me the rest of your story then."

"There's no place around here to go," Abby answered. "Tell you what, you have some time to yourself and I'll make us something nice. Six or seven sound good?"

"Seven would be fine." It sounded like she'd accepted my apology.

"Then I won't disturb you."

"Thanks."

I trudged up the stairs to my room and closed the door behind me. The heat and sudden tension had given me a headache. I took two Advil tablets from my toilet kit and washed them down with water from the sink. Then I fell back on the bed and stared into the ceiling.

Deep inside I had seen what was coming. Halfway through Abby's tale I actually felt it. There really was a spirit in that cabin, and no matter how much I tried to ignore it, there had been some weird sense of a connection. As Abby spoke I started to feel like someone else was there. And they were speaking to me just as Abby said they would, whispering silently in my ear, *"This is your story. This is your story."*

The pieces started falling together as soon as I calmed down and allowed them to. There would be no Choctaw Indian bride to speak of later. She didn't exist. A bastard child born of a single encounter between a white Union soldier and a black Mississippi slave was the missing link I'd been searching for. But why the story of an Indian bride? Even I could figure that one out. In the 19th century, it was better to explain one's mulatto skin color as the result of mixed blood with a Native American from a so-called civilized tribe, than with a Negro. And did the captain change his name from Fraser to Sexton because someone found out he'd fathered a child with a slave?

I had to know what happened to the captain and Abigail. I was so close to putting it all together, but I had to know the rest of their story and I needed to see the proof that Abby had promised me. I locked my fingers together behind my head, closed my eyes, and daydreamed of what the outcome might be.

Hours passed while I tried to sort out my feelings of the new revelation. I was ashamed that for even a moment I'd been angered with the idea that I might have African American ancestry. How dare me! I didn't think I had a racist bone in my body. Or did I? As for the rest of my family, I knew there would be some who would refuse to believe it. For them, I'd need evidence for convincing and Abby had yet to produce any. Then I realized all I'd heard could simply be some old Southern family's fairytale that had been handed down through the ages. It had probably been told over and over so many times by different storytellers, there was no way to know how much of it was actually true. I had to see the evidence and I couldn't wait any longer.

My original plan was to organize my thoughts alone and maybe take a nap, but my brain was pulsing with questions that had to be answered. When it finally became unbearable, I jumped out of the bed and headed out the door to find Abby.

As I began down the stairs I heard someone playing the piano in the big library across from the dining room. The song was one of my favorites and it made me smile.

"I knew you couldn't wait until supper time," Abby said from the piano bench when I poked my head into the library.

I raised my finger to my lips and motioned for her to keep playing.

"Sorry," she said, "but I'm not very good with an audience."

"Then I'll help you."

Abby shifted over and I squeezed onto the bench next to her. Her body was warm and it felt good to touch her.

"Do you play?" she asked.

"A little," I confessed.

"Do you know this piece?" she asked as she gestured toward the sheet music on the stand above the keyboard.

"I know it well," I answered. "It's one of my favorites. My father played the piano and put himself through school giving lessons. He taught me and it stuck. He did it because he loved it. I think I did it to impress the girls."

"Did it work?" Abby asked.

"It did for my dad, according to my mother."

"Well, let's see if it works on me."

I didn't know how to respond to that, but it kind of felt good thinking about it.

"Ready?" Abby asked.

I looked at her and nodded. And though we were simply sharing a piano bench, I suddenly felt like I was about to make that first exciting drop on a great rollercoaster ride. Something was happening to me. I wasn't just ready to play a simple Beethoven sonata that I'd mastered when I was in junior high school. I was ready to learn the truth about my ancestry. And, I was ready to have a life again.

Abby laid her right hand on the keys and I placed my left hand beside hers. She then nodded a four count, and we began to play the 2nd movement of Sonata #8. As the soft rolling melody enveloped us, I gently leaned into her and she into me. Then the music stopped.

We both looked at each other and I knew. "Have you been waiting for me?" I asked.

"Uh huh," she said with a disarming smile. "You did take longer than I thought you would."

"I'm sorry."

"Kiss me and I'll forgive you," she said.

I'd never felt so close in my life to standing at the edge of a cliff and being compelled to jump off of it. Any other time on any other day, I'd have been too afraid. But on this day I grasped Abby's hand, and jumped.

"Does this mean I'm your girlfriend now?" were Abby's first words.

"Sure," I answered, relieved we weren't going to immediately jump into some crazy deep conversation about how we were going to try to manage a relationship.

"Well then, is my new boyfriend ready to hear the rest of his family story?"

"Uh...yeah," I replied. The truth was, I'd completely forgotten about it.

"Would you like something to drink first?" Abby offered. "Ever tried a Mint Julep? They're very refreshing and very Southern."

"Does it have any booze in it?" I felt like some alcohol was definitely in order.

"You like bourbon?"

"Is it cold?"

"Very."

"Make mine a double," I answered.

"I'll be right back." Abby rose and gently pushed me back into the piano bench when I tried to get up to help her. "You stay right here."

I couldn't help but watch her walk out of the room. I wondered if the slight sashay with each step was for my benefit. Or could it be she was just naturally the kind of woman that made men like me have to look, even as we desperately tried not to.

When she returned a few moments later with our drinks, I had moved to one of two old high-back velvet chairs across the room. Abby handed me one of two large chilled pewter cups and then sat in the chair next to me.

"Don't swallow that mint floating in there," she warned.

I took a precautionary whiff and followed with a sip "This is good," I said and took another drink. "You'll have to give me the recipe." As I took another sip I noticed an old faded book resting on a nearby coffee table. "Do you just leave that stuff out for decoration?" I asked.

"No, not hardly," Abby answered like it was a silly question. "That copy is priceless."

"I bet most the stuff in here is priceless," I added, scanning the room of antiques.

"Depends on who you're talking to, I guess," Abby said. "The chairs we're sitting in for instance. Probably as old as this house. In this condition I bet you'd have to pay a lot of money for these in a nice antique store. But they're priceless to my family. I think I actually had an aunt keel over and die in one of these."

255

"That's kind of creepy," I said, suddenly wanting to find another seat.

"Point is, these chairs and most of the other things in this house, have a story behind them. To anyone outside the family this is just old stuff, like you said. Some really nice old stuff, but it's still just old stuff. I like it. It gives me something to hold on to that I know one of my ancestors also touched. Do you have anything like that in your family?"

"Not really," I answered. "I have a couple of ceramic goldfish that used to hang on my grandmother's bathroom wall. When she died I took them because I knew they'd always remind me of her. I could have taken a piece of jewelry or something that would make a decent family heirloom, but I chose ceramic fish. I'm quite a class act aren't I?"

"I think that's cute," Abby said. "You took something that meant something to you, instead of something you thought would have some monetary value. That's admirable."

I blushed at the compliment.

Abby continued, "What if I told you I had something priceless to give you? Would you be interested?"

"Sure, but it can't be that valuable if you're just giving it to me."

"Oh, it's valuable. To me, it's the most precious thing in this whole house."

"And you want to give it to me?" I asked. "What's the catch?"

"You probably learned something today that will forever change the way you think of yourself. You may not realize that now, but it's true and I think you know what I'm talking about."

"Yeah, I do," I admitted.

Abby took a deep breath, sighed, and stood up from her chair. "When I first talked to you on the phone and realized I might know who you were looking for, I never imagined I would ever, and I mean ever, give you a piece of my history. But now I think I want to give you something because...," she paused for a moment, gathering her thoughts. "I think...it's...it belongs to us both. But I think right now, it would mean more to you."

"I don't want to take anything from your family," I said.

Abby ignored my insistence. The issue was closed. She then asked, "When you were up in your room did you wonder what happened to Captain Fraser and Abigail?"

"That's *all* I could think about. They had a child didn't they?" I asked, already knowing the answer.

"Yes, Abigail did have a son," Abby confirmed, "but the captain never knew of him. John Fraser was your great-great-grandfather and I've already traced his lineage back to Scotland for you." Abby reached over to the coffee table and retrieved a large manila envelope full of papers. She handed it to me, saying, "You've got some interesting ancestry in that line. You're going to be impressed."

"I...I don't know what to say," I replied as I peeked into the envelope. "Thanks." I leaned over and embraced Abby. She smelled really good. "But what happened to him?" I asked, pulling away from her.

"Major John Chesterfield Fraser was killed during the Battle of Five Forks in Virginia, on the first day of April, eighteen sixty-five," Abby answered solemnly. "He almost made it. Eight days later, on the ninth, Lee surrendered the Confederate Army."

"I thought Fraser was a captain?" I asked, suddenly confused.

"He was, but after he left Abigail he found another regiment from Indiana and was promoted. He died commanding that regiment, leading from the front of his line. That wouldn't have happened to a man without great courage. You should be proud."

"And his son and Abigail?" I was now desperate to know. "What happened to them?"

"Abigail gave birth alone and named her baby John, after his father. When the war ended, my people came back to the plantation and found her still here keeping things up. They were so grateful that she'd saved some things, particularly that Bible over on that stand, they started treating her like family."

I looked across the room and saw a large open Bible displayed on a brass stand. "That's it?" I asked. "That's the one he read to her?"

"The very one," Abby answered.

I nearly jumped from my seat and rushed across the room to examine it. Afraid to turn its fragile pages, I leaned closer to get a better look. "This is beautiful."

Abby got up from her seat and walked over to me, taking my arm as she pressed her body into mine.

"Major Fraser basically willed everything he owned to Abigail," she said. "A copy of the deed transfer for his Clay County, Indiana, property is in the paperwork I gave you. I think he knew it would draw suspicion if a recently-freed black woman just showed up one day in Indiana with the deed to his land, so it looks like he played a little trick on his county recorder's office."

Abby walked back to the manila envelope, removed some papers, and returned to my side saying, "When I contacted the people up in Clay to get copies of any old records they had on the property, they sent me these two deeds." Abby handed me one of the papers and continued. "On that one on December third, eighteen sixty-four, John Fraser sold his property to someone named John Sexton."

I briefly looked over the document copy and could see it appeared to be a record of a property sale between a *John Fraser* and a *John Sexton.*

Abby then handed me the second paper and said, "Two days later, John Sexton amended his new deed to indicate the real owner was to be his wife, Abigail Sexton. Your great-great-grandfather basically sold the property to himself using the name of John Sexton, and then had Abigail's name put on the new deed as if she was his wife."

"No shit," I mumbled under my breath as I scanned the second document copy.

"And look there," Abby said pointing to a section of the paper. "Look what it says on the line that asks for the new landowner's nationality."

The line had *N. American* written on it.

Abby and I looked at each other. "Are you thinking what I'm thinking," I asked.

"I am if you're thinking somewhere along the road that 'N. American' was confused between 'Negro American' and 'Native American.' Someone probably knew Abigail had moved north from Mississippi where Choctaws were from and who knows? A couple generations pass, a little gossip takes hold as truth, and the next thing you know you are what you look like. If by then everyone in the bloodline was Caucasian and looked white, what difference did it make if one distant relative was another race?"

"Or someone cared a lot and took advantage of an opportunity," I imagined out loud.

"That could also be very true," Abby answered. "Racism didn't just disappear because the war was over."

I didn't care either way. I just wanted the truth and I was convinced that I now had it. "This is amazing," I said again. "Is there more?"

"I don't know anymore about their son, but you should know the story from there. I do know a little more about Abigail."

"So tell me," I begged.

"Remember she couldn't read or write, so there was no reason for Major Fraser to try to correspond with her, right?"

"Okay."

"Well, after my family came back, as the story goes, she spent almost all of her remaining days here being taught to read by one of my great aunts named Elsa Mae. This was such a big deal to Abigail that it was remembered and passed on from generation to generation. They really came to love her so much for her loyalty, it's no wonder eventually one of us was named after her."

"You were named after my great-great-grandmother," I confirmed aloud.

Abby shook her head in playful disappointment. "You're just now figuring that out?"

It really was fairly obvious at that point and I felt kind of stupid for not catching on earlier.

"Anyway," Abby continued, "everyone just assumed that she wanted to read because she was going to be free soon, but that wasn't it at all. One day she just stood up in the middle of a lesson right here in this room and told Elsa Mae, "thank you," and never came back for another.

Abby walked back across the room and took the antique book that I'd noticed earlier from the coffee table. She then walked back to my side and handed it to me. "The only reason why Abigail wanted to learn how to read was because the father of her child had written something just for her in this."

My hands began to tremble and my throat tightened. I could suddenly feel the ghosts of Abigail Sexton and John Fraser in the room, their presence was all around us. I looked at Abby for direction and she nodded for me to open the book.

"Don't be afraid of it," she said. "That's our history in there."

I took a deep breath, exhaled, and first read the cover- *Leaves of Grass, by Walt Whitman*. Then, carefully opening the fragile text to the first page, I found these faded words written in the sweeping cursive hand of my great-great-grandfather:

My Dearest Abigail,

I came to you a spiritless warrior, far from my home and eager to die. I believed that God had forsaken me-with my every breath taking vengeance upon me for killing brothers in his name. But I know now it was providence that I was delivered to you, just as the Lord has delivered so many to the final verse of their own great faith test. You have breathed life back into me, if only to sustain my journey to meet my destiny in God's glorious battle with evil. I will go now into that fire a Guardian of your freedom with you as my Angel. Let your liberty be my reward and the source of my peace in the hereafter.

Most sincerely,
John

"Oh my God, this is all true," I whispered, my knees almost buck-ling beneath me.

Abby stood by, tears filling her eyes as she watched me absorb the revelation.

I carefully placed the book back on the table and stepped away from it. "This is just...wow, I don't know what to say." I was nearly speechless. "Didn't she take the book with her to Indiana?"

"Oh, yes," Abby answered. "She loved John Fraser and basically lived as his widow for the rest of her life, but as a Sexton. She requested in her will that the book be returned here to be a part of this estate, so here it's been. I think she knew someone would someday come back looking for it. She was an incredible woman, John. You really should be proud."

"Like I said, I'm totally lost for words."

"Tell me you believe in destiny," Abby said.

"I don't know what to believe anymore," I answered. "I mean, man, this is incredible."

"Do you believe they were destined to meet?"

"My great-great-grandfather obviously did," I answered as I con-tinued to try to grasp the moment.

"What about you?" Abby asked again. "Do you get how beautiful their story is? You don't have to be a woman to get it. Please John, tell me you understand how remarkable this story is."

I looked into Abby's eyes and smiled. It was all coming together-the places, the names, the feelings I had when she looked at me. "Yeah...I think I get it," I told her. "I think I understand it all."

AFTERWARD

The ending to my story is that it's really just a beginning. I returned to Seattle and Abby and I tried the long distance dating thing. It was a disaster. After a few months and two brief return trips to Mississippi, I confessed to the guys at work what had happened and gave them two options. I was either done and I was cashing out, or they could let me work from a satellite office and I'd show up when they needed me and during tax time. Thank God they wanted me to stay on.

Abby didn't realize what I was worth until I moved in and paid for the remodel of one of the upstairs guest rooms into a nice office. I think she thinks I'm a lot smarter now. I was also able to help chip in a few bucks with the rest of Abby's siblings and find their mother a nice retirement home in Jackson. She refuses to live with any of her kids and likes the activities they have for the old folks up there. I see a lot of Abby's mother in her- passionate about life and kind of feisty.

So for now it looks like it's just going to be us, the dog, and lots and lots of crickets. Megan hasn't flown out yet to meet Abby. We're still in negotiations about how all that is going to go down. I think Megan pictures us being out in the middle of nowhere, far from shopping malls and movie theatres, which we are. I'm not sure I wouldn't share her same concerns if I was a Southern California teenager. Getting those two together is going to have to happen sooner than later though, because we have some big plans for next summer. Abby and I are getting married in the big house. Sure, it's going to be hot as hell in Southwest Mississippi in July, but that's what the lady wants. I sure love her and Roger does too. Megan will someday.

My best memory of the first time I met Abby was when I first met the woman she was named after. After that day we spent in the old slave quarters at the back of the estate, Abby took me out to a small cattle pond after dinner. It was at the back of the plantation where my great-great-grandparents, Abigail Sexton and John Fraser, had once sat together. We spent the rest of the evening drinking wine, roasting marshmallows, and laughing at each others' stories from a blanket placed next to a fire. When we awoke the next morning covered with dew, I knew she was the one.

During the night I remember I had a spectacular dream of a vast plateau covered with a golden field of wheat swaying lazily in the wind. In the distance was a woman standing at its edge, shielding the sun from her brow. At her side was a small boy in faded denim overalls clutching her leg. Before them, a river at the basin of a long green valley wound its way to some faraway storybook place- the kind of place that is best left to dream of than spoil with actual discovery. The woman and her child had no sign of fear or anticipation in their eyes. Their faces only told of peace and satisfaction- expressions of hope finally answered.

As they stood together looking out into the sunset, I began to feel like I was being drawn into the picture. My shirt sleeves started flapping in the breeze and I could feel the gentle brushing of wheat stalks against me. The sensation was weightless as though I was floating, yet my feet were soundly on the ground. I was afraid to take a step forward, thinking I might be released from the gravity holding me to earth, so I chose to stand quietly, safely, and watch the scene unfold.

Then, though I'd made every effort not to disturb the living portrait, the woman with her white linen dress flowing behind her like a sail let loose from a passing ship, turned to me and smiled. I could see in her eyes were the answers to all of life's questions. In her grace was the spirit of absolute salvation.

Now I wanted to go to her. I could tell she had something for me, but I was somehow unable to move. At first I was angry, and I fought with the power that was gripping my body, but it was no use. I was too weak to escape. I looked back toward the woman, her dress still billowing wildly in the breeze, and wished she could see my struggle and would come to my rescue. But she and the boy stood fast.

Then slowly, the woman raised her hand as if to bless me and I suddenly felt a mysterious warmth surge through my body. I closed my eyes and spread my arms, the more I submitted to her power, the greater the rush of her spirit flowed through me. And when the ritual was over, I opened my eyes again and was suddenly free of all my past disappointments, cleansed of doubt and despair and now feeling safe and protected from future harm.

The woman in the distance, her destiny seemingly completed, then looked down to her child and whispered something gently to him, yet I could hear the words as if she were standing right next to me softly speaking into my ear.

"We done good," she said quietly to the boy. "Now it's time tuh be on our way."

And with those last words, the mother and child slowly turned away from me and began their final journey to that far-away destination, a place reserved for Guardians and Angels, and hearts filled with hope.

Thomas Wade Oliver was raised in Kansas and now makes his home in Southern California.